STOLEN SPIRITS

Thank you for being part of my team Bill. I appreciate your input & ideas!

Penny ☺

PENNY ROSS

Copyright © 2014 Penny Ross

All rights reserved. No part of this publication may be reproduced or transmitted in any form or by any means, graphic, electronic or mechanical, including photocopying, recording or by any information storage and retrieval system now known or to be invented, without permission in writing from the publisher, except in the case of brief quotations embodied in reviews.

This novel is a work of fiction. Names, characters, places and incidents either are the product of the author's imagination or are used fictitiously. Any resemblance to actual persons, living or dead, is coincidental.

Published by Butterfly Dreams Publishing, Manitoba, Canada
www.butterflydreamspublishing.com

Summary: Contemporary murder mystery with Indigenous characters and voices – Cree – Fiction – Canadian – Saskatchewan – Missing and murdered Indigenous women of Canada.

Library and Archives Canada Cataloguing in Publication

Ross, Penny, 1962-, author   Stolen spirits / Penny Ross.

Issued in print and electronic formats. ISBN 978-0-9869033-6-6 (pbk.).
--ISBN 978-0-9869033-7-3 (ebook)
ISBN: 0986903361

    I. Title.

PS8635.O696S76 2013　　　C813'.6　　C2013-905791-9
　　　　　　　　　　　　　　　　　　　　　C2013-905792-7

Cover design by Cathy Wickett
Printed and bound in the United States

STOLEN SPIRITS

PENNY ROSS

Butterfly Dreams Publishing
Manitoba, Canada

Dedicated to the Missing and Murdered Indigenous Women and Girls of Canada and their Families

CHAPTER 1

Sunday Evening

"No," Diane cried as she threw her arm up to shield her eyes from the eerie sight.

"What?"

The sky darkened as a cloud covered the full moon. It was dusk and the effect was twilight zone-ish. Had Diane picked up on something Stacey couldn't see?

Stacey slowed then grabbed Diane's arm to stop her forward motion. "You've been strange all night. What's up?"

"I don't know. It's hard to describe."

"So try."

Diane shook her head. Stacey was stubborn. If Diane didn't tell her they'd stand here all night. Then again, the way she felt, maybe that was best.

"Let's sit over there."

Diane sauntered over to the swings. The school grounds provided a good spot for a chat. As they idly rocked back and forth, Diane admitted, "I have this weird feeling I can't shake."

"Yeah, so?"

"Have you heard the expression '*someone walked over my grave*'?"

"Uh, maybe. I don't know. It sounds gory."

"Whatever. This is something like that. Only worse."

Diane had Stacey's full attention.

"The hairs on the back of my neck," Diane shivered then rubbed her arms, "They won't stay down and I have goose bumps." Diane stroked her neck. "I'm cold, like something inhuman is breathing down my neck. I can't warm up even though it's August."

"That's weird."

"There's more. I cried tonight for no reason." Diane rubbed her eyes. "Mom was talking to me. I don't remember what it was about. I burst into tears. I was like, embarrassment much? Mom took me in her arms then rocked me like a baby. I longed for comfort. Part of me never wanted to leave her. Then I hugged my sister and brothers. I wish I could have hugged my dad but he's not around since she took off and dragged us with her. I think everyone thought I was crazy."

"Wow, that's strange." Stacey's eyes darted over her shoulder. The conversation gave her the heebie geebies.

"Yeah, I know. I left though. I shouldn't have cause I know it's gonna get worse."

"What? What is?"

"Yeah, well, I know, and don't ask me how, but I just do. I know something bad will happen tonight. Scary bad, like you read in the paper or watch on TV." Diane wrapped her arms around herself.

Stacey shivered. "But, how can you know that?"

"I just do. The worst part is this will happen no matter what. It's like fate or chance. I can't do anything about it. When the moon covered that cloud it confirmed my fears. I'm powerless to stop it."

Stacey frowned.

"I know, I know, it sounds freaky." Diane rushed to explain before Stacey voiced her thoughts aloud. "Sometimes I sense things. I can't explain how or why I know, but I do. I could have some ability. Could be because I'm Cree."

"What's that got to do with anything?"

"Well, in any culture there are stories passed down from one generation to the next. Some people have powers. Not that I'd pretend to be an Elder. I'm not old or wise. I don't have a special gift like chosen ones or a true leader. Yet I feel things. I guess you'd call it intuition. I don't know."

Diane flashed Stacey a long, hard stare. "You with me so far?"

"Yes," Stacey whispered.

"First Nations and Inuit people talk about tricksters like Wisahkecahk (wee-sah-keh-chock or wih-sah-kay-jock), Nanabush or Raven when they tell creation stories. There are stories about the moon."

Diane smiled, yet her eyes were sad, distant. Her head felt heavy on her neck.

"So what do tricksters have to do with the moon?" Stacey rubbed her face as a shiver coursed down her spine. "What are tricksters anyway?"

"Tricksters are supernatural, like mythical figures, you might call them shape shifters."

"Whoa, is that why they have so many names?"

Diane stared at Stacey. She shook her head, confused by the question. "So many names," Diane repeated. "Oh, I see what you mean. No, it depends on who tells the story."

Diane pumped her legs, back and forth, back and forth. Her swing rose higher and higher.

Stacey pumped her legs in unison.

Diane shook off her gloom. "My grandmother, she's Cree so when she refers to trickster it's Wisahkecahk. The Ojibway, or Anishinaabe trickster is Nanabush. Then Raven is around British Columbia groups. There's other names but those are the ones I remember."

"Wow, you know stuff."

"Nah, not much. My grandparents tell stories, especially my grandmother. She likes to tell creation stories about how things came to be in this world. She talks about animals and nature, how the sky and everything here on earth are gifts for the people. Grandmother's into that sort of thing."

Stacey smiled. She liked the direction the conversation had taken.

"Now if I want to explain the moon to you I'd have to bring Wisahkecahk into it. That's how it makes sense. Trickster can be a creator, transformer, joker, truth teller or destroyer. When I check out the moon tonight I see Wisahkecahk gazing down at us. Coyote could be howling right now to get moon's attention. Coyote likes to cause trouble," she added with a tight smile.

"When cloud covered the moon I saw something pass in front of it." Diane closed her eyes, shook her hair back then flashed her eyes open. "If this was a trickster tale, I'd say cloud covered moon so no one can see moon come down to earth to ask coyote to be quiet. Coyote would agree to moon's request. He wants moon to think he's listening. In reality, coyote likes moon to visit him. When coyote wants moon to come closer to earth for a visit he'll howl again. That's the way coyote is."

"Hey, did you make that up just now?"

"Yeah, so?"

"You could be a storyteller one day, like your grandmother."

Diane shrugged.

"What did you see pass in front of the moon?"

Diane turned away then mumbled something Stacey couldn't hear.

"What? I couldn't understand you."

"It was Wisahkecahk."

"Yeah, so?"

Diane took a deep breath then turned toward Stacey. "Tonight, Wisahkecahk was the destroyer," she whispered.

"What does that mean? What are we going to do?" Stacey's voice rose as she caught Diane's tone.

"We have to be on our guard, extra careful. I don't want to be around strangers." Diane clenched her jaw then spat out, "There could be a psycho out there killing teenage girls."

"What?" Stacey shrieked. She threw her feet down to stop her forward motion. Dust flew up as she jumped off the swing to confront her friend.

"Relax." Diane shook her head then jumped off the swing mid-pump. She landed with a graceful leap a few feet in front of the dirt, safe on the grass. As she turned to Stacey she added, "I'm sure it's not as bad as that. I just wanna be cautious, take it easy."

"Yeah, okay, sure, sounds like a plan." Stacey ground her teeth, a nervous habit from childhood days.

Stacey replayed the conversation over in her head during the next few days.

If only she'd listened to Diane.

Diane could have had special powers.

Too late for regret, the deed was done…

CHAPTER 2

TUESDAY MORNING

Marti's thoughts were focused on the victim. Was she in the wrong place at the wrong time? Was it misfortune, fate, chance, a case of mistaken identity?

The writer in her longed to know, was something deeper responsible? In novels, the killer could be any number of supernatural beings. The range was broad and covered mystical, all-knowing beings from the netherworld, mythical spirits with demonic powers, legendary beasts, monsters, reptilian creatures, those brought back from the dead like zombies, the list went on and on.

Or, one could attribute the garden-variety, crazy, homicidal lunatic to any number of deaths. It made one dizzy to think of the possibilities. In real life, the killer was often someone you knew or had crossed paths with on occasion. It wasn't as sensational as a novel, movie, videogame or TV show. Yet, the result was the same… deadly.

The possibilities, although inconclusive, could provide hours of dialogue for a storyteller, teacher or professor. The topic, although grisly, was intriguing. It was enough to keep teens and young adults captivated on a sunny August morning.

Marti formulated her first paragraph. Aloud she murmured, "Stars alight across the sky. The moon bobs out of reach. For all intents, it was an ordinary evening. Yet perched on the horizon, drifts a sinister force. Will we be faced with the customary mischief linked with a full moon? Or, will grief and destruction, accompanied by a darker evil, darken our thoughts tomorrow?"

She shook her head, "Needs work," Marti uttered.

As she followed the directions given to her, Marti's thoughts turned to those of the family. Had they been forewarned of this day, would their actions reflect the nameless, headlong force that rushed towards them? If one could predict something in advance, an unspeakable event, how would one spend their last moments with a loved one?

Who knows what cosmic wonders course through everyday lives?

Was this meant to happen?

Or was it pure chance?

No one knows with certainty.

After all, who can predict?

Death.

Or worse yet…

Murder.

He hadn't done anything wrong, it just happened. Nothing he could have prevented. He was a victim of circumstance. Yeah, that's what he was, a victim. Innocent since he hadn't intended to kill her.

Then why was he guilty and confused? The feelings were alien to him, not words he'd use to describe himself. He'd dreamt of her last night, more of a nightmare. Bizarre, distorted images coursed through his mind. They'd left him mystified.

He'd woken abruptly. Her face swam before him. Heavy-lidded from lack of sleep he saw her in his mind's eye. Indistinct features floated toward him. It was the dead girl. The one he should have buried from prying eyes. Covered beneath yards of dirt and grime her shape would have been less noticeable, easier to forget.

The form he imagined was vindictive, out to seek revenge. He felt it. The shape wandered through the mist, intent on finding the person responsible for its lifeless state.

Why else had it come?

Didn't something like that go to heaven or hell when it died?

Why was she tormenting him? It hadn't been his fault. She should be focused on the other side she needed to move to. Why bother him with remorse or accountability?

He rolled his neck and shoulders then closed his eyes. He hoped to drive her image from his mind. Instead, twisted, bizarre thoughts raced toward him. They tracked him. The shadow hunted, relentless in pursuit. Her bloated body floated. Blood dripped from torn fingertips.

He heard background noise, drip, drip, drip…

The sound fluid, it flowed from the tap. His eyes flew open. With horrid fascination he watched it course to the ground. The colour was a bright, vibrant red.

His hands flew up to cover his ears as he tried to erase the sound. He stretched then laced his fingers across his belly. He refused to worry. That would get him nowhere. The deed was done. There was no turning back.

As he reflected back on last night's nightmare he recognized the need for action. It was essential he find something to occupy his time.

After work he'd come home, figure out what to do next. He needed a plan, something concrete to drive out the crazy thoughts.

Yeah, that's what he needed, a plan.

⋏

Brian gulped down his cereal. He didn't want to be late for work. It wasn't the best summer job but it was better than nothing. Besides, it was August so they were almost done entertaining kids.

"Did you read about that girl they found in the newspaper Ed?" his mom asked as she dished out breakfast.

"Yeah, I did. Sounded grisly."

"She was the same age as Brian. Did you know her?" his mom asked as she turned toward Brian.

"What?"

Brian's dad cut him off before he could tune into the conversation.

"Come on Sissy, what are the odds Brian knew her. It was a random killing, nothing to do with us. Don't bother the kid. Let him finish his breakfast and get out of here."

"Thanks," Brian muttered as he spooned up the last morsel. "Later," he added as he grabbed his backpack then ran out the door.

※

"Hurry up, I've gotta talk to you before the kids arrive." Cindy grabbed his arm. "Did you hear about Diane?"

"Nope, what's up?"

They hurried toward the recreation center.

"What about her?"

"She's dead, murdered."

"What?" Brian screeched to a halt.

"I can't believe it. Didn't you check Facebook this morning? Everyone's talking about it. This can't be happening." Cindy leaned toward Brian then ran her hands through her hair. "It's true," she whispered. Her voice rose. "It was in the paper. Stacey's a basket case. She can't focus. Muttering it's her fault, something about premonitions, superstition and the moon. I don't know. It was a weird conversation."

"What?" Brian repeated. He'd said that a lot this morning. "Start over, I'm confused."

A car pulled up with two kids and their mom.

"Great, just what we need, stupid kids, here early again for a fun day of camp adventure," Cindy griped. They watched the kids pile out of the car.

"Why do the rowdy ones always come early? Let's get the kids organized. While they're busy we might get a few minutes to ourselves. Hey, how about the park? We'll walk down there. We can talk while they're on the play equipment. Argh," Cindy grunted as one of the kids grabbed her arm then began to pull her toward the entrance. "Sammie, how many times have I told you that's not the way to get my attention?"

Brian caught the door before it slammed shut. He rushed to catch up to Cindy.

"I love my job, I love my job," Cindy muttered. She rolled her eyes at Brian then plastered a fake smile on her face.

Car doors slammed outside. It was the start of a new camp day.

⋏

"Why should we let her near the crime scene?" Pitt was puzzled as Worthington pointed out the woman exiting her car.

"The boss said we had to. She's a writer, crime maybe, or mysteries. Apparently Van Naught loves her books. He wants us to cooperate. He says she's sharp, remembers facts. Might be able to help us out. I guess she's assisted with cases in other cities like Vancouver, Winnipeg and Toronto. She's from B.C. According to Van Naught she asks great questions. He thinks she'll address angles we might not think of."

"Great, an amateur crime fighter and a woman to boot. She's easy on the eyes though," Pitt admitted as he checked out the woman headed their way.

Worthington shook his head at his partner.

"Don't let her hear you. We don't want to piss her off or Van Naught will send us back to patrol."

As she walked toward the train yard Marti noted an abandoned auto wrecker place on her right. It was fenced in and there was no sign of life, not even a dog barked. She wondered if anyone ever went in there. She'd have to ask the detective if they'd checked it for clues.

After introductions, Marti walked around the site with Worthington. When he got called away she took the opportunity to nose around the area on her own. Marti liked to get a feel for a place. It helped with background for the story.

CHAPTER 3

Barry walked along swinging his lunch box to a lively tune in his head. Today had gone well, better than he'd expected. No one yelled or gave him hell for anything. It was a pleasant change. He smiled. He wanted to curl up in his blanket, think over the days' events. It would be great to relax after his first day of work. Today, life was good.

All he had to do was figure out that other thing. He frowned. He'd be fine. Everything would be back to normal in no time. All it took was a bit of planning.

As he neared home, Barry's steps slowed. Why were so many people around? Why was yellow tape everywhere? Something was up, likely unpleasant. His stomach knotted up. Uneasy now, Barry paused. What should he do?

Marti had circled the perimeter of the area, careful to stay out of everyone's way. People scurried about, anxious to find clues while evidence was fresh. She knew the first days were critical. After that, the odds of solving the crime decreased. It was Tuesday, late afternoon. The body had been dumped early Monday morning. The killer could be anywhere by now.

Something caught her eye, something out of place. Marti scanned faces as they rushed past. No, it wasn't one of them. It had to be someone else. Slowly she spun in a circle, careful not to draw attention.

There it was the guy who stood by the abandoned auto wrecker site. He appeared to search for someone, or something. Was he lost?

Marti strolled toward him. She struck a natural pose, as if she were out for her daily walk and just happened upon the scene. She sauntered up to him.

"Lot of people bustling about," Marti commented.

She pegged him to be in his thirties. He had washed out eyes and pasty skin like someone who'd been indoors for a long time. His body was tinted. If he'd been a character in a comic book, Marti would ask the illustrator to brush stroke him a pale, nondescript colour. No, as she stared at him, Marti decided he needed a pencil rub and a touch up to enhance his colouring.

Marti frowned. There was no doubt. The man's appearance was off. He was like a puzzle jumbled up. There was something about him, his posture maybe, the way he held his head. What was it?

Marti raised her thumb to her chin then began to tap. Absentmindedly now her mind had gone to another place. Was the description she'd given accurate enough for a page of her story? Was this man worthy of a character in her novel? Only time would tell.

Marti watched the man stare off into space as he took everything in.

She raised her eyebrows then gave a satisfied nod. Marti realized what had struck a chord. The man seemed beaten, like a dog hit repeatedly. Marti imagined he was the type of person who strove for invisibility so others would leave him alone. He was visibly shaken at the troops gathered nearby. Braced for bad news, he knew something unpleasant had happened.

Marti almost slapped herself in the forehead. Of course he knew something bad had taken place. It was patently obvious. Police cars surrounded them, marked and unmarked. Yellow tape covered the area while officers and photographers milled about. They gathered evidence, pointed, took pictures, measured distances and talked in low voices.

She was surprised more spectators hadn't gathered. This man was the first she'd noticed. Then again, there were no houses nearby. Everything was far away. They were at an abandoned railway yard. Nothing else was around except the auto wrecker place.

Why had this man stopped by? Marti decided it was time for questions.

"Do you live around here?"

"Huh, what did ya say?" he mumbled, startled out of his fog.

"I wondered if you live nearby?"

"Ah, yeah, guess so."

The man was skittish, like a young colt about to bolt at a moment's notice. Marti smiled. She had to remember that line. It was a great description for her story.

"What's going on, why are all these people here?"

As she met his gaze, Marti was surprised by the clarity. His eyes weren't washed out like she'd first thought. She forgot the question he'd asked. "Pardon?"

"I asked why all these people are here, what's up?"

He stared at her, intent.

"Oh." Marti was oddly surprised by the question. Why had she expected him to know what happened?

She shook her head, unnerved for a moment. A voice in her head whispered, "Keep him talking, he's the key. Don't lose him." Marti always listened to that little voice. It had never failed her in the past.

She straightened her back. Her gaze sharp, Marti rose to her full height of five seven. If she could have read Barry's mind, it would have surprised her. She wasn't used to people who paid attention to detail.

With silent contemplation, Barry conducted his own analysis of Marti. Her face was attractive. She had high cheekbones and full lips. Her long hair framed her face while her bangs were wispy. She had big, wide eyes, brown and crinkly around the edges. Her eyes were warm, friendly.

Barry wasn't good at guessing a person's age. He thought she was older than him though. She was interested in Barry for some reason, like she wanted to get to know him. This was odd since most people ignored him. As he watched her, she seemed to grow taller, snapping to attention.

Marti flashed the man a welcoming smile. She sensed his friendly appraisal. He stepped back as if unnerved by her spontaneity, like she'd centered an unwelcome spotlight on him. Marti was relieved when he returned her smile. It was important she gain his trust.

"Want to guess what happened here early Monday morning?" Marti held her breath. Her *'Spidey sense'* tingled big time. This guy knew something.

"Hmm, I'd say there was an accident. Or someone got hurt since the place is crawling with coppers. Yup, something bad happened here, that's what I'd say."

"Yes, you're right."

Marti beamed at him.

He grinned back, like a schoolboy who'd gotten an answer correct for the teacher. He rocked back on his heels then nodded.

"Yup, if I was to guess further I'd say someone important got hurt. That's why there's so many of them."

He gestured towards the police then licked his lips. He glanced over at Marti, eager for further encouragement.

Marti gave a dreamy nod. This man was a picture-perfect character for her story. Was he the villain, a common spectator or a secondary character, certainly not the hero?

"Who was it?"

"Hmm." Marti focused on the man. He was eager now, desperate for a morsel of knowledge. His curiosity was piqued. Drawn to the mystery, even though he'd shown no desire to know anything earlier.

If he'd known Marti better, he'd have recognized she had a way about her. People were interested in what she did and said. Events, an everyday occurrence, something normal or routine became fascinating because Marti was there. She was the ultimate storyteller, able to weave a story with only a hint of an idea.

"Well." Marti leaned toward him. She lowered her voice to a conspiratorial tone. "Did you read the newspaper this morning?"

The man flinched as if she'd hit him. He backed away like a guilty child caught at a wrongdoing. He held up his hands, quick to shake his head.

"No, no I didn't." He shook his head again, for emphasis.

Marti's skin tingled. Something was up. The man's reaction was over the top for such a simple question. Then again, he might not read well.

"That's okay," she reassured him. "I'll tell you what it said."

Marti glanced over her shoulder to ensure no one was within earshot then dropped her voice. She wanted to regain his trust. Marti moved closer to gauge his reaction to her story.

"There was a young girl hurt bad the night before last."

He nodded, wide-eyed at the information. She'd confirmed his initial analysis something serious had happened. That should bolster his confidence.

"This poor girl, I can't tell you her name, was only fifteen years old."

She lowered her eyes, gave a sad nod.

The man imitated her movements.

"Man that's terrible. Snuffed out in the, what do ya call it, heyday of her youth."

He glanced towards Marti for confirmation. What an odd way to put it she thought. Unfortunately, he was right on the mark. Marti sighed then nodded. She was about to continue when she thought of something else.

"Oh, we haven't introduced ourselves." She flashed a bright smile then held her hand out. "I'm Marti Rose."

He took the hand offered. Pumped now, he gave a hearty shake then thrust out his chest. "Pleased to meet ya Marti." He grinned. "Name's Barry."

Marti raised her eyebrows. She leaned toward him, ear cocked as her body language persuaded him to give her more.

He shrugged then coughed up his last name. "Barry Moore."

Marti rewarded him with a wide smile. Her eyes danced merrily.

Barry watched her expression as he gave his name. Marti's face lit up like a Christmas tree illuminated for the first time. He felt proud. Marti made him feel like he'd done something extra special.

"Pleased to meet you Barry."

Marti linked his hand through hers as she began to walk toward the auto wreckers.

Barry felt like he was out for a stroll with a new friend. It felt foreign. He didn't have many friends.

"So Barry, tell me something about yourself." Marti's movements were slow, unhurried. "You tell your story then I'll tell mine."

Barry couldn't believe Marti wanted to swap stories with him. He couldn't help himself. Her enthusiasm was contagious. Barry began to talk about his life, a rarity indeed. He had never done anything like this. He liked to fade into the background. With little prompting, he opened up to Marti, a man happy to share the intimate details of his life.

"Started a new job today," he boasted, secure in the knowledge Marti would be impressed with this bit of news.

"You did, how wonderful," she exclaimed as she patted his hand.

"Yup, be a big change. But a man's gotta pull his own weight. Ya know what I mean?"

"Oh certainly, it's a necessary part of life."

"Exactly, yup, definitely something a guy had to do."

"So where do you work?"

"Hmm, oh, it's Sears, you know the big one close to downtown. It has like a catalogue centre or something in it."

Barry seemed satisfied Marti was interested in his life but not too attentive. She was relieved he'd opened up so readily. She'd achieved the right balance of curiosity.

"I think I know where that is. I'm not from here but I thought I passed it the other day. I've ordered things online from Sears."

"Yeah, guess a lot of people order online. I work in the parcel section."

"Really, how exciting." Marti made sure her voice held the right note of enthusiasm. Now that Barry had told her where he worked she just needed to know where he lived. "Do you send out the packages or put them together?"

"I get to put the plastic wrapping on the packages. They come down this chute. The person ahead of me checks with this list to see if the name of the person on the package matches with the contents. Follow me so far?"

He nodded encouragement.

"Yes, do continue." Marti flashed a broad smile.

"After that guy does all his checks and stuff he passes the parcel to me. Then I get to use this machine."

Barry gave a visual demonstration of how he held the parcel.

"The plastic covers everything nice and tight like. Then I hand the package in plastic to the guy next to me. He puts the address and a whole bunch of stamped things on the package and then," he paused, "It's ready to go. We send it on its way, off on another chute."

Barry patted his hands briskly, like he'd just sent a package off.

Marti noticed a few nicks on his hands. She grabbed one then touched it gently.

"Did you get these today?"

"Yup, ain't nothing." Barry was quick to brush her worries aside.

"You should put hand lotion on them every evening so they don't get too dry or your hands may start bleeding." Marti knew she sounded like a mother giving advice to a child. She couldn't help it, once a mother always a mother. "The job sounds wonderful."

Barry brightened. "Yup, it's all right. I like it."

"Great."

They'd walked past the auto wreckers towards one of the streets nearby. With a sharp turn Marti steered them back in the direction of police cars parked on the perimeter.

"So what do ya do?"

"What do I do?" Marti echoed. "I write books. I'm here to visit my sister and her family and attend a fundraiser this weekend. I'll go with my sister Marni."

"Wow, your names are kinda the same aren't they?"

Marti laughed. "Yeah, you're not kidding. When our parents called one of us when we were young, we'd both answer."

"Are ya twins?"

"A year apart. We're close though. Always have been."

As they neared the crime scene Marti thought she better make a move. She wanted to make sure she didn't lose her tenuous tie to Barry. If he knew something about the murder she wanted to find out what it was.

"I've enjoyed talking to you Barry." Marti turned to face him.

Barry nodded. "Yup, I've enjoyed meeting ya too. I've had a fantastic day." Barry gazed toward the crime scene. "Gotta head home, I've got people waiting on me." Barry wasn't sure what people, or what home, but it sounded good.

"Hey," Marti cried out as if she'd just thought of it. "Would you like to meet for lunch tomorrow? My treat. I like to check out local restaurants. How long do you get for lunch break?"

"Half an hour, we're part of the union ya know."

"Hmm, that's not long enough for lunch. We'd likely need more time."

Barry's mind raced. Marti had asked him out on a lunch date, on his second day of work. It sounded good. He never went out for lunch with people.

"Well ya know, I bet I could stretch it out to forty-five minutes. I could skip my morning break. Would that be long enough?"

"That would be perfect. I'll make sure you get back in time so you're not late," she promised. "I'll wait for you in the parking lot at noon."

"Well, guess I oughta head off." Barry turned to go. "Hey, I just thought of something. Ya were gonna tell me more about why these coppers are here. Ya never finished the story." He wheeled back to face Marti.

"The young girl I mentioned was murdered a few nights ago. Her body was found over there." Marti pointed to one of the nearby railroad cars.

"She was a friend of my niece." Her last comment seemed unnecessary.

Barry stilled. His eyes widened while fear darted across his face. It was as if he'd gone somewhere else when she mentioned murder. Marti thought he took the news rather hard for a stranger. Or had he? Was her little voice right? Did Barry know something?

Marti stared at him. She wished, not for the first time, she could read minds. It was more effective to know a person's thoughts than watch their face, hoping for clues. If he were a character in Marti's book she decided he'd be one of significance.

Barry followed Marti's finger, shocked to his core. There had been a murder here…two nights ago. He'd been sleeping in his car not what, maybe three hundred and fifty feet away. He gulped, as his mind raced. What did it mean?

He shook himself. His eyes darted about. It had nothing to do with him. He'd been asleep. Everything would be okay. No one knew he'd been nearby. Man, lucky he'd stayed at Leon's last night otherwise those coppers might be questioning him right now.

Barry gave a guilty start then turned back to Marti. He narrowed his eyes. She'd questioned him. Why? No, that was different. Marti was a new friend. But why was she here?

Marti watched Barry's face, intent as she searched for clues. Numerous emotions tumbled across it. Shock, followed by something that could be fear or guilt.

When he narrowed his eyes at her she watched him shake himself. He seemed to gather his wits. His face became a mask. Barry became a stranger again, his thoughts and feelings closed to interpretation. Marti was convinced he knew something. He was afraid, especially now that she'd mentioned murder.

Barry noticed Marti watching him. It wasn't unpleasant. She seemed to search for something but he didn't know what.

"Why are ya here then?"

She leaned towards him.

"As I mentioned my niece was a friend of the girl that was murdered. Plus, well, this part is rather exciting."

Her eyes darted over her shoulder to make sure no one was nearby. Satisfied, she added, "I write mystery and thriller novels. I base my books on real crimes. When the police chief heard I was in town for a fundraiser he tracked me down. He's a fan of my novels and asked me to check out the crime scene. Encouraged me to help them out. I guess I've gotten a bit of a reputation as an amateur crime solver."

Barry noticed Marti opened her eyes wide when she said this. Like it was a surprise anyone referred to her that way.

"Wow," Barry said, awed by her news.

"Yes, that's how I feel. I'm not used to it yet."

"Guess not, wow."

Barry reached out. His hand shook as he touched her shoulder. She was real flesh and blood. Wow, a real amateur crime solver and a writer. She'd talked to him like a friend. Barry got goose bumps when he thought how his sister-in-law would react to this news. She loved to read murder mysteries.

That's where he'd go, to his brother's house. He had something interesting to share. Maybe they'd even like this visit. Barry smiled, anticipating a potential welcome from his sister-in-law.

"So ya've solved murders before?"

"Yes, well just helped. I've been included in a few cases," Marti murmured, downplaying her involvement.

"Hey, maybe tomorrow or another day if ya have time ya can tell me about some of the other crimes ya've solved."

"Perhaps, yes, maybe, we'll see."

Barry hesitated then asked the question he'd been dying to know.

"So, do ya know around what time they found her body?"

Marti stared at him, caught off guard at the direct query. She was surprised. The question signified more than a casual interest in the crime. She shrugged off the nagging, suspicious thought. It shouldn't hurt to answer him. The information had been in the newspaper. It was public knowledge.

"This morning, just before 10:00am."

"Who found her?"

"A man from the neighbourhood out jogging with his dog. They were running along that road." She pointed. "The dog veered off in this direction then began to bark. When his owner couldn't get him to come back he wandered over to investigate what the dog had found. It was the body."

Barry gave a slow nod while he gazed off in the distance. He appeared relaxed. Then again, he could be masking his features.

Marti shrugged. His questions were harmless. None of the information she'd given him was new. It was in the paper.

"Well, thanks for the info. Better be off. See ya tomorrow."

Turning, Barry walked back in the direction he'd come from.

Marti watched his progress. He paused then glanced at the auto wrecker site. His step faltered. What was over there? She couldn't ask Barry directly but was curious as to why he'd pointedly checked it out. She filed it away for further consideration.

CHAPTER 4

Barry felt like whistling while he walked, so he did. Funny he hadn't felt this good in a long time. Not since before… no don't go there. It would only make him sad again. He shook himself like a wet dog after a rainstorm as he tried to erase imaginary droplets and self-doubt.

Man he'd been lucky the other day. He'd left for Leon's on Monday shortly after 9:00am and taken a change of clothes with him. Leon had invited him over and he'd spent the night there since there was a good bus connection from Leon's place to Sears. They'd dickered about in Leon's garage working on one of his cars for most of the day. After supper and a few brews they'd hit the sack early. This was the first time he'd ventured back to his car since the murder.

As Barry thought of Leon he grinned. Hey, Leon was a friend. He was getting to be a mighty popular guy now that he thought about it. His grin turned to a frown as he thought of the murder.

If he'd been at his place this morning someone might have seen him leave. What if the coppers had come before 10:00am? Barry would have had to hide out, miss his first day on the job. Otherwise he'd be stuck talking to those coppers right now. Man, lady luck had shone down on him.

He should lay low for a while though. Until this thing blew over. Then he could head back home. May as well phone Megan. Ask if he could stay at her and Mark's place for a few days. It was worth a try.

Barry walked down one of the side streets until he hit Dewdney Avenue then headed towards the nearest store where there was a pay phone. There weren't many of those around anymore what with everyone having a cell phone.

"Hey Megan, it's Barry."

"Yeah," she replied.

Megan didn't like Barry, said he was a loser and a bum. Told him that right to his face and everything. Man, she was cold.

"Yeah, well the reason I'm calling is I was wondering if I could stay at your place for a few nights?" His words were rushed. He spoke quick, before he could change his mind.

"What?"

Barry shuddered at the hostile tone. "Yeah, ya see I was just by my place." Barry mumbled, took a deep breath then continued, "There's been a murder right next to it at one of those railroad cars. So I can't go to my place right now and…" he trailed off, unsure what to say next.

"A murder," Megan yelled, paying attention now. "Did anyone see you?"

"Na, I was talking to this lady but none of them cops seen me. Man, they were crawling around everywhere. It was funny watching them."

"We'll be eating in about a half hour, hurry up and you can tell us about it when you get here."

"Great, see ya."

Barry grinned as he hung the phone up. That had gone better than he'd expected. Megan even invited him for supper. She hadn't complained about him asking to stay there. What a super day.

※

Marti wandered over to Detective Worthington. She didn't mention Barry since she didn't want him spooked by the police. She'd talk to Barry by herself tomorrow. She wanted to find out if he knew anything. Her little voice thought Barry was important and that little voice was never wrong.

"Have you got time to go to a coffee shop? We could talk there," Detective Worthington suggested.

"Sure, sounds like a plan."

After tea and coffee arrived, Worthington mentioned the two suspects they had in custody.

"They claim they're innocent. We don't have any evidence to contradict their statement. They're brothers, one is sixteen and the other eighteen. They live in Estevan but came to Regina to visit their sister. Their story checks out, the sister says they dropped by Sunday night around midnight to get a key. They came back about an hour later and stayed the rest of the night."

"Where were they for that hour?"

"With the victim."

Marti raised her eyebrows.

"Yeah, I know it sounds bad but without evidence we can't hold them."

He shook his head.

"They had two young ladies in the car when they went to their sister's apartment. One of the girls was the victim while the other was her best friend." He glanced at his notebook for the name, "Stacey Lowe."

"Hmm," Marti commented.

She'd seen Stacey a few times with her niece Cindy.

"Do you know her?"

"Yes, she and my niece Cindy are good friends."

"Do you know a lot of your nieces' friends?"

Marti shrugged. "I guess. I've met a few since I'm an author and they read my novels. Some have brought books for me to autograph. My daughter is a year younger than Cindy so she hangs out with Cindy and her friends when we visit."

Worthington nodded then signaled the waitress for more coffee.

"We talked to Stacey yesterday and the story given by the two brothers matches hers. Stacey and the victim, I'm sorry we don't want to release her name yet to anyone outside of the family. Although you probably know her name anyway."

Marti nodded. Cindy, terrified after hearing about the murder, found out through her teen hotline the name of the victim. It was Diane, a close friend of Cindy's.

Cindy called Marti immediately, begging her to help solve the murder. To avenge her friend's death was how she'd put it. Marti knew teens liked to exaggerate things. Tragedy and drama were their lifeblood. As an author, Marti had that in common with teens since conflict, heartbreak and misfortune were necessary ingredients of a worthwhile story.

Moments after Marti ended her conversation with Cindy she'd gotten a call from the police chief. When he'd asked for help, she'd readily agreed.

"Did you know the victim?"

"I signed a book for her last time I was here. I only met her once. She was pleasant. Quiet, very pretty." Marti shrugged. "Cindy claimed she was star struck. She didn't talk much, stared mostly while Cindy and I spoke."

Worthington glanced at his notes. "The two girls went out for the evening like they usually did. Headed down to the exhibition grounds. They liked to meet their friends there and scope out cute guys."

He stopped when he saw Marti's face.

"They're only fifteen. I hope they weren't in the habit of hanging out with strangers. My sister and I have read the riot act to Cindy and my daughter Andrea. We don't want them hanging out with strange men. There are tons of wackos out there waiting to take advantage of girls their age. I should know, they're fodder for my stories."

"Yeah, well I wish more parents were like you. Maybe we wouldn't have so many young girls disappear or show up murdered." He glanced at his notes. "Two nights ago the victim insisted on taking a bus to the exhibition. Stacey said she'd had one of her premonitions."

Marti nodded.

"Do you believe in premonitions and such?"

Marti hesitated then thought of her sister. "Yes, certain people are blessed with them."

Worthington nodded. He didn't agree with that nonsense but knew some people were famous for premonitions, intuition, listening to their little voice and those sorts of things. He wasn't about to argue with Marti or get into a philosophical discussion about the subject. She was a writer. She probably met all kinds in her line of work.

"Stacey said as they walked down the street Diane… Damn, sorry," he apologized. "Well, now that I've said her name I guess it'll be easier."

Worthington shook his head.

Marti felt sorry for him. It was obvious he thought it was unprofessional to let the victim's name slip. She already knew Diane's name but that didn't make it better.

"As they walked down the street Diane cried out then pointed at the sky." Worthington focused on his notes, refusing to catch Marti's eye. "A cloud had covered the moon. It was full that night. The sky seemed to darken for a few minutes until the cloud passed. That's when Diane said she had a premonition. Something bad, real bad was going to happen that night. Stacey tried to laugh it off but Diane was sure of it. They took a bus to the exhibition grounds."

Worthington took a sip of coffee. "Diane insisted they leave the exhibition grounds to catch the midnight bus. It was the last bus of the evening. They don't run after that on Sunday nights. Stacey said they half ran, half walked to Albert Street. It's a fair distance," he noted for her benefit. "As they neared the corner they saw the last bus go by."

Worthington's voice held a note of finality.

"If only they'd caught that last bus," Marti uttered. What a waste of life. How could someone murder a young girl like that? What possible reason could a person have to kill someone? Her eyes widened as she thought of the many scenarios she created for her killers. She sighed. Marti hated when real life mirrored fantasy. She much preferred the make believe world of her crime and mystery novels to this stark reality.

The detective broke into her musings.

"Stacey said Diane lost it. She moaned, cried and whimpered. She insisted they get a taxi since they'd missed the bus. Diane pulled out her cell phone and called information to get the number for a taxi. Stacey was standing near the corner when a dark green Grand Prix pulled up at the curb. Stacey talked to the guys for a minute then jumped in the back seat. Diane had no choice but to join her."

He shook his head. "It was the two brothers from Estevan."

"Why did she get in? Why would Stacey get in the car when Diane had insisted she wanted to get a taxi?"

"Yes, well even if it wasn't them it looks like they were part of the fatal circumstances," Worthington agreed. "Stacey said the guys had driven around for the last hour searching for their sister's apartment. They'd only visited during the day so they got turned around in the dark. That's why Stacey got in the car. She thought they could help the guys find the apartment. Diane navigated and got them to their sister's place in a few minutes. Stacey said she could find her way anywhere in the city."

Pausing in his narrative, Worthington cleared his throat, took a sip of coffee then glanced out the window. Following his gaze Marti noted children playing across the way, oblivious to the unpleasant side of life. They watched the children bounce their ball against a wall, laughing at one another's antics. Marti smiled at their innocence then sat up straighter when the detective resumed his story.

"Diane was antsy while one of the boys was in the apartment. Kept whispering she wanted to go, now. She pleaded for Stacey to leave, said she'd pay the entire cost of the taxi."

Worthington glanced down at his coffee cup. "Stacey wept while she told this part. I guess she feels guilty even though she had no way of knowing Diane would be murdered.

One of the brothers returned to the car with a key to the apartment and the boys agreed to drive the girls home. Diane's mother moved quite a distance from their old house this summer. Left the dad I think. Stacey and Diane aren't in the same neighbourhood anymore. From what Stacey said, typically Diane was dropped off first. Stacey drove alone with whomever they'd gotten a ride with. Stacey's house is a few miles east of Diane's current location."

Worthington moved his chair, scraping it clumsily on the floor. "The other night Stacey insisted on being dropped off first. She said Diane went berserk. Diane was focused on her premonition, how something bad was going to happen. Poor kid."

Marti wasn't sure which one he referred to but felt it applied to either one of the girls in this instance.

"When Stacey got out of the car Diane jumped out. She pleaded with Stacey to wake her Dad, to drive Diane home. Then she begged Stacey to walk her part way. Stacey was hysterical by this point in her story. It was the last time she saw her friend alive. Stacey told Diane not to worry, said it was late then shoved her back in the car. As they drove away, Diane was seated in the front, between the two boys."

Snapping his notebook closed the detective pushed his chair back.

"That was the testimony Stacey gave yesterday. When we showed up at her house I thought she was going to have a stroke. She was beyond upset. Lucky she's young, she'll bounce back."

"Of course Stacey was distressed. She lost her best friend, in such a brutal manner. Stacey was with Diane, just before it happened. It's tragic, beyond words."

Marti shook her head while a few tears leaked out. Worthington glanced away, giving her a moment to compose herself. Marti swiped her cheeks. Now was not the time to get emotional.

Worthington cleared his throat signaling the waitress for the bill.

"I know this has been difficult. We appreciate any input you can give us on this case. If you're up to it I'd like you to come to the detachment. I want to show you the victim's possessions. I imagine you'd like to see what we've collected."

Marti sighed as she gathered up her things. "I'll follow you there."

CHAPTER 5

The plastic bag held a red sweater that had seen better days. The T-shirt had a popular band on the logo. Andrea had one like it. Marti shook her head then began to reconstruct the articles in front of her, piece by piece. As she swayed slightly, Marti acknowledged this was more of an effort than the usual cases she was involved in.

Was she up to it?

What if it had been Cindy or Andrea?

Marti massaged her temple. It was counterproductive to picture Cindy or Andrea as the victim. She had to focus on the task at hand and concentrate. She had to summon the writer, researcher and investigator in her. Now was not the time to be a mother.

Detective Worthington had moved off to chat quietly with another officer in the corner. It gave Marti a moment to compose her thoughts. The stress of the day had gotten to her. Her stomach was in knots and she felt lightheaded, not grounded. It was hard to detach from the situation.

Marti grabbed the printed inventory list, intent to sort the details into an ordered series. She grabbed a pen and her notebook from her purse then leaned down to transcribe the list for herself. Murder, was often chaotic and disorganized, messy, yet there was always some consistency in the pattern. She just had to find it.

These items provided clues. Shrouded in secrecy with a sheer layer, they were unclear to the naked eye. She had to sort through the mundane to come up with the gems hidden beneath. As Marti copied the list something nagged at her. There was an item missing, something no teenage girl would leave home without.

Marti grabbed the plastic bags, jostling them to see if any small items were enclosed in the clothing. She glanced at the catalogued articles for make-up. The usual paraphernalia was there, except for one.

"Detective," Marti called as the officer he'd been talking to left the room. "Can you join me please?"

"Sure, what's up?"

"Is this the entire list of Diane's belongings?"

"Yes, everything found at the site was brought here then itemized. It hasn't been checked yet for DNA, fingerprints or the other host of tests evidence goes through. I'll send it off shortly. Why? What have you found?"

"It's not what I found that bothers me, it's what seems to be missing."

"I don't follow."

"The clothing, shoes, purse and its contents. It's all standard teen stuff. When I check over her make-up though, I don't see lipstick, lip-gloss or lip balm on the list. I don't know any teen girl that doesn't wear that. So where is it?"

"Hmm, just a sec, I'll get us some gloves."

The detective came back with a box of latex gloves. Marti donned hers then waited while Detective Worthington began to empty each bag.

Clothing, shoes, purse, cell phone and make-up had been categorized in each plastic bag.

"Maybe she kept it in one of her pockets," Marti suggested.

Detective Worthington shook his head to indicate there was nothing in the jeans. He passed her the pair to double check.

They went through everything laid out on the table in a systemized, orderly manner.

"Nope, doesn't appear to be here," Detective Worthington declared.

They returned everything to the appropriate bags then checked out the inventory list one last time.

Lipstick, lip-gloss or lip balm had not been entered.

"I'll ask Stacey if Diane wore lipstick or lip-gloss," the detective said as he took off his gloves then made a note in his notebook.

Marti pulled off her gloves, threw them in a nearby garbage can then made a similar note in her book.

"Wackos often like to keep a trophy from their victim." Marti's eyes met those of the detective.

He gave a slight nod.

It wasn't much, yet Marti knew a requirement of detective work was precise thought, measurement and an eye for vigorous detail. The time to ponder and reflect would come later when they'd pieced more of the puzzle together. The smallest detail could lead to an arrest. They had to find everything that didn't add up, quick.

The missing lipstick could be their first clue.

▲

As Barry walked in the door Megan called out, "We're in here Barry, hurry. I'm dishing out dinner."

"I'll just wash up and be right there," Barry yelled as he stopped at the washroom. He smiled into the mirror. Wow, this was the best welcome he'd ever gotten from Megan.

When he entered the kitchen everyone was seated in their usual place. His spot beside Jason was set with a plate, cutlery and glass. He beamed at everyone.

"Thanks for the invite Megan. I really appreciate it."

"Oh, no problem Barry," she said with a wave of her hand. "You're family."

Barry and Mark exchanged a smile. Megan had used this expression a lot but it usually ended with a sigh and frown. Today was different though.

"Mom said you were at a murder scene," Randy mumbled as he shoveled food in.

Megan grabbed Barry's plate then began to ladle food onto it. He was grateful since the boys ate fast and gobbled down everything they could shove in their mouths. There weren't a lot of leftovers in this house.

"Pass your uncle the salad Jason," his mom ordered.

"Mm, smells great," Barry praised as he eyed the lasagna on his plate. "Thanks Jason," he said as he received the salad.

"Randy, garlic bread," his mom motioned.

Garlic bread was added to his plate that had rapidly filled up.

Barry took a bite of lasagna. What a treat. Megan was a fantastic cook.

"Um," he said aloud, "You're the best cook Megan," he praised.

Megan blushed. "Thanks," she mumbled. "Kind of nice to hear that once in awhile. So, eat up then tell us about this murder."

Everyone began to talk at once. The boys loved to speculate on crimes. They watched TV, read the paper and played video games that revolved around crime solving. They were crime crazy.

Barry listened to the talk swirl around him. He heard a lot more about the murder since everyone had read something about it. Even Mark added his two cents. Murder was a favourite topic at this table. Barry's ears perked up at a comment Randy made.

"It was actually a jogger and his dog that found the body," Barry corrected. "The dog wouldn't quit barking. Just barked and barked until the guy checked what the dog had found. Turned out it was the body. That's what Marti said anyway."

Four sets of eyes turned to Barry. He had everyone's attention now.

Barry brushed his hands off then leaned forward a bit. "Ya should have seen the coppers crawling around the place. Man, there were tons of them."

"Who's Marti?" Megan demanded.

"Oh, that woman I told you I met at the crime scene. She's the one that told me about the murder, Marti Rose."

"What?" Megan shrieked. "No way. You've gotta be wrong about her name."

"Nah, it was definitely Marti. Cause her sister's name is Marni and I said how similar the two names are. Then she told me a story about when they were kids. When their parents called one of them both came running since their names are almost the same."

"Freaking unbelievable," Megan screamed. She jumped up then ran out of the kitchen.

Mark shook his head at Barry then scowled. "This better be good news not bad."

"Yeah," Jason and Randy agreed as they stared, wide-eyed at their uncle.

Barry gulped. Oh, oh, what had he done now?

Megan bounded back into the room with a book in her hand. "Check it out," she commanded. "Was this the woman you met today?"

Barry glanced at the picture then nodded. "Yeah, that's Marti. She has bangs now though, they're kind of wispy."

"Wispy bangs," Megan repeated. She began to play with her hair. "How do you guys think I'd look with bangs?"

The guys mumbled then shuffled their plates around.

"You'd look great," Barry offered when no one else said anything intelligent.

"Ya think?"

"Yeah, they'd suit your face."

"Mark, I should get my hair cut, maybe colour it lighter while I'm there. What do you think?"

"Great idea Megan."

Randy and Jason nodded.

Barry grinned. Everyone liked to keep Megan happy. A cheery Megan made everyone's life easier.

Megan turned back to Barry. "So, tell us everything Marti said to you."

Everyone leaned toward Barry, eager to hear his story.

Barry was excited. He thought his heart was gonna burst from being so happy. He lapped up their attention. With great fanfare he told his tale. When he finished Jason and Randy jumped in with their viewpoints. They knew crime.

"I read Marti Rose was coming this weekend for that fundraiser," Megan said as she got up then went to the fridge. "Anyone want dessert?"

"Yeah," they chorused, "Mm, looks great."

"Love it, keep the compliments coming," Megan joked as she placed a cake on the counter.

"Boys, clear the table," Mark commanded as Megan grabbed small plates.

Barry jumped up to help. Within moments they'd cleared the table. They moved everything into the sink and on top of the cupboard.

Megan served up dessert. "You're lucky you got to meet Marti Rose. I'd do anything to meet her."

"What are ya doing for lunch tomorrow?" Barry asked as he scooped up cake.

"What?"

"Tomorrow, are ya free for lunch? I'm sure Marti wouldn't mind if ya joined us."

"What?" Megan shrieked. "You're going for lunch with Marti Rose tomorrow? No way, you're joking, right."

"I wouldn't joke about that," Barry said as he took another tasty bite of cake. "Yum, you're a great cook Megan."

"Thanks. So, Marti Rose invited you for lunch tomorrow? Why?"

"She likes to try out local restaurants. I guess there must be one near Sears she wants to check out." Barry shrugged. "We got along great today, guess she wanted company for lunch tomorrow."

"Hmm." Megan arched her brows at Barry.

"What?"

"Nothing, it's just, well, odd a famous author would want lunch with you. After all, you're a total stranger."

"Maybe she wants to date him," Jason suggested. "On TV, guys get asked out by girls all the time."

Jason turned to his uncle. "Was she eyeing you, or you know, flirting or anything?"

Barry frowned. "No, she wasn't like that. I'm pretty sure she's older than me. She treated me like a mom or aunt." He showed them his hands. "She grabbed my hand then told me to put lotion on these cuts I got at work today."

"Maybe she wanted to hold hands with you but didn't like all those cuts," Randy suggested. "Girls have smooth hands and like to use hand lotion. There are lots of ads on TV that show girls with nice hands. They use tons of lotion." Randy grinned then nodded at his uncle.

"When we went for a walk she put her arm through mine," Barry noted. He linked arms with Jason to demonstrate what Marti had done.

"Where did you go for a walk?" Megan asked.

"Oh, just down the street and back. We were getting to know one another."

"Hmm, I don't know Barry, I find this odd. No offense but I don't get why she'd want to meet you for lunch. I better come. See what her motive is."

"Sure Megan, you just want to meet her," Mark joked. "You should take your book along, see if she'll autograph it for you. If you're checking her out for Barry, you might as well make it worth your while."

"Hardy, har Mark, very funny." Megan turned back to Barry. "Where are you meeting her tomorrow?"

"In the Sears parking lot. She said she'd pick me up since we only have forty-five minutes for lunch."

"Hmm, guess that's where I'll meet you tomorrow then. I'll get one of the girls at work to answer the phone while I'm gone."

"Wow, lucky you," Mark said as he threw Barry a playful punch. "Lunch with two beautiful ladies tomorrow."

"Yeah, what a week," Barry agreed. He chuckled. "First I start a great job, then I meet Marti Rose and she turns out to be a famous author. I get invited for this fantastic supper and get to visit my favourite people. Tomorrow, I've got a lunch date with two beauties. Wow, it doesn't get any better than that."

"Hey Dad, since Uncle Barry is here we should play baseball. Huh, Dad, what do ya say, can we?" Randy begged.

"Sounds great," Mark agreed. "Hey big bro, you up for some baseball with the boys?"

"You're on. Man, this night gets better and better."

"Boys, rinse off those plates for your mom and put them in the dishwasher. Uncle Barry and I will get the gloves and stuff from the garage. We'll meet you outside."

"Thanks for supper Megan."

"No problem Barry, anytime," Megan said as she moved toward the cupboard to get some wrap for the lasagna. "I'll put some blankets on the couch for you. Oh, and I'll leave some hand lotion for you in the boys' bathroom. You should put some on those cuts before you go to bed. I'm going to pop over to Wendy's after I clean up Mark."

Mark laughed. "Of course you are hon. Make sure you're casual when you mention your lunch date tomorrow with your favourite author."

"Of course," Megan quipped, "Casual is my middle name."

Later that evening Marti shared the conversation she'd had with Barry. Marni was fascinated when Marti mentioned her inner voice, how Barry could be the key to this whole case.

"What was he like?"

"Young, somewhere in his thirties I'd say, unsure of himself and afraid."

"Afraid of what?"

"I don't know. Life maybe, but it was more immediate than that. The police made him nervous. That's not odd though since a lot of people are edgy around the police. With just cause since they often bring bad news."

"Yes, I guess that's true."

"I asked Barry out for lunch tomorrow."

Marni frowned. "Is that wise? Should you be alone with him? What if he has something to do with the murder or…" her voice faded away as the words Marni didn't utter aloud filled the space.

"Yes, I've thought of that of course." Marti waved her hand as if to brush the thought aside. "I don't want to lose contact with him though. Barry could provide some clues. Right now we're pretty short on those."

"Did you get his address or phone number?"

"No, I didn't. I found out where he works though. How's that for a start?"

"A fine piece of detective work, Sis. I suppose tomorrow you'll casually give Barry your cell number. It's only natural he'll return the favour by passing on his number."

"Yes, the thought crossed my mind. I might invite him to watch that noon interview I'm scheduled to do as well. Thought he might get a kick out of being in the audience."

"Good idea. Who wouldn't be thrilled to watch a famous author in action? Want me to join you for lunch tomorrow, provide backup?"

They laughed at the corny phrase they'd heard countless times on cop shows.

"Sure Sis, it's a date."

CHAPTER 6

WEDNESDAY

As she got ready the next morning, Marti called Detective Worthington. Something bothered her about the Estevan boys. She blew on her tea eager for it to cool while she waited for the detective to pick up.

"Morning Detective Worthington, it's Marti Rose calling."

"Morning Ms. Rose."

"Please, call me Marti."

Worthington cleared his throat.

"I have a question, detective," Marti rushed to add. She knew he didn't have time to waste on pleasantries. "Where did those boys from Estevan go after they dropped off Stacey the other night?"

"Well, originally they were going to drive Diane straight home. Instead they decided to scare her. They pretended they weren't going to take her anywhere near her house."

"What? Why? What did that accomplish? Why did they confess that to you?"

"They could have decided honesty was the best policy. They scared Diane just to be mean, I couldn't get any other reason from them."

Marti huffed but didn't interrupt again.

"The boys took Diane on the other side of the railroad tracks, across from where her body was found. They drove aimlessly down side streets while Diane pleaded for them to let her out of the car. Don't know why she wanted to get out on that side of the tracks. The houses are pretty run down."

"It's obvious isn't it?" She'd jumped in to interrupt again. A thought had entered her mind, crystal clear.

"What's obvious?"

"Stacey mentioned Diane was jumpy all evening. Diane was nervous, jittery and weepy. She had premonitions and was worried something terrible would happen. Those boys were bad news. When they taunted her, they scared her witless.

Those boys were cruel. They knew Diane didn't want to get back into the car when they dropped off Stacey. They fueled her insecurity, terrified her." Marti banged her hand against the table, spilling her tea. "People like that make me mad! Give me five minutes alone with them. I'm sure they did more than they've admitted."

"Hmm, you could be right. What they did was mean spirited. I wonder if they did more than they've admitted. I'll call them in again."

Marti took deep, calming breaths. Now was not the time to lose control, she needed to maintain a professional distance. Voice steady she asked, "What happened next?"

"They drove around for awhile then turned down Dewdney Avenue since Diane told them she lived around there. They claim she pointed out one of the houses on a side street. They laughed at her, said she lied about where she lived. It's not an affluent area."

"I'm not familiar with that part of the city."

"Well, a kind description would refer to the homes as *'fixer uppers.'* They drove down one of the side streets. They teased Diane, joking about whether or not she lived in this house or that one."

"They sound heartless."

"The boys drove near the spot where Diane was killed. They confessed they enjoyed scaring Diane. They pretended to drive to a secluded area of the field. They wanted *'a bit of fun,'* yes, that's how they phrased it. I just checked my notes."

"They sound like monsters."

"Yeah, wouldn't want them as my kids that's for sure. It sounds like they managed to frighten her because when they turned onto a field of grass, Diane went berserk. She kicked, screamed her head off, did some major scratching, you should see the hand of the younger brother. Reminds me of a victim of a cat brawl. She shoved, elbowed, punched. Caught them totally off guard."

"Ha, serves them right, jerks. Good for Diane." Marti grinned. "Must have been hard on their ears, a car screamer is never pleasant."

"The driver said Diane pressed her foot down on top of his on the gas pedal. When he braked to decrease speed, she elbowed them again, screamed louder, kicked, then, listen to this part, it's my favourite, she reached across the passenger, fumbled for the door handle then flung the door open."

"What?"

"Yes, Diane threw open the door, jumped out across the passenger then rolled away from the car."

"Wow. I wonder if Diane was a gymnast?"

"Not sure, no one's mentioned it. Probably isn't relevant," the detective mumbled.

Marti wondered if he'd add a note about her gymnast comment. "Did they leave her alone after that?"

"They claim it was the last they saw of Diane. They have scratches on their arms and on the younger guy's left hand. It confirms she did strike out at them. Oh, and the driver has a red spot on his cheek. That could have been from an elbow or one of Diane's punches landed just right."

"Can't you hold them when you call them in again, Detective? They admitted they were the last people to see Diane alive. Their story sounds plausible but they could have chased her, dragged her back to the area then killed her."

Marti pondered the sequence of events in her mind. Then it dawned on her there had to be more since the detective hadn't answered her. He was quiet. Marti doubted she'd been the first to question the boys' story. Suspicious now, she asked, "There's something you haven't told me, isn't there?"

Worthington cleared his throat.

"The autopsy confirmed Diane was raped before she was killed."

"Oh," Marti uttered. She stared down at her tea. An image of a younger version of Andrea and Cindy running on the beach, arms clasped played out in her mind. It brought a slight smile to her face. That's what she wanted, to preserve their innocence as long as she could. Rape and murder was something Marti wrote about yet prayed never touched anyone close to her. Diane's death had narrowed the gap. The senseless violence was right there, splayed open for all to see. How would her daughter and niece deal with the harsh reality of Diane's brutal murder?

"Blood tests and semen samples have been conducted. I don't want to bore you with the particulars."

"I've done research on the subject for previous novels. No need to go into further detail. I'm familiar with the process."

"Great, suffice it to say the semen found in the victim didn't match either of the boys. We had no choice but to cut them loose yesterday. I won't be able to hold them today but I can call them in for further questions."

"Hmph," Marti grumbled.

"Every section of the crime scene has been examined. The forensic team came up with zilch to link those boys to the murder. There was no trace of them at the site."

Marti sighed. If this were a novel she would have left some small item unaccounted for, either as a red herring or a clue. Unfortunately, real life didn't work that way.

"The forensic team dusted the entire car. They found Diane's fingerprints where Stacey indicated Diane was seated. Her prints were also in the front seat area. There were only faint traces of hair and skin from Diane in the car, consistent with a person who'd ridden in both the front and back seats. There was none of her blood anywhere and," Worthington turned a page, "No traces of semen."

"Hmm." Marti nodded as she absorbed the information. She'd sort, compartmentalize then analyze the facts later. It was part of her thinking process.

"When people come into contact there's always contamination. That means minute traces of material are transferred from one person to the other. The guys found significant traces of Diane on the passenger's left arm, hand and clothing but only minute traces were found on the driver. Her fingerprints were on the steering wheel and passenger door handle, which is consistent with the struggle and story they told. One thing was odd though. I've noted it with a star."

"What was it?" Could this be one of the clues that would mean something further down the road? Marti held her breath while she waited for Worthington to continue.

"Diane's right hand was plastered with the passenger's fingerprints. He must have gripped her hand by force. The medical examiner asked if they'd been arm wrestling. We know she was under duress. Why arm wrestling though? The boys haven't explained it to our satisfaction. There must be more to that part of the story."

Marti imagined a shrug at the other end of the line.

"We're not sure what to make of that piece of evidence. The boys deny she gripped the younger one's hand like that. They've lied but it's not enough to hold them for murder. It raises a red flag though."

Aha, Marti thought, the missing clue, the small, unaccounted item that would come into play.

"So they've been caught in a lie. Pokes a hole in their story doesn't it? If they've told one falsehood one wonders if the rest of their tale is true or an elaborate concoction?"

"I'll call them in again for a follow up. See if I can get one of them to tell me about the handgrip. I'll keep you posted."

"Thanks, I appreciate that."

Marti pondered the sequence of events again. What had the passenger of that car been up to? Diane struggled for some reason. Evidence showed the little jerk had gripped her hand with force. He must have pressured her to do something against her will. What was it?

Marti frowned, shoved her chair back, rinsed her teacup out then decided to run out to the drug store before their lunch date. She needed supplies.

⊥

Lunch with Barry was an event.

Marti and Marni entertained Barry and Megan with stories of their youth.

Wide-eyed, Megan complimented Marti on her books then asked her to autograph a few.

"I hope it's all right that I brought these with me," Megan murmured as she watched Marti sign with a flourish.

Marti grinned. "I appreciate your support Megan. Did you choose these books for a special reason?"

Megan fingered one of the books. "I love all your novels. I have every one you've ever written. This one had me hooked from the beginning." She turned to include Barry and Marni in the conversation.

"I love how your characters are everyday people. Like this one with the jewelry heist, it was a minor part of the story but it was something I related to."

Marni raised an eyebrow.

Megan giggled. It came out as a squeak. She brushed hair from her face. "That didn't come out right. I'm not a thief nor do I know any thieves. I mean the way it was written made me feel like I had a connection with the characters. Does that make sense?"

Marni laughed. "Perfect sense, yes I know what you mean Megan. Marti has a flair for that. I think that's part of the reason she's a successful author."

"What's the story about?" Barry wondered.

Megan leaned toward Marti. "Have we got time to fill Barry in? Could you describe it Marti?"

"Sure, I'll give you the short version. The scene Megan mentioned was about a local jewelry store robbery. The police couldn't figure it out but one of the main characters did. The owner of the jewelry store got robbed on a regular basis. Every few months he reported a number of expensive items missing. There was no sign of forced entry so the police thought perhaps shoplifters frequented his store." Marti glanced at the clock then reached into her purse.

"Marni, can you pay the bill?" She passed her wallet to her sister.

"Oh, no, I should pay," Megan insisted.

Marti waved her offer away. "Don't be silly. I invited Barry for lunch. I'm glad you joined us. Now where was I?"

"The police thought shoplifters frequented his store."

Marti flashed Megan a smile. "Right, the store was robbed for almost a year when the police asked Eddy to assist with the case. Eddy is a character in the story," she explained to Barry.

"Eddy talked to the owner of the store. He hung out there daily to get a feel for the number of customers that came to the place. It was a quiet jewelry store, not many people came by."

Marni returned to the table.

"We should go, I'll finish the story on the way out," Marti said as she grabbed her purse. She gave Barry a polite nod as he held the door open for her.

"Eddy got to know the customers. They were mostly adults and older people who came to check out the merchandise. Some were regulars who came for coffee and a chat with the owner."

They walked toward their cars.

"Eddy thought these weren't the type of people who would shoplift. There were no robberies during the month Eddy hung out at the jewelry store. One day when Eddy visited Arty, the owner, the pieces of the puzzle came together.

Arty liked to chat while he did detailed jewelry work. Arty mentioned a friend who used to be his partner. His friend had inherited money and wanted to invest in the jewelry store. He wanted a secure venture."

They stopped beside Marti's rental car.

"Arty's friend left the money in the store for a few years. He needed it when he made a bad investment and had to come up with fast cash. Arty gave it to him and they remained friends. The friend still visited on a regular basis."

"You'll love this part," Megan said as she turned to Barry.

Marti smiled. "That was the end of Arty's story. Eddy thought it was coincidental how Arty's ex-partner visited every few months and jewelry pieces went missing around the same time."

Barry nodded, "Oh, I gotcha."

"Eddy had Arty check the calendar. The date of his friend's visit coincided with the last robbery. His friend had a key to the place and knew the security code. He helped himself to whatever he wanted on a regular basis. He'd visit Arty during the day and case the place for new items. He'd come back that evening to steal what he'd taken a fancy to that day."

"Arty's friend was always in financial difficulties," Megan elaborated. "He thought he was entitled to jewelry pieces since he'd been a former partner."

Marti chuckled. "Yeah, he forgot to mention that to Arty though."

"That's one of the reasons I love your books Marti. Ordinary details combined with mystery, intrigue, wow, what a combination." Megan glanced at her watch. "Whoa, we better get back to work."

"Yeah, guess so," Barry agreed. "Thanks for lunch, gotta get back before we're late."

"Barry." Marti touched Barry's shoulder before he got in the car. "Here's my phone number in case you want to get in touch. It would be nice to get together again."

"Oh, can I give you our number Marti?" Megan babbled. "Barry's staying at our place."

Marti smiled. "That would be lovely Megan. Thanks. You know Barry," Marti added as if she'd just had the thought. "If you think of anything that might help with the case we could use the assistance, phone anytime."

"Yeah, can't think of anything right now. I'll mull it over in my mind. If I come up with anything I'll let ya know."

"Great, bye," the women chorused as they got into Marti's car.

"Thanks again, bye."

"Bye, nice meeting you," Megan gushed as she jumped into the driver's seat.

CHAPTER 7

"What did you think?" Marti asked, as she eased into traffic.

"Barry seems nice enough. He could be a stalker though. You'll have to watch him, make sure he doesn't latch on to you. He's like a stray dog searching for an agreeable owner. I don't think he has many friends. He was excited by the lunch date. His sister-in-law Megan is a big fan. It's nice to see he has family."

"Yeah, I was surprised Megan showed up. I thought he might not have family. I like how Megan gave us their number. It seemed more natural than me asking for it. I'll call later, mention the noon interview. See if Barry can come." Marti frowned. "Hmm, he probably can't since he just started that job."

Marti stopped at a red light. "For a man of his age, Barry appears younger, like he hasn't done anything with his life. He's unsure of himself."

Marti tapped her fingers on the steering wheel. The light turned green. "When I mentioned the newspaper and the article about the murder, Barry got defensive. Almost as if I'd asked him whether he could read."

"Hmm, that's interesting," Marni agreed. "Barry's the opposite of Megan. She's an avid reader judging by your book sales alone. Hey, your interview, is it tomorrow or the next day? You said I could watch the show. I'll see if Cindy can get part of the day off from day camp. She'd be keen to be in the audience. It might perk her up."

"The *'Interviews at Noon'* show. Can you grab my phone? All the info is in there. Check my calendar, I'm pretty sure it's Friday."

Marni searched through Marti's purse.

"It's in the side pocket."

"Oh, yeah, I see it now. Hmm, you're right, it's Friday, day after tomorrow. You have to be there at 10:00am for make-up and preliminary questions. It says Peggy S. will meet you there. Who's she?"

"She's involved with the *'Families of Sisters in Spirit'*. She arranged the interview then called my publicist to see if I'd join her. When we spoke on the phone Peggy confessed she's terrified to be on TV. She wants me to do most of the talking."

"Well Marti, not everyone's a famous author used to interviews on TV and radio. How many have you done? Do you even keep count?"

Marti shrugged. "Nah, I just go where my publicist sends me. What station is the interview at?"

"CTV News."

"Where's that?"

"They're out on Highway #1, a few minutes east. Do you want me to come with you? I could give you directions."

"Nah, I'll find it. Come closer to noon with Cindy. I have to tape another show when we're done the live interview. If you come with me you'll have to hang around for hours."

"Oh, is that this other note? Remember *'Indigenous Circle'* it says."

"Yeah, CTV News has a weekly show. They asked if I could do *'Indigenous Circle'* after the noon hour show. We'll focus more on the topic of missing and murdered Indigenous women and girls since it's in my upcoming novel. The *'Interviews at Noon'* show is specific to the fundraiser on Saturday."

"Right, gotcha. You'll promote the fundraiser along with Peggy S. first then focus on your novel during the second interview, and that one's taped. Will you talk about your novel in the first interview?"

"Yes, I'll read a scene from the novel. It's about a girl who's missing. Then I'll see where the interview takes me. As long as we promote the fundraiser we're golden."

Marni touched Marti's hand resting on the steering wheel. "I'm proud of you Marti. Not everyone would contribute money towards a non-profit organization like *'Families of Sisters in Spirit.'* You're doing the fundraiser for free, interviews and donating a portion of your upcoming book sales. You rock big sister."

"Thanks Marni. Hey, I bet Megan would jump at the chance to be in the studio audience even if Barry can't come. I'll mention that to Barry when I call."

"Ooh, fantastic idea, I'm sure she'd love to come. Are you going to mention Barry to the detective?"

Marti shuddered. "Are you kidding? He was terrified when he referred to the *'coppers.'* He was nervous and jittery when he watched them at the crime scene."

"Nervous, like guilty?"

"No, I don't think so, maybe," Marti shrugged. "I don't know to be honest."

"Yeah, after meeting him I get it. I don't think he's dangerous. Just in case though, promise you won't be alone with him? I didn't get the sense he's a killer yet he could know something. If he does, you're going to have to tell the detective about him."

"You're right. I'll make sure I've got you or Megan around when I talk to him again. How's that sound?"

"Perfect, he doesn't strike me as a mastermind who can kill two of us at once. On the other hand, Megan is smart. She could be in on the caper."

"Hardy, har, you're funny."

Marti's phone interrupted Marni's retort. As Adele blared from Marti's phone she said, "Can you answer that?"

"Sure. Hello, Marti Rose's phone," Marni chirped.

"Oh, hello Detective I'm Marni, Marti's sister. She's driving right now. I'll put the phone on speaker, just a sec."

"Hi Detective Worthington, Marti here."

"Are you and your sister alone in the car?"

Marti raised her brows as she answered. "Yes."

"There's been another murder. There's something I want you to see. I don't want to get into it on the phone. I'm headed to the crime scene now."

Marti sighed. "Can you give me directions? I'll drop my sister off then meet you there."

When Worthington mentioned the site Marni said it was nearby.

"Why don't I drop you off then come back when you're ready to leave?" Marni suggested. "I want to drop by my friend Gwyn's shop."

"Sure, that works. Which friend is Gwyn? You have so many friends I have trouble figuring who's who."

"Gwyn has the nutrition shop. She specializes in natural vitamins, minerals, herbs, herbal teas and homeopathic remedies. She teaches yoga in the evenings. I've taken her classes, not lately though."

Marti smiled. "Let me guess, you put your heads together and discuss herbs, flowers and those amazing plants of yours. I bet you don't come up for air for hours. I envy your passion for identifying wildflowers and scrounging around the dirt in your herb garden."

Marni laughed. "Don't forget the hours I dedicate to getting those plants indoors before first frost." She shook her head. "Why were our ancestors the first peoples of the coldest country in the world?"

"I don't know. I guess First Nations people never thought to check out warmer climates. Your house has the essence of summer year round though. You've created the brilliance of sun with your flowers and greenery."

"Yeah it keeps me warm even on cloudy, chilly days. I love to gaze at the riot of colours."

"Combined with your dried herbs, those plants and flowers provide a haven for the senses. I could use some of your peppermint tea later to soothe the stress of these nasty murders." Marti shuddered. "Tell me more about your garden. I don't want to think about the murder until I get there."

"Sure Sis, you know back in the days of our ancestors we would have learned about herbs and medicines from our Elders and the local medicine woman. We were fortunate Grandma knew about herbs and wildflowers."

"Yeah, I should have listened to her stories more about the natural elements like you did. I was more into the ancestry and stories about her residential school days. I thought the gardening and herbs were just a chance to muck around in the mud and sniff smelly roots." Marti laughed. "When I watch you though, it's restful and soothing. I could use that some days."

"Let's start with the peppermint tea when we get home. I'll put on music and we can sit in the garden. That's sure to lighten the mood," Marni promised.

"Turn right here, that's it," Marni announced as they pulled up at an auto wrecker's site. "Call when you're done and I'll pick you up. Gwyn's shop is less than ten minutes away."

Marti grabbed her purse, unbuckled her seat belt then slid out of her seat. As Marni passed her on the way to the driver's side they exchanged a quick hug. "Love you. We'll get you relaxed again as soon as you're done," Marni promised.

"Love you too Sis, thanks."

⋏

"It's different than the one we found yesterday," Worthington noted as he met Marti near the entrance. "I know you're part of those groups. This girl turned up on the national missing persons list so that's why I called you."

"Thank you. I appreciate the call." Marti was curious as to how he knew she was involved with groups dedicated to awareness of missing and murdered Indigenous women and their families. She didn't ask though since it wasn't the time.

"The girl was seventeen. She's from a northern community." He shook his head. "So many young ones leave home to head to the city. I wish they'd stay with someone they trust. She's been missing for three months. Her family are headed this direction, they'll be here tomorrow. Glad I didn't have to make that call."

Worthington filled Marti in on what he knew while they wandered to the far side. "I don't know if you want to see the body." He frowned. "She was badly beaten and the bugs have gotten to her. It's not a pretty sight."

Marti shuddered. "I think I'll skip it." She gazed around. "Have there been other bodies dumped here in the past?"

The detective glanced at his notes. "No, it's gated and there are two guard dogs so it's hard to get on the property." His eyes met Marti's. "The dogs were poisoned. One died. When the owner arrived this morning he found the dogs near the entrance to the gate. He rushed them to the vets. While he was there he got suspicious so he came back to check out the yard. That's when he found the body."

"So the body hasn't been here long?"

"No, it was moved here last night. The victim was killed somewhere else. She was left outdoors before they brought her here."

As they approached the crime scene Marti was relieved to see the body covered. She wouldn't glimpse it by mistake. People scurried about as they took pictures, measured or talked in huddled groups. A few flashed a curious glance their direction but most ignored them.

Marti shielded her face with her hand. The sun was hot today. She should have worn a hat. "This seems far back to dump the body. You'd think the killer would have put it closer to the front of the site."

"Yeah, the killer might have hoped it wouldn't be found right away. Guess he doesn't have dogs though. The owner knew something was off right away. People don't poison dogs. This is the first time anyone has harmed them. It was a red flag."

"He didn't bother to put her under any cars. That would have hidden her. Odd he took time to find a spot in the back then just threw her out in the open."

"Yeah, killers aren't known for their smarts."

Marti turned to Worthington. "Do you think I could meet her family tomorrow? I'd like to give them my condolences. I know people they could turn to for support. There are online groups that provide comfort to families in their time of need. People who have faced what this family will."

Worthington shrugged. "I don't know. It's not something we encourage." He glanced at Marti. Something in her face made him add, "I'll see what I can do. Maybe I could introduce you as a consultant. That would explain why you want to meet them."

Marti nodded. "Thank you. I'd appreciate that." She turned her back to the body. "If you find anything that might locate other missing women please contact me. I realize this crime may not be solved before I return home." Marti rummaged in her purse then pulled out a business card.

Worthington winced then took the card she held out to him. "Yes, well, odds are." His voice trailed off.

They talked a few more minutes than Marti called her sister for a ride. It was hot and she longed to sit in the shade of Marni's garden.

⋏

After they'd settled themselves under the shade of the gazebo, Marti shared the scant details she'd learned at the auto wreckers.

Marni poured tea then raised her brows to indicate the large sack by Marti's feet.

"I bought supplies this morning. I need to get everything down on paper. It's part of my process." Marti grinned. "It works when I'm in creative mode, on a writing roll, or have my amateur crime fighter hat on."

"Sounds like this time it's a combination."

"Yeah, sometimes they overlap." Marti sighed. "This one is more personal than usual. I need to distance myself. This should help."

Marti leaned down to remove the items from her carrier bag. She placed them on the table, took a sip of tea then leaned forward to peer at the blank sheet of paper. "The best way to start is to write something down, anything. Once I've marked something on the page, on foolscap, a journal, a new document in my computer or on poster board like this, I feel I've accomplished something. It's not significant but it's a beginning, it has potential."

Marni nodded. She loved to watch her sister create.

Marti grabbed a coloured marker. As she bent over to write she glanced at her sister. "Oh, sorry, is it okay with you if I get started? I want to get it down while it's fresh."

Marni grinned. "I'd never stand in the way of a genius at work. I'll get my book from the house."

As Marti scratched away at her poster boards, Marni got caught up in her book. Neither tracked time until Cindy slammed the back door.

Cindy pecked her mom and auntie on the cheek then collapsed into a chair. "What a day," she griped, "Those kids were insane. Lucky Brian was there to keep me company or I'd go nuts by myself."

Cindy worked at a summer day camp with young children. Without fail when she returned home she grumbled about work and the kids. Everyone knew Cindy loved the children.

Marni marked her place with a bookmark then turned to her daughter. "At times like this Cindy, stress undermines the pleasure we enjoy from activities."

Cindy shrugged. "Yeah, I guess. Did you find anything new today Auntie Marti?"

Marti glanced up from her sheet. "Not really, I've recorded my thoughts so that often helps with clarity." She didn't mention the second victim found as Worthington said the two cases weren't related.

"Can I look at it?" Cindy pointed to the poster board.

Marti stared at her niece then glanced at her sister. "What do you think?"

Marni's eyes widened. What did she think? "Is it specific to the murder or an outline for another story?"

Marti shrugged. "Like we said before, a little of both. To answer your unspoken question though, yes, I think you and Cindy should read it. It's factual and you know most of it already."

Cindy jumped up then bounded over to stand beside her aunt's chair. Marni leaned across the table to peer at the sheet. Long moments passed while they read what Marti had written.

"It could have been me," Cindy gulped. Tears ran down her face as she blurted, "This is so unfair. What did Diane do to anyone? Why would someone murder her?"

"The police will find her murderer," Marti soothed. "They'll interview everyone who knew Diane and figure out what happened. Criminals always make at least one mistake. It might take time but the police will find the inaccuracy. They'll catch the killer."

Marni watched Marti and her daughter. She didn't join in the conversation since she had nothing of value to add. Like Cindy, Marni knew nothing of crime. Marti had spent her life immersed in the subject. It showed as she answered her niece's questions then expertly steered the subject in another direction.

"I should start dinner," Marni announced as she glanced at her watch.

"We'll be right there to help," Marti promised as Marni gathered the mugs and her book to take inside.

"Oh, how was your visit with your friend Gwyn?" Marti asked as Marni turned to go.

"A visit with Gwyn is always interesting. I'll tell you about it inside." Marni's face lit up. "I want you to meet her tomorrow."

At that precise moment, Gwyn was occupied...

CHAPTER 8

Ragged breaths, they came in short, painful bursts. A hand tightened. It squeezed, painful, constricting, too little room in my lungs. I couldn't run anymore. Mental note: add cardio to my routine. How was I this out of shape? What teen couldn't run full speed for a few blocks?

I'd gotten away from those hormone-induced assholes. Now I needed a break. I wished time stood still. All it took was a moment, a crack in the flow, a mere brief instant to achieve avoidance. The other option totally sucked. I couldn't surrender to further humiliation, captured by two morons. I'd rather die…

With a nervous glance over my shoulder I spied their vehicle headed toward the railroad cars. They were slow, careful to navigate bumpy ruts and uneven grass. Certainty and dread dogged me. In a moment they'd turn to head back my way.

I anticipated their relaxed movement as they tracked my unsteady progress. I felt their awareness, giddiness, confident of the ability to overtake me when the mood struck. They weren't in a hurry. This cat and mouse game would carry this chilling diversion to a new level. They were in charge. I was at their mercy, powerless to escape their clutches.

I had to outsmart them. I couldn't outrun a car. I had to make it to the houses off in the distance. At least a block away, the illusion was unreachable.

I paused near the fence, my chest heaved. One precious moment, time to rest before they rounded the corner. I held my hand out. Detachment replaced surprise when I noted no shakes. My hands were steady. I'd gone beyond fear to a place you went when you'd been frightened nearly to death. Was this stage preferable?

I shrugged. They were heartless. I had no illusion when their car caught me I'd be trapped in their headlights. Like a deer disoriented by the suddenness of the oncoming instrument of death I'd be poised to run yet powerless to move.

I tried to convince myself they were only silly boys out for fun, harmless really, not intent on bodily damage. That was the only way to look at it. The sinister side was too unrealistic, too fantastic to consider. I couldn't go there. Their approach was imminent. Almost time for that final burst of energy. I gathered my resources, ready to spring into action.

When they rounded the corner I madly dashed into the middle of the field towards the safety of houses. I screamed like a banshee. Had I been an actress the part of a hysterical female would have been mine. Wouldn't they expect me to be frightened and panic-stricken? I'd act the part. If I lulled them into complacency an opportunity could open up.

They failed to disappoint, roared up behind me, revved their engine and yelled out their windows. I didn't expect to be hit but they came damn close, too close for comfort. I zigzagged while they hounded me. I was near enough to hear coarse suggestions, lewd promises of what they'd do when they caught me.

Fat chance, I'd rather die…

Amazing how your mind works, to welcome death over what they suggested. Now that I've reached this state I'm sure the alternative wasn't worse. This one is final, irreversible. People don't realize what the end means, until it's too late. I never understood...

I hate melodrama but this is my moment to shine, so to speak. How often does one get a captive audience at this stage? Whoever you are, thanks...

Gwyn longed to answer yet the voice needed no prompting. The girl continued while Gwyn listened, eager to project empathy through her thoughts.

So where was I in my little tale? Oh yeah, I remember. After what seemed like forever but was only a matter of moments I emerged onto the street, houses in throwing distance now. They were within reach. I searched for one with trees or bushes bordering it then bee-lined toward them. With a sudden burst of energy, propelled by the likelihood of escape, I lunged forward.

It caught them off guard. They hadn't anticipated I'd have enough oomph to carry me forward and across the street. Short of hitting me they had no recourse but to let me get away. If they'd had one brain between them they would have jumped out of the car to pursue me on foot. Fortunately they were dumber than stumps, unable to think that far in advance.

I gave them the finger then dived into the bushes. They cursed me from the car while I laughed at their stupidity. Heady from the thought of renewed freedom I turned then negotiated my way between houses.

Ever cautious, I peered over my shoulder then crossed the street. I'd traveled a few blocks without sign of pursuit. I let my breath out slow aware of the need to act normal.

I saw Murray's house ahead, lit up like a Christmas tree. He had no guilt about turning on every light whether he went into a room or not. He was the electric company's idea of the perfect tenant. Music blared as I approached. Murray enjoyed noise, the louder the better. He liked everyone in the area to know about his good time. Not exactly a favourite in the neighbourhood...

I entered the back door. No one noticed me. There were only three guys. I would have guessed from the racket Murray had a houseful of guests.

I longed for the solitude of my bedroom. Only a few minutes more I told myself. Another illusion!

Now that'll never happen. If only I'd been nicer to mom and dad. I won't see them again until they die and come here. Why, why did this happen to me? What did I do to deserve this?

Gwyn heard sniffling noises. Intent, she listened, quiet while she meditated in an altered state. The voice came back, muffled, in pain…

They played caps in the living room, drunk and stoned as usual. Great, it'd take time and persuasion to get a ride home. Maybe I should suggest a walk to my house. Not that any of them were capable of that either but it was worth a try.

"So ya decided to come didjya?" Murray slurred, catching sight of me in the doorway.

Hunched over, Mark and Don grinned stupidly in my direction, beyond recognition. They didn't remember me most days since they were dumber than dumb.

"Yeah, thought I'd drop by and see how everything was going."

Cautious, I perched on the edge of the couch.

"What took ya so long?" Murray took a swig of beer then delivered a loud belch.

His friends hooted, snorted then giggled.

I forced myself not to sigh or shake my head. It was useless to annoy them. I needed someone to get me home. Those two creeps could be lurking outside. I glanced around the room, took my time to answer.

The place was a pigsty. Food, beer bottles, dirty dishes and clothing littered the floor. I'd never seen the place cleaned up. This was the way Murray lived. As

I glanced in his direction I wondered why I went out with him. Why give him the time of day when it seemed an effort? Why bother?

Then he smiled. Murray's face lit up as he focused on me. It must have been an effort considering the shape he was in. I knew why I put up with it, why I hung around.

Murray made me feel special. A glance was all I needed. Elevated, enriched by the experience, the knowledge he cared was what mattered. That was enough. It was always enough…

I smiled at him then said, "I got here as fast as I could."

No need for sordid details. Murray likely wouldn't care enough to do anything about it when he was in the middle of a game. On the other hand, he might have gotten pissed at the two jerks then roared off to look for them. That would have been worse than indifference. Drunken righteousness wasn't something I craved.

Then again, things might have turned out different if I'd told him…

I sat back quiet, until they finished the round. Every once in a while, Don muttered something, voice slurred. Loud music drowned him out. That was okay since Don didn't make sense the best of times.

With a casual glance at my watch I noted it was past 1:30am. I hoped my mom wouldn't be up again. She'd blow a gasket when I walked in late. I hated her scenes. She'd yell, threaten then harp about danger, partying and the unknowns out there in the wee hours of the morning.

Mom had no concept of the trouble I'd managed to get into. Early or late in the evening, it didn't matter. I'd had close calls in the middle of the afternoon. Time was irrelevant when you got caught up in the moment.

Mom didn't have a clue what it was like out there in the big bad world. Lucky, or she'd have locked me up when I hit my teen years. She was so out of touch I didn't know where to start. Her reality was far from the truth. No need to clue her in. Ignorance was bliss.

Now I'd give anything to see her. I'd let her yell all she wanted. She could keep me locked in chains if the mood struck her. She was right… it is dangerous out there. My mom was right and I was wrong. I couldn't take care of myself. I wasn't as smart or worldly as I thought.

Look what happened…I'm dead, wandering around. I'm stuck. I don't know where this is. Why am I here? I feel close to everyone. I can almost touch them. I reach my fingers out to grasp those I love or whisper their name. They don't hear or feel me though. What's the point of that?

This isn't what I thought heaven or hell would be like. Where are the other spirits? Why am I alone? Aimless, I've wandered for days. Shouldn't someone show me the ropes? Why am I here? What's wrong with me?

Gwyn heard sobs, heart wrenching, grief stricken moans, weeping. She longed to reach out, comfort the voice. Without warning the cries faded away…

"I want to help," Gwyn called. "I can't show you the ropes but maybe I can help guide you or something…"

More sobs then the voice.

"Hey, who's there? What's that noise?"

"I'm here," Gwyn shouted.

"Jeesh, what's with the moaning? You sound worse than me. Is this where everyone hangs out? Hey, maybe I'm not alone…"

"Aieeee, aieeee, huh, huh, aieeee."

"Whoa, you're wrecked. The rocking back and forth, hunched shoulders, moans. You're in rough shape. Hey there, dead girl, I'm here, in front of you. Open your eyes."

Startled, Gwyn raised her head. The voice wasn't talking to her. There was someone else, another dead girl.

"Yeah, dead girl, over here, wow is your skin blotchy. How long have you been crying?"

"Aieeee, aieeee."

"Okay, okay, enough with the chanting and gnashing of teeth. You have blood on your lips. Did you bite them? Come on, I understand the need to thrash about and the flow of tears. I can handle moans and groans but can you cut out the screams? My ears hurt. Cut it out."

Gwyn heard more sobs followed by a scurrying noise.

"Hiding, yeah that's real mature. Hey, you, dead girl, I can see you. That little bush isn't big enough to cover you. Come on, talk to me. Who knows, maybe you'll feel better."

Gwyn heard a loud sigh.

"I'm close to the bush. I'll sit here, nearby. La, la, la. I'm not much of a singer more of a talker. Seems we're the only ones here. Might as well get to know one another."

Gwyn heard loud gulps, labored breathing, a few moans followed by sniffles.

"That's better, yeah, you can get it under control. Take a moment, we've got time, hah, like all the time in the world."

The crying was quieter now, subdued.

"Why don't I tell my story first? Then you can tell yours, you know how you came here. How you died or got killed or..."

"Aieeee, aieeee, huh, huh, aieeee."

"Whoa, calm down, no need to scream. Remember the ears, you're too loud. Come on now, you gotta know you're dead. Don't tell me it's a surprise. Hmm, yeah, okay, so I guess it is."

The sobs started up again.

"Man, you're not the best company you know. You're worse than my sister. I thought she was a crybaby. Now I'll never see her again."

Gwyn imagined the girl's red-rimmed eyes as they filled with tears.

"How old is she, your sister?"

Gwyn heard more sobs then they quieted down to sniffles.

"Hey, great, a question, yeah, my sister is thirteen. She's a pain in the ass. Was, no I guess is, she's not dead. I am."

There was an indrawn breath.

"Okay, let's get past this. How about you? Any sisters or brothers?"

Great heart-wrenching sobs were the answer. The voice sighed.

"Gee, who would have thought, more tears. So, how about introductions? I'm... Diane."

Gwyn's eyes flew open. Disoriented, her gaze flitted around the room. It was Diane, she was the voice; the dead girl had identified herself as Diane.

"Diane, are you there?" Gwyn shouted.

Her voice echoed then the room became tranquil again. Gwyn was alone, in the shop, seated in her regular meditation spot. In her wooden chair, back against the wall, light subdued. Gwyn fingered the cotton of her white robe.

Diane, the girl murdered, the one Marni had mentioned hours earlier, had come here, to communicate with Gwyn.

Why? What did Diane want? Who was the girl with her?

CHAPTER 9

As he walked to the house Detective Worthington thought how life could throw you a curve ball hard. He imagined the distress on Stacey's face. His job was to hassle her, make Stacey dredge up painful conversations, while he hoped for that glimmer. Anything to help find Diane's killer.

Worthington sighed, squared his shoulders then rang the doorbell.

He watched Stacey open the door, momentarily taken aback at her pallor. Pain and shock had taken a toll. Dark circles highlighted the fairness of her skin. In spite of the summer, Stacey was pale, pasty white, like a ghost who never went out in the sun.

The detective was unaware Stacey never tanned. Her skin burnt bright red or got pink as a lobster. It was Diane who had adored the sun.

"Is your mom home Stacey?"

She gave a dull, half-hearted nod.

"Could I come in and talk to you?"

She held the door wide open.

"Could you tell your mom I'm here?"

Stacey returned with her mom who appeared years younger than the teen.

This tragedy, nightmarish to Stacey had to be brought to a close. Once the killer was found it would help ease her pain. With luck Stacey could go back to being a teen again.

As he stared at her, Worthington knew Stacey might never fully recover from this. He stifled his sigh then said, "I'd like to ask Stacey about that night."

"Sure if you think it will help. Is it okay if I go back to my painting?" She indicated the hall behind her.

"Of course, if Stacey doesn't mind."

Stacey had moved to a spot by the window. Shoulders slumped, head flopped forward, body propped up by the wall Stacey stared out at a little boy who played with a ball.

"I'm sure she'll be fine."

Raising her voice she addressed her daughter. "Stacey, I'll be right down the hall painting, okay."

With a jerk, Stacey was back. Eyes unfocused she stared past them. "Yeah, yeah, sure," she mumbled.

Worthington closed his eyes. It was hard to imagine Stacey would be fine like her mother thought. His eyes flashed open. Best to get down to business, his job was to deal with this in a dispassionate, professional manner.

He should have brought Marti. It might have made things easier for Stacey. Too late now, he was already here.

"I'm sorry to take you back to that night Stacey but you might remember something important. Talking could trigger a memory."

"It doesn't matter, that's all I think about anyway."

Red-rimmed eyes flashed toward him. Then her attention skittered somewhere else, where only she could see. Grief etched spider lines around her eyes and forehead. Her voice shook.

"If only I hadn't made Diane get into that car with those guys. How could I know Diane's premonition meant death? Who would do that to her? Was it those guys from Estevan?"

Worthington shook his head. No need to keep it from her, they'd been released.

"What about the people we talked to earlier that night at the exhibition, was one of them tied to the murder? Do you think that's possible? Most were our friends. Could they have murdered Diane?"

He let Stacey ramble. She didn't wait for answers, hodgepodge, her words were jumbled.

Stacey shook her head. Her mind felt fuzzy like she'd stumbled into a vat of cotton. Entering through her eardrums it voided rational thought. She felt encased, useless and dried up like a tiny ball of fluff. With a dazed and distracted air, her words formed the basis of a story.

"The moon that night was some big deal to Diane. Man she was moody. She got freaked out when clouds covered the moon. She was jittery, not herself. Premonitions, superstitions, I don't know. How could Diane know she was going to die? It's too freaky to think about."

Stacey crossed her arms. She pursed her lips then leaned down to rifle through her purse. Triumphant, she dug out lip balm then applied it to cracked, chapped lips.

"We didn't meet any strange people at the exhibition. Yeah okay, some of them are weird but they're not killers. Diane talked to Murray, her current boyfriend, about an hour before we left. I don't know what Diane sees in Murray. He's older than us, you know. That's alright but he's not very bright and Diane, well she's destined for great things, was…"

Stacey stifled a sob.

"Murray's a loser. He does drugs and is drunk more than sober. I think he works at Sears in the warehouse. He drifts from one job to the next."

"That's good, you never mentioned Murray when we talked before."

"I didn't, hmm."

"Can you describe him for me?"

"Sure, uh, Murray's good looking, hazel eyes, dark hair. He's tall, I mean real tall. You have to hold your head back when you talk to him." Stacey angled her head back. "He's like this giant that stretches up to the sky." She tried to smile. It faltered as her lips wobbled then skittered back to a frown. "He held Diane in the crook of his arm. He'd lean her backwards when they talked so they'd gaze into each other's eyes. It was dreamy watching them."

Stacey sighed then shook her head, brow puckered.

"I'm not sure what they talked about that night, usual stuff I guess. Now that I think about it I heard Murray say they'd get together later. I don't know if he meant the next day or that night. Diane never mentioned she'd see him again but she'd been in a hurry. That was because she wanted to catch that damn bus we missed.

If only we'd caught that bus." Stacey stuffed her hand in her mouth then turned away.

When she turned back, face tear-stained she whispered, "Diane would be alive if we'd caught that bus. Or, I should have waited for her to call a taxi. She'd be here, right now. I didn't want to wait though. I watched that bus go by and thought, 'So what, we missed the stupid bus.' She's dead. My best friend is dead. Who would have thought missing a bus or not getting a taxi could mean death… that's so, that's so…" Tears rolled unchecked down Stacey's cheeks as her voice trailed off.

Worthington watched her stare dully outside. Had she lost her train of thought? He put his hand out to touch her arm but jerked it back when Stacey's shaky voice resumed her story. She reminded him of a sleepwalker going through the paces, oblivious to those around her.

"Murray was with his two loser friends. They'd done drugs and would do an all-nighter. Murray bragged about the beer they'd drunk. They were anxious to get home to drink more."

She shook her head then sighed. Her head leaned forward as if too heavy on her neck.

"Why do we hang out with guys like that? What a waste. Then again what's our alternative? None of the guys we know are in the keeper category. Except for Brad of course, he's different."

Stacey talked aloud yet not directly to him. Worthington felt intrusive but wasn't keen to stop her rambling. Better for her to talk he reassured himself, healthier to get it out instead of bottling it up inside.

"I wonder if Diane still liked Brad? There'd been a spark between those two, something that might have lasted." She groaned.

"What a shame. He was at the exhibition Sunday night with his latest trophy hanging on his arm. I went to get a drink and saw Diane and Brad chatting together. His latest airhead talked to a group of friends while Diane and Brad were intense, heads bent close. Maybe they made arrangements to meet later? I hope they saw each other again before she died. They were soul mates. What do you think?"

She didn't wait for an answer, just rambled.

"Brad's normal compared to other guys we know. He's okay, blonde with blue eyes and a quick grin. Not my type but Diane went out with him earlier in the year. He's into poetry and uses different words when he talks, not like a teen. He's not much of a partier either. Girls surround him even though he doesn't flirt. Diane liked his sense of humour. She said he listened when she talked. Sensitive to her needs was how Diane put it."

He asked for Murray and Brad's last names then wrote them down for reference. She resumed her story before he'd laid the pen down.

"We talked to Terri and Sky that night too. They couldn't have had anything to do with Diane's death. It's not as if other girls kill each other for no reason. We're not best friends but we hung out and got along most of the time. As well as teen girls get along."

A brief fleeting smile crossed Stacey's face.

"What about Tony? He's stranger than strange. He's drunk or stoned most of the time so the idea of him planning a murder is far-fetched. Maybe it was an accident though. Was this pre-planned?"

Worthington ignored her question. "Who's Tony?"

"Oh nobody, just a guy we know. He's uncoordinated and unorganized, scattered I guess. It wasn't an accident was it?"

He shook his head.

She hung her head, gave a heavy sigh. "Huh, I didn't think so. How do you accidentally murder someone out near the railroad tracks? Have you figured out how Diane got there?"

Worthington casually picked up his pen then wrote Tony with a question mark beside his name.

"Wait, I just thought of something." Stacey slammed her hand against her forehead. Her eyes widened as if jarred by the sudden impact.

"Murray lives nearby, a few blocks from where she was found. What if he had something to do with her death?"

He gazed steadily at Stacey, noting her eyes were crystal clear now. It was a lead Worthington couldn't ignore…

⬥

While Stacey talked to Detective Worthington one of the suspects was busy knocking back beers in a bar with friends.

One look at his blurry-eyes was enough to convince people he'd been on a bender again. They were wrong this time, driving had reddened his eyes. Unkempt, gritty, unshaven, clothes wrinkled, he emitted a manly yet unclean odor.

They'd driven for two days, were headed south toward Mexico. They'd decided it was best to lie low, til trouble died down. Then they'd head back home.

The drive through the States had been sweet. None of them had ever been that way so they'd been interested in everything. They'd taken a back road in the early twilight hours to avoid the border crossing. No passports, no trace of them, an acquaintance knew where they should cross.

Bars were different than in Canada. There were special names for drinks. Yesterday he'd ordered rye and coke and gotten a puzzled frown. Then Mark offered up Canadian Club and the waitress nodded then walked off. Had to mention the brand name here, now that was a bit of trivia his brother Pete would be interested in. He had to remember to tell Pete when they headed back. Whenever that was. This was one fine mess they'd gotten into this time.

Murray sighed then made an effort to listen to Mark and Don's conversation. Oh yeah, same as usual, how to pick up women. They eyed up girls sitting at the bar, arguing about whether or not to wander over and offer up lively convo.

Murray didn't care what they did. It was all the same to him. One girl was identical to the next now. He should swear off women, they were trouble sure as hell, didn't take a genius to figure that one out. Take the two he'd gotten involved with back home, talk about a nuisance.

He shook his head. Well, one was a nuisance. The other one had turned up dead. This stuff depressed him. No wonder he drank.

Idly Murray took another swig of beer. He glanced in the direction of the bar. One of the trio nearby caught his eye in the mirror. She gave a slow nod. Murray took it as an invitation, stood then wandered over to sit beside her. His two buddies joined the group. He'd made the decision as per usual. What else was new?

If he'd known the police considered getting a search warrant for his house Murray would have been nervous, anticipating the worst. As it was he tossed beer back, relaxed as he began to sweet talk the girls.

Murray had always been a favourite with women, even when he was in a sorry state. There was no accounting for taste…

CHAPTER 10

"Brad, I know it hurts. If you talk about it you'll feel better. I'm here for you," his mom said.

Brad, Diane's one true love, the guy she'd dug for years then managed to hold onto for mere months was taking her death badly.

"When we read about it in the paper I thought it was a teen who got in trouble with crazy guys. When Stacey called I couldn't believe it was Diane. It can't be true. It's like something from a TV show or a book. It's too out there. This doesn't happen in real life."

"I know honey, I know."

"How am I going to get through the funeral without breaking down? It's tomorrow. Everyone will think I'm a sentimental fool. Why did I break off with her?"

Eyes wild, Brad appealed to his mom.

She nodded, arm firm around him.

"Diane was someone special, you know one of those people you meet once in a lifetime. I thought we'd get back together. We'd settle down. Who knew what might happen? It could have been a forever thing. Now there's no future, no hope. I'm like a boat adrift at sea, floundering. Does that make sense?"

"Yes honey, it makes perfect sense."

"That article they wrote. It was brutal. They made Diane sound like a loser. They implied even though drugs and alcohol hadn't been involved that night, Diane was often drunk or stoned like she absorbed it through her skin. It bugged me. She wasn't like that. She was pure, believed in God, talked about spirituality, liked nature and animals, and…"

He trailed off, at a loss to describe what Diane had been to him. How could he make others understand?

"I know Brad, people who knew Diane would never think that. They'll remember the good things, the fine qualities you saw, the real Diane."

Brad met his mother's eyes, anxious to believe her.

"Do you think? I don't know. It seems people don't care what she was like. It's easier to assume Diane was a troubled teen, no good, better off dead than growing up to be a burden on society. The article mentioned she was Cree, implied she wouldn't live long no matter what. How could people be so mean and wrong about her pure heart?"

He raised a tear stained face to his mother, begging her to make it right somehow, to soothe his troubled soul.

"Well honey, culture is a topic people don't always agree on. It's easier to ignore the goodness in individuals and broad stroke with a brush. Labels are often used for this or that type of person based on colour, race or creed."

"Diane was a rare flower. She had drive, ambition, was excited about everything. Like little things, you know I watched her follow insects around to see what type of flower they chose to land on. How many people care about that?

She had this ability to see deep inside you. She'd share her innermost thoughts, search within you for that special mystery. When I was around Diane I felt we'd reached this heightened level of understanding. There were no masks or deception. Our emotions were exposed not covered up and hidden away. She wasn't a normal teen, jaded, uncaring."

Brad sighed. "Diane cut through all the crap. She was gentle, sensitive, kind and genuine, she had amazing qualities. Now she's gone, snuffed out, she was an angel taken from us. I want her here now."

"I know honey."

"You know what I crave?"

"What?"

"Her spirituality. Diane would know how to get through this. She told me about her spirit ancestors, the importance of respecting one's Elders and the bond of kinship. At a stressful time like this Diane's relatives will flock to the family's side to provide support and reassurance. I wish I could be part of that.

Diane's beliefs were sound, grounded in the certainty everything would work out for the best." Tears poured down Brad's face. "It didn't though, nothing worked out the way Diane thought it would. She's dead, taken from us before she had a chance to live her life to the fullest. Why, why her?"

Brad put his head in his arms as he wept.

His heart had been broken. His mother stroked his hair as she hoped support and love would heal him.

Wednesday Evening

While Brad poured his heart out, Stacey and Tony joined a crowd of schoolmates who pretended to mourn Diane. Tony, one of Diane's true friends had talked Stacey into joining him, to witness the social event held in Diane's honour.

Stacey stared at Tony as he poured himself a drink then headed over to the gang in the back yard. She'd just arrived and felt disassociated from those around her. Most of the crowd had partied throughout the day, conducting their own private wake for Diane was how they'd put it. In reality, it was another excuse for enjoyment as they drank, popped pills or smoked up, whatever it took to forget.

Stacey watched Tony approach a crowd of people. Short and wiry, constantly on the move, Tony liked to be surrounded by others. He hated to be alone. Stacey thought of him as a social animal. He craved the company of others to ease his own feelings of helplessness, fear and loathing.

A friendly guy, there were times when Tony would fling off in a bizarre direction less in tune with those around him. Then he'd become unapproachable and depressed. Diane and Stacey were used to his weird behaviour but didn't like it any more than those that ridiculed him.

The peculiarity of Tony's temperament made others wary of him. Diane hadn't minded him though so Stacey got to know Tony more than she cared to admit. Stacey knew how important it was to conform. Tony was different and classmates treated him with distrust and suspicion. He was regarded as strange. Tony's frequent outbursts and inability to behave how his peers expected kept him on the fringe of their group, not on the outs yet never one of the chosen few.

Today, Stacey was thankful for Tony's quirks. Since she'd latched onto Tony everyone brushed them with the same paint stroke. It meant she could wander around, think private thoughts and not get caught up in awkward conversations about Diane.

Rather than dwell on the death of her best friend, Stacey focused on Tony. He laughed and joked with classmates. Complicated, Tony didn't fit any set mold. He was charming though and the kids accepted him in limited doses.

Today, Tony was part of the group as they mourned the death of a classmate. Stacey watched him work the crowd as he paused to listen to a story, joined in, or delighted others with his own account of facts. They knew Tony had been chummy with Diane, not as close as Stacey though. They'd given her a wide berth sensing she didn't want to talk to them. They knew better than to approach her.

Tony knew Diane's likes and dislikes, had been privy to her secrets. This made him a minor celebrity at the party. Teens were enthralled by the gossip he repeated, the suppositions, list of suspects, outlandish ideas he concocted. Tony was in fine form. He rose to the occasion and didn't disappoint his audience.

Eventually Tony wore down, like a Duracell bunny on its last leg. Stacey glanced at him as he plopped down beside her. Like a dam burst from its barricade his words tumbled out.

"I've been trying not to think about Diane too much."

Stacey nodded. She understood.

"It hurts. I don't like the way I feel. I can't get her out of my head. I mean the last time I saw her."

Stacey jerked her head, wiped a tear away, but Tony didn't notice. Too caught up in his own thoughts Tony missed Stacey's silent misery.

"I saw it, was conscious of it, the fear I mean. I saw it in her eyes. She was unwilling to admit something bad was going down. Diane knew it was inevitable. I can't get past it. Diane grasped what was coming. I almost recognized it. If only I'd known it for what it was…"

Stacey stared at Tony as he trailed off. She wanted him to shut up yet part of her wanted him to continue, painful though it was.

"Diane sensed it. She recognized the evil and hatred. She knew she'd get caught up in the web of deceit as it spun out of control. She couldn't stop it, the spinning, spinning…"

Stacey stared at him, open-mouthed.

What did Tony mean? Did he know who the killer was? Did he know what happened? Her throat closed up. Stacey couldn't get the words out to pose the questions.

Tony muttered, more to himself than her.

"We had that in common you know. Well, that, and more."

"*What, what did you have in common?*" Stacey wanted to shout but the words were stuck in her throat.

"Diane was uncanny in her ability to identify the bullshit. Diane saw through me you know. She had clarity and understood us all. She accepted me for who I am." Tony paused, held his hand out toward something only he could see. "Diane knew me. Realized what I'm capable of. The depths of depravity, absence of morality, indecent acts, none of those mattered to her. Diane was a true friend. Now I have to figure out what to do on my own. I need a plan."

As Tony whispered his last words, Stacey leaned forward to hear them. Dumbstruck by his comments Stacey pondered what he meant. What plan? What did he mean, Diane realized what he was capable of? It sounded sinister and final when Tony said it. It reminded her of something the killer said in those old, hokey movies her parents watched. If this was a movie the music would go *'du, du, du, dum'* and the picture would fade out.

Wild-eyed Stacey's gaze darted around the yard. She half expected a camera crew at her elbow. Were they part of a new reality show?

Had Tony been involved in Diane's death? Did he know something?

Stacey's troubled stare landed back on Tony. As she studied him she realized she couldn't voice her doubts aloud. The words were stuck in her throat.

They sat in silence, spectators to the nearby partiers, alone with their troubled thoughts.

"*No, no, stay away,*" floated by on the breeze.

Tony turned to Stacey.

"Did you hear that?"

"Um, what?" Stacey whispered. She brushed a lock of hair away then sat on her hands to stop them from trembling.

"You did, didn't you?"

They watched trees sway dizzily, rocked by a sudden breeze.

"Yeah," she admitted, reluctant.

They were quiet, not sure what to expect.

Stacey broke the uncomfortable silence. "Do you think it was her?"

Tony raised his chin. "Yeah." His voice got firmer. "It had to be. It was her voice."

"But, how...?" Stacey trailed off, unsure of her next words.

They sat there for a long time, quiet, waiting.

Stacey wanted to talk about what they thought they'd heard. She didn't know how to form the words though. It must have been wishful thinking. Trees rustling could sound like a voice. That was it.

Stacey focused on Tony's earlier words.

Could he be the...? No, it was impossible.

Did he know who had...? No, how could he?

After awhile, Tony got bored, or restless, Stacey didn't know. She watched him wander off then got up to follow at a safe distance.

Terri and Sky, two classmates, talked in low voices in a quiet corner of the yard. The topic was Diane's murder. In hushed tones, with abundant theories and healthy speculation they discussed what might have happened.

"Do you think she knew the guys who murdered her?" Sky wondered. "I mean how gross to be with someone than find out when it's too late they're this barbarian who likes to butcher people."

"Yeah like what if there's a serial killer in town? Would they mention it in the paper?"

Terri loved farfetched ideas. She had a tendency to take things past the limit of reality. She had already managed to stir the group of teens into a fear-crazed frenzy. Theories became more fantastic by the moment. None of it based on fact.

The two girls eyed the guys with suspicion, ready to distrust anyone with the slightest provocation. The booze and drugs didn't help. It contributed to their heightened sense of fantasy. Sucked into a vortex of cynicism and doubt they were ready to pounce on anyone who struck their fancy.

Tony wandered in their direction at the peak of their distortion. Hands in pockets Tony sauntered over to see if the girls needed more drinks. His timing couldn't have been worse. Terri and Sky verbally attacked Tony, mistaking his good intentions for a confession of guilt.

How they arrived at their conclusion was never determined. Their misguided accusations overruled Tony's vigorous objections they were wrong. The loud, forceful claims Terri and Sky suggested were reminiscent of Salem witch-hunts of long ago. Hysteria, panic and scathing accusations have been the basis of dark periods in history. Reminiscent of people burned at the stake for unproven acts, the girls' ridiculous comments became reality in the eyes of the partygoers.

The seed was sown. Tony's life took a decided downturn at the party. In the eyes of his peers he became a suspect in Diane's murder.

Stacey was silent as she listened to Tony's denial. Fear and distrust clouded her tear stained eyes. Moments earlier she'd questioned his innocence. Was it possible he'd had something to do with Diane's death?

Tony turned from the girls, angry.

Stacey caught his glare and shuddered.

Tony's face was that of a stranger, distorted. Stacey imagined evil oozed from his pores. Questions raced through her mind. Why did Tony's expression mirror rage and fury? How well did she know Tony?

The evening ended with an eerie reminder. Stacey stilled as she heard, "*No, no, stay away,*" float by on the breeze once more.

CHAPTER 11

THURSDAY

"She escaped from two sinister teen boys with raging hormones to a place she felt safe. The guys she turned to were coarse and drunk. I sensed her helplessness. They didn't sound like the type of people one would turn to in a time of need. I'm not sure how this ties in with her death though."

"You're sure it was Diane you dreamt or communicated with?" Marti confirmed.

Gwyn met Marti's stare.

"After Marni left yesterday I meditated. It's part of my routine. A girl entered my thoughts. I heard her voice. I thought she addressed me but when I answered she left. She said her name was Diane. I don't think it was a dream but I'm not sure since this hasn't happened to me before."

"She didn't tell you who the killer was?"

"No, it was clear these were events before her death. What time did Diane die?"

"The coroner placed her death at 2:30am."

"This was 1:30am. She thought her mother would be waiting up since it was past curfew."

They stared at one another.

Gwyn, Marti and Marni had systematically outlined the series of events. Marni took notes as Marti pumped Gwyn for information. Gwyn had experienced something, a dream or connection with Diane. Suspended in time, she'd heard the voice of a dead person. Diane had shared her story, the events that transpired before her death.

If only Gwyn had gotten more…

They still didn't know what happened that last hour.

"Diane was vulnerable, genuinely afraid. She was anxious and terrified as she ran from those boys then depressed as she realized she'd never see her family again. She was heartbroken. I felt her despair, it was real."

Gwyn ran her hands through her hair.

"Do you think Diane gave me information so I could pass it on to you? She must know Marni and I are friends. She must have sensed Marni would bring you here today. What if something Diane said has direct bearing on the case?"

Marti glanced outside the front window of Gwyn's shop. Geraniums stood in pots outside the door, lining the front border of grass. Hanging wisteria and ivy draped from the windowsill. The effect was pleasing, homey and inviting.

Marti tore her gaze from the colourful array outdoors. Her wandering eyes idly roamed the interior of the room. Marti didn't want to discuss the case, to tie the events to a spirit. Reluctant to answer Gwyn's question she inhaled the exhilarating aroma of the shop.

Nutritional packs, vitamins, herbs, healing candles and specialty teas created an aura of harmony and wellbeing. As she took a deep breath, Marti absorbed the overall effect. While she tuned in to the serene music she silently acknowledged her sister's assurance Gwyn's shop would imprint upon her senses.

Hesitant to admit anything as of yet Marti fixed her gaze upon Gwyn. Curled up in her wicker chair, Gwyn embraced her surroundings as she relaxed against the plush cushions. Her expression dreamy, she reminded Marti of a cat lapping up rays of sunshine. Her teacup sat forgotten on the table while a moccasin encased toe tapped in time to melodious sounds of a flute.

Enormous blue eyes tinged with violet stared into Marti's forcing her to focus on the direction of their conversation. She felt trapped, compelled to answer Gwyn.

Marti's gaze slid from Gwyn to contemplate her sister instead. Caught up on her notes, Marni's chin rested on her hand as she stared at a display case. Marti longed to postpone the moment when she had to answer Gwyn.

Was it possible Diane could help with the case? What message had she sent? Could Diane communicate with Gwyn from whatever place she'd been transferred to? Marti was hesitant to agree with Gwyn's assumptions since they seemed '*way out there.*' Marti knew Marni believed in spirits though. She had always been in tune to otherworldly activities while Marti preferred order and logic based reasoning.

Marti sighed. Her sister had brought her to Gwyn for a reason. Her instincts had been on the mark as someone had conveyed information to Gwyn about the murder. There was a slim chance Diane was out there, eager to help. Marti couldn't ignore the possibility.

"Yes, I have to admit Diane could tell us something. I don't know how you converse with spirits but we'll need to figure out what her message is. If we continue to transcribe notes based on your, hmm, what was it exactly?"

Marti wasn't sure how to address what Gwyn experienced. She didn't want to alienate Marni and Gwyn or belittle something they passionately believed in.

As if sensing her sister's unease, Marni jumped in to rescue her. "Gwyn were you in a trance-like state, awake or asleep? Can we interpret what she told you like a dream?"

Marti flashed her sister a grateful smile.

Marni grinned back then launched into one of her favourite topics. "Dream interpretation is one of the building blocks that forms the foundation of our friendship." She nodded toward Gwyn. "We've discussed the importance of dreams, they form the basis of who we are."

Marni moved her hand from her chin to make a sweeping motion. "Dreams may imply something indirect. Theorists have written how dreams express current anxieties and misgivings. Was it that kind of dream?"

Marni answered her own question. "I find that unlikely since you have nothing to do with the case. You're not anxious about it. Dreams can afford crucial insights about oneself or other people. If that's the case there could be something relevant to Diane in the dream, a clue perhaps as you've suspected."

Marti turned to Gwyn. "Was this a dream?" She tapped her fingers on the chair, impatient to hear the answer.

"Yes, it was like a dream but more than that. It was outward channeling."

"What's that?" Marti asked as her gaze darted toward her sister again. Marni nodded at Gwyn.

Marti frowned. At times, her sister was an enigma to her, eccentric and unconventional.

Marni possessed a strong belief in spirituality and reincarnation. Harmony and the inner self formed the basis of her identity. Mysticism was one of Marni's passions, she read everything about the subject she could get her hands on with enthusiasm bordering on obsession. Marti suspected her sister dabbled in Wicca. She'd done research on Wicca for one of her books and knew it was a lifestyle alternative. Marti made a mental note to ask her sister about it later.

"Outward channeling is control of the mind. You clear all thoughts then allow your mind to drift. One needs to reach a state of serenity, open to a vision." Gwyn's smile was fleeting. "It's similar to meditation yet more. One might sense images, see a white flash of light at the edge of your vision or experience a free floating consciousness."

"Have you ever felt or sensed someone like this before?"

Gwyn stared at Marti.

"No, I haven't communicated with someone like Diane before, but yes, I've connected with a spirit."

Marti tore her eyes from Gwyn unsure if she liked the direction the conversation had taken.

"What sort of spirit?" she whispered.

"A guide. Someone you maintain contact with daily, like a presence to assist in communication. As one becomes skilled, with daily practice one becomes aware of spirits while in a relaxed state. After a while I noticed one particular presence visited me repeatedly. That was my guide."

"You see this guide daily?"

"Yes."

"How long did it take to find this presence?"

"I don't know, let me think, it would have been, a few months."

"So, now you've seen Diane too? Yet it didn't take a few months."

"No, I didn't see her. I heard her voice. I assume it was her voice. I don't know since I've never met her. Before she faded away though she told someone her name was Diane."

Marti tensed. "Someone, what do you mean? Was someone else there with Diane? You never mentioned that earlier."

"I didn't?" Gwyn shrugged. "I thought I did. There was another dead girl with her. She showed up near the end." Gwyn sighed. "The poor girl was racked with tears, she couldn't stop sobbing. It was heart wrenching to listen to. Diane tried to talk to her. The girl chanted and cried uncontrollably. At one point Diane mentioned her sister and the other girl asked a question." Gwyn tapped her chin. "Let me think. What was the question?"

Marti leaned forward.

Gwyn waved her hand. "It was her sister's age. The other dead girl wanted to know how old Diane's sister was. She broke down though when Diane asked if she had any brothers and sisters."

"Hmm."

"What did she chant?" Marni wondered.

"Pardon?"

"The other dead girl, you mentioned she chanted and cried. What did she chant?"

"Oh, it was loud and constant." Gwyn's voice rose, "Aieeee, aieeee, huh, huh, aieeee."

"The other dead girl could be First Nations as well," Marti noted. "That sounds like something from a drum ceremony."

"It had more depth though. Her grief was intense. The chanting was mournful. She was in agony, distressed, shattered. I can't chant like she did, my intensity is off."

Marti nodded. "That's to be expected. You're not dead. So," she paused, "Why would you see, I mean hear, Diane when you typically communicate with your guide? Then there's the issue of this new girl. How does she fit in?"

Marti didn't expect answers. She liked to pose questions out loud. It was part of her process. She wasn't clear about how channeling worked though so was grateful when Gwyn answered her.

"It's complicated but in simple terms I think Diane is trapped here. She can't progress to the other side. She's a ghost. Her spirit was stolen when she was murdered. That's why I communicated with her. Perhaps my guide led her to me. I don't know how the other dead girl fits in though. I'm new to all this."

Marti forced herself to be open to the possibility of what Gwyn suggested. She took a deep breath to clear her mind of doubt. The promise of something unknown poised before her; nectar as sweet and clear as a bubbling brook. Gwyn believed what she said was true. Marti didn't doubt her motives, merely her conclusion. The guide could have an ulterior reason for bringing Diane to Gwyn.

What could that be? How could a spirit place Diane in Gwyn's path? Then again, would Diane wander then coincidentally come into contact with Gwyn? That seemed more farfetched.

Marti silently acknowledged Gwyn's logic. If she was involved in outward channeling, Diane could have entered the sphere of her consciousness or dream state.

"Something doesn't add up here," Marni noted. "Diane is Cree like our people. The Cree believe when your life has been taken from you like Diane's was, her spirit will go to the other side without delay. Why has Diane's spirit stayed nearby and not advanced?"

"Her spirit was stolen from her, against her will." Gwyn stroked her chin. "As I mentioned I think Diane is trapped here. She needs help to move on."

Marti nodded. Her fingers itched to record the questions that skittered through her mind. Would Diane communicate with Gwyn again? Would she help solve the mystery of her death? Who was this new dead girl? How did she fit in to the puzzle? She wondered if she'd have time to write any of this down when they got to Marni's house. The scene was clear in her mind.

"Gwyn, do you think Diane will come back? Do you think she'll tell you who the killer is now that you've established a connection with her?"

Gwyn's expression was unreadable. "I don't know, she might. If she does I'll call Marni, or you, right away."

"No one was around when you meditated?"

"No, why?"

"You need to be careful. You could be in danger if Diane identifies her murderer."

"I'm at less risk than you since I'm not interrogating people."

Marti acknowledged the truth of the statement with a tight smile.

"I'm not in charge of the investigation, Detective Worthington is. Besides, we don't have a clue who the murderer is so they shouldn't be nervous yet."

"Don't be lulled into a false sense of security. If the murderer finds out you're involved you could be at risk. Anyone who's read your books knows you always get your man, or woman." Gwyn laughed.

Gwyn launched into a discussion of one of Marti's novels with Marni. Marti found it interesting how people felt they knew her since they read her books. Gwyn warmed to her immediately, like they were old acquaintances. Of course it helped that Marni and Gwyn were longtime friends.

Was Gwyn a witch? If she was, could Gwyn read her mind right now? Just as she had the thought, Gwyn broke off her discussion with Marni to flash her a grin. Marti shuddered. That was unnerving. Had Gwyn read her mind? She shook her head then wrapped her arms around herself. It was coincidental Gwyn beamed at her.

Marti's thoughts bounced around. As Marni noted, why had Diane not advanced? Her spirit was stolen from her. She should have gone without delay. Their First Nations ancestors regarded energy and spirituality with an open mind. To accomplish a sense of peace and wellbeing was something one hoped to achieve. Would

Diane ever reach that state of harmony and serenity? Did she need their help to get there?

Marti heard her name. She shook her head to re-focus on the conversation.

"Marni has one. Marti, I'd like to give you one." Uncurling her legs, Gwyn stood. She stretched her arms high like a cat arching its back.

Marti glanced at her sister who flashed her a broad, mischievous grin.

Gwyn led them over to a display case. Light bounced back and forth illuminating objects within, creating radiant prisms, vivid rainbows of colour.

Gwyn pored over gemstones. She'd pick one up, peer at it then discard it with a shake of her head. Her hand hovered near one of the crystals. She didn't grasp it at first yet her hand returned to it repeatedly. Finally she succumbed to the invisible force. She held it with the tip of her fingers while they watched the light create a kaleidoscope of colours. Then she clutched the crystal fiercely and began to chant softly.

Marti glanced at her sister. Gwyn continued to chant with rhythmic, ritualistic monotony.

Marti watched Gwyn's movements. In spite of her earlier anxiety Marti was curious to hear about the chosen crystal. Marti knew her sister believed crystals had healing properties and were charged with spiritual powers. She understood the importance of rituals and beliefs. After all, her ancestors had adopted ceremonies handed down throughout generations, carefully cultivated by tradition.

Gwyn gently passed the crystal to Marti. She placed it reverently into her open hand. Tenderly cradling the gemstone Marti stroked the edges. The flashes of light mesmerized her as they burst from the stone. Sunbeams joined the bright, carefree glow to glint twinkling fire. It was a vibrant, energized dance of streaks and sparkles.

Marti felt the strength of the crystal. Energy radiated heat as if part of an explosion from a newly lit fire.

Marni leaned forward to whisper. "Power and force of belief can carry a person forward. You need only be convinced what you hold in your hand or carry on your person is enough to ward off evil, conflict and wickedness. Crystals can be a talisman. The belief is they have magical powers. They protect whoever wears or carries them. They heal, change attitudes and do more."

Marti nodded.

Gwyn added, "Crystals have their own spirit. If you talk to them and ask for help they'll assist with your request. The prayer I chanted was an appeal for protection."

Marti smiled. Her ancestors knew the power of crystals, gemstones, herbs and other natural elements. She'd been raised by her grandmother on tales of medicine men who believed in the forces of nature.

"Grandma told stories of First Nations people who believe supernatural powers are personal beings. The believers would seek to establish relationships with benevolent guardian spirits. Once a link was recognized, guardian spirits became like family members assuring them of help in times of crisis."

Marni nodded. "Yes, remember the Pacific Northwest band of people Grandma told us about? They handed guardians down in families from one generation to the next. This First Nations clan was responsible for remembering their guardian spirits. They had rituals where they offered food, treats and other items they thought they'd like. Gwyn's guide could be similar to the guardian spirits of the Pacific Northwest First Nations band."

Marti grasped the crystal tighter. Grandmother believed in the power of mother earth and offered prayers to spirits when she gathered herbs. Ancient beliefs were tantamount to truth in the First Nations world. Guardian spirits took an immediate interest in a person's health and ensured them a long life. Could the power of the crystal be equated with the strength of guardian spirits?

It was another viewpoint, one Gwyn and Marni believed in. Since crystals are natural it made sense they contained energy and innate power.

Marti's family had numerous traditions and beliefs. An image of her grandma with the medicine bundle she'd worn around her neck flashed before her. Fascinated by the bundle, with childlike curiosity Marti had questioned her grandmother endlessly about why she carried it and what was in it. Hers contained oddly shaped stones, shells, bones, teeth, dried flowers, roots and plant slips she picked while walking. Grandma said it protected her from evil and destructive spirits, those that might harm her.

Their grandmother had been a healer, knowledgeable about the healing powers of plants, roots, flowers and herbs. The girls had absorbed their grandma's stories like a sponge. Marni was fascinated by the spiritual qualities of plants and herbs while Marti was more interested in their practical use. Marti remembered grandmother offered gifts to the earth in her rituals. It renewed her spiritual relationship with mother earth, the source of life.

Touched and appreciative of Gwyn's offering Marti understood why Gwyn felt she needed the crystal. Marti believed in the goodness of people even though she wrote about those who had murder and mayhem in mind. She didn't consider herself jaded.

People who viewed kindness and reverence for mother earth and all God's creatures with contempt sickened her. Concerned for her welfare, Gwyn had presented her with a gift she believed would protect Marti from evil spirits or dangerous individuals.

Murder was nasty. Who knew how complex the deep, dark secrets that lurked in the recesses of a killers' mind were. To unravel this mystery, Pandora's box could be opened. Marti believed murderers embraced the evils of the world.

Marti glanced at her sister. She knew she wasn't as spiritual as Marni, nor could she boast accurate premonitions about the future like Marni could. She had an intuitive streak though. It had served her well in the past. With Marni and Gwyn's guidance, Marti hoped she'd have an accurate sense of the best direction to pursue when it came to Diane's killer.

Aloud she mused, "Why do you think Diane happened to be where she died? Murder is complex. It takes logic, digging and background research to figure out why a person commits murder. So far, the police haven't made sense of why Diane was there."

Marti turned to Marni. "I've listened to you and Gwyn. It makes me wonder, was Diane meant to die? I heard you mention we're in a certain place at a particular time for a reason. What was Diane's reason?"

Marni grabbed Marti's hand. "Oh honey, you can't believe Diane was in the wrong place at the wrong time. Fate was not responsible for Diane's murder. That's not what we meant. It was a brutal, cold blooded killer, not chance."

Marti shook her head. "You're right. I don't know why I've let emotion get in the way of logic. What explanation is there to take a life, to intentionally cause harm? It's contrary to our values and beliefs. I'm grasping at straws, hoping there was some *'way out there'* reason this happened."

Marni stroked her sister's hair. "This murder hit you harder than you care to admit. It's affected you deeply." She glanced at Gwyn. "We'll help ensure your sense of self remains intact, to safeguard you and our families against the evil you've encountered."

Gwyn nodded.

Marti sighed as her sister finished the soothing motion then removed her hand from Marti's hair.

"You're right, I'm out of my depth on this one. I think it's the age of Diane and the location since you and Cindy live here. I don't want this to be some random act of violence that could have affected one of our daughters."

She shook her head. "I'm fearless when I get involved in these cases. I charge forward with a relentless need to assist the authorities. The words write themselves when I sit at my laptop to transcribe another Marti Rose mystery. This one is different. I appreciate any help the two of you can provide."

"Gwyn, why don't you tell Marti what type of crystal this is?"

"It's a black tourmaline. I picked it for you to provide protection. Expose yours to the sunlight to energize it. It's new so you need to remove negative energy it might have. The first thing you want to do when you get to Marni's house is place it in a nonmetallic container filled with distilled water and a pinch of salt. Have you got rock salt Marni?"

Marni shook her head no.

"I'll give you some to take home."

They watched Gwyn pour a small amount of rock salt into a plastic bag. "Take the container of water and salt and put it in the fridge for a day. Then take the crystal out and place it on a sunny ledge. Do this for three days. That will cleanse it. Hmm, wait…"

Gwyn wrinkled her brow. She pulled on her lip, deep in thought.

"You know what, put off the cleansing until after you catch the killer. Soak it this evening. When you get up in the morning put it on a sunny ledge. It will be cleansed enough. Take it with you when you leave Marni's house. I've cleaned these recently and removed negative energy. This one has sufficient force.

This is being used for powerful protection. You'll need to cleanse it when you catch the killer. Their negativity will soil your crystal. It's important to use it now though. Put it in your pocket or in a pouch you attach to yourself. How does it feel when you hold it?"

"I feel its strength. It gives me a sense of rightness." Marti smiled as she stroked the stone. "I feel comfortable with it."

"Good, then it will work for you. Be careful. I've read your books. Murderers don't discriminate when they kill. People who pose a threat are in danger. Be aware. Don't put you or your loved ones in the killer's path. Crystals won't protect you from a gun pointed at your head, or fingers around your throat as they squeeze your lifeblood."

Marti shuddered, as an icy chill ran down her spine. The room felt eerie as if they were no longer alone. The talk of spirits, guides and murderers had gotten to her.

"You're right. That reminds me." Marti leaned across the display case to search for gemstones. Marni had one. It didn't hurt to get Andrea and Cindy a crystal though…

CHAPTER 12

Worthington led with the unpleasant news.

"The cause of death was asphyxia. She was suffocated or in this case strangled to death by her assailant. Results of the autopsy are back."

"So is it safe to assume whoever raped her strangled her either during or just after the, umm, act?" Marti shook her head. It was a typical question. There was no need to be uncomfortable with the term.

"Yes, and there were three or four people, that. Well, you know…" The detective's words trailed off.

Marti shuddered. "You won't tell her parents those details will you?"

"Yeah, we have to."

Marti watched Worthington squint then shake his head. As he glanced up he added, "The autopsy revealed something noteworthy.

It could help identify the killer. Of course they'd have to find more than just the ring but...I've seen less lead us to a murderer. We'll keep an open mind. It could help."

Marti shook her head. Was the detective rambling? "Could you be more specific?"

"She had a gash on the top of her cheek, just under her eye." Worthington indicated the spot. Then he reached across with a quick movement to imitate a person backhanding someone.

Marti touched the spot on her cheek as she imagined the gash.

"It could be a ring, something chunky. The murderer was right handed."

Marti fingered the spot again. It was bony. "Not much flesh there. I wonder how high Diane's cheek bones were?"

"Similar to yours I'd guess. That's why the gash was deep. When a ring hits bone it's jarring."

"The killer would have felt the blow as well then."

"Yes."

"Good, I hope it hurt him."

"There's more."

Marti wasn't sure if she wanted to hear more. Something that used to intrigue her had become sordid and dismal. Would murder mysteries and crime become a chore instead of the enjoyable pastime they'd been? She shook her head. Now was not the time to examine her motives as a writer.

"The boys from Estevan admitted what they'd done to Diane. It tied into why she jumped from the car."

"What?" Marti leaned forward. She'd outlined a number of scenarios and written them down in her notes. None made sense though. Even if Marti used one as a red herring it couldn't be too preposterous. Fans hated to be tricked on purpose. Clues couldn't be scattered haphazardly on a path to nowhere. There had to be a logical conclusion. Marti was impatient to hear what happened. Her earlier pessimism evaporated.

"We got a confession." Worthington's grin was brief. "I won't go into detail how we got it."

Marti wrinkled her brow. Was the detective stalling?

"The younger one in the passenger seat admits he had Diane in an arm wrestling grip. He was trying to get her to, ahem."

Worthington stopped to clear his throat.

Marti rummaged in her purse for a mint. She passed it to the detective.

"Thanks." He took a moment to unwrap the mint. "He had his pants unzipped and his private parts exposed."

"What?" Marti yelped. It was the last thing she'd expected.

Worthington wouldn't meet her eye. "Yes, I guess he wanted her to touch it. She wouldn't though. Hence the arm wrestle grip."

Marti was speechless.

Her mind grappled with the scenario. Her fingers itched to write the scene out, quick, while it was fresh in her mind. She rummaged in her purse for her notebook and pen.

"Do you mind if I write something down? I need a few minutes." Marti was already bent over her notebook, scribbling madly.

She barely noticed as the detective murmured. "Sure, take your time. I've got phone calls to make."

The door closed behind him.

Marti scrawled notes as her mind played the scene in sequence. It had to be believable. Yet there was something otherworldly about it. She could play up that angle as well. A scene with Diane musing what happened from the other side could be in order.

Marti jumped when the detective returned. Immersed in notes she was oblivious to the outside world.

Marti mumbled, "Has she crossed over?"

"What?"

Marti glanced up. She lay her pen down then crossed her arms. "Diane. My sister Marni has a friend."

Worthington raised an eyebrow.

Marti sighed. "Okay, yes Marni and her friend Gwyn believe in spirits and other things…" She trailed off, loath to go into too much detail. "Suffice it to say we discussed why Diane has not gone to join those who have peacefully accepted their fate.

Marni and Gwyn came up with an alternative. What if Diane is stuck between here and there? She could seek retribution. I know it sounds out there. I don't believe farfetched scenarios exist. I have to admit I've written some though. There have been instances…" She trailed off then squared her shoulders. "What do you think?"

"This sounds specific. Have your friends felt Diane nearby? Is that why you ask?"

"Gwyn sensed her or someone. Gwyn thinks Diane is watching, waiting, poised on the brink but unable to cross the chasm. She feels Diane's stolen spirit is trapped here. Gwyn communicated with her yesterday."

She filled Worthington in on her conversation with Marni and Gwyn. Marti appreciated how he didn't scoff at their ideas.

"Gwyn communicated with Diane so they think she's nearby. Is that right?"

Marti shrugged. She wasn't sure what it meant.

"Did Gwyn get the sense Diane wants to help?"

"Could be. If Diane is still here there must be a reason she hasn't left yet."

Marti gazed at the detective. "Imagine if a victim gave a first hand account then lead you to the killer. Justice would be enacted every time." She laughed. "Wouldn't it be handy if victims came back to tell the authorities who killed them. It would simplify matters."

Worthington chuckled. "It would make my job infinitely easier." Then he squared his shoulders. "The reality is we sift through evidence, analyze facts and talk to anyone who might have seen something."

"Yeah, I know. Clear thinking, concrete facts and unemotional decisions solve a case. One has to guard against feelings. They tend to cloud or distort issues. I can wax poetic in my novels though." She shook her head. "I often describe the murderer at the victim's funeral. No one knows it's the killer of course. You can't make it too obvious."

She paused as she noted Worthington's raised eyebrows.

"They're often nearby when a victim is laid to rest. Is it to gloat, watch the reaction of loved ones or ensure their horrific deed is carried out to a gory conclusion? Or is there another reason we can't fathom?"

Worthington shook his head.

Marti grinned. "I know. How can we relate to a killer, get in his or her mind? We can't. That's a good thing. I prefer to be guided by pure intention."

She waggled her fingers. "It's fun to write about them though and speculate as to intention. People love to read about the force of evil."

Worthington ignored her last comments. "I agree clarity and purpose are preferable to ignorance and emotion. Speaking of emotion, I have a favour to ask. Have you got a half hour to spare?"

Marti glanced at her watch. "Sure, I have to pick up my sister and niece for the funeral but I've got time."

⁂

Ron was quiet as he approached. He realized he should make noise, the guy hated when people snuck up on him. He belched loudly then thumped his chest. Oblivious, the guy continued to work on the car. It was his baby. He preened over it, cleaned, fixed, painted, waxed, polished, the list was endless.

Ron coughed when his friend ignored him. He received a grunt in return.

"Lookin' good, been working on it all morning?"

"Yeah."

Oh, oh it was gonna be one of those days. Ron paused, uncertain. He wasn't sure if he should bring the subject up or not. Nervous, he jerked his hand across his brow then brushed the hair away, it forever fell into his eyes.

Ron had the frame of an athlete. Over six feet tall he held his body erect, years of martial arts had taught him more than discipline. It had enhanced his natural grace and coordination. His hands, a lethal weapon, combined with a razor sharp mind, made him a deadly foe.

Steel gray eyes focused steadily on his friend. He chewed his lip, thoughtful. Ron calculated the odds of getting info out of him today. Would he make more sense than the other night or go berserk again? It was hard to say. He'd never been easy to figure out.

Ron went for the plunge.

"I'm worried about the girl in the newspaper. You know, Diane was her name."

No answer.

"I know we talked about this the other day. I think we should call the police and give them anonymous info. She was alive the last time we saw her. Even though we roughed her up a bit, and did, well, you know. She was still alive."

Ron paused as he thought back to Sunday night. A nagging suspicion had entered his mind. He couldn't shake it. What if?

Nah, he couldn't have.

Or could he?

After a long silence Ron asked, "Where did you take her after you dropped us off?"

No reply.

It was too quiet. Birdsong ended, dogs stopped barking, children ran indoors. There was not a soul around. An unnatural hush descended as if they were the only two left on earth. Ron's breathing sounded ragged in his ears as all sound died away.

Ron gulped a mouthful of air. He held his breath, hopeful as he awaited an answer. He paused, ready with a reply, anticipating an innocent explanation.

The alternative was more than Ron was prepared to face.

Tense now, he turned, unsteady. Ron stumbled, the unspoken reaction of his friend revealed more than words.

He couldn't tell the police.

Ron knew the killer. Evidence would point to him as an accessory to the crime.

It was more than he could bear…

⋏

Hunched over his barstool, dejected, Murray nursed his beer. He should have done something. Murray couldn't shake the thought. What kind of man was he? His bleary glance took in a nearby calendar.

"What day is it?"

He couldn't believe the date on the calendar or the one the bartender uttered.

"It's Thursday, August 26th."

"No way."

Unbelievable. Less than a week ago his life had been on track. Well, as much as one could expect it to be. Now it had veered off in some crazy direction. Murray felt like he'd flung forward into unknown danger.

Murray never suspected it was the day of Diane's funeral. If he had it might have explained his intense feeling of loss.

"What a waste," he mumbled brushing a tear away. She hadn't deserved it, totally unjustified that's what it was.

So where did that leave him and the guys? What should they do? Flight seemed reasonable at the time but what now? They needed a plan.

Murray hunkered down lower on the stool. Thinking gave him a headache. Weary, he passed his hand over his face then sighed. His life wasn't too far in the dumpsters.

After all, he was alive.

It was more than he could say for Diane...

CHAPTER 13

Their eyes slid in Marti's direction as Worthington made introductions. The mother frowned then murmured, "Your name sounds familiar." She broke off as her youngest child pulled at her skirt.

Marti felt the detective tense beside her. They hadn't thought of Marti's fame when Worthington agreed she could meet the family.

He cleared his throat. "As I mentioned, Marti can give you more info later. I'm sure right now you'd like to see your daughter."

The mother groaned low in her throat.

Marti jerked her head toward Worthington. She was sure he hadn't meant for his remark to sound callous yet it had come across that way. This family would never see their daughter again. Viewing the body was not the same thing.

Worthington led the group down the corridor. He paused in front of a door then glanced at the children. "I don't think," he began.

"Oh," Marti rushed forward. "I should take the children with me. We can wait over there while you go in." She smiled at the mother.

The mother gave a slight nod then gently pushed the two youngest toward Marti. An older daughter rocked back and forth on her feet.

All eyes turned to the teen. No one said a word.

"I need to go in," she uttered.

Her father took her hand then wrapped his other arm around his wife's shoulder. They were ready.

Marti led the children down the hall toward a bench. "They shouldn't be long," Marti whispered as they sat down. Marti searched for something to add. "I have a daughter a few years younger than your sister."

"Sisters," the boy who Marti pegged to be around eight corrected.

"Sisters?"

"Rosie and Rosemarie are twins."

Marti glanced back toward the room. "Twins." Her voice shook as she added. "We didn't know. I always wished my sister and I were twins. She's a year younger than me."

She had the children's attention now.

"What's your name?" the little girl asked.

"Marti, what's your name?"

"Anna. His name is Junior."

"No it's not." He turned to Marti. "It's Will, but I like Junior so everyone calls me that."

"Great, nice to meet you Anna and Junior. Let me see if I can guess your ages." Marti squinted at the children as if deep in thought. "I think Junior is eight and Anna would you be six?"

They nodded.

"Rosie and Rosemarie are seventeen," Anna offered. "They think they're grown-ups but dad says they need to act like adults before he calls them that. He always says that, doesn't he Junior?"

"Yeah, that's why Rosemarie ran away. She said dad should quit treating her like a kid. Do you think Rosie will run away too? We wouldn't like that." Junior grabbed Marti's sleeve as he asked the question. Anna squirmed forward then leaned toward her brother while they waited for Marti's answer.

Marti gulped. "I don't know your sister Rosie so I can't say for sure what she'll do." The children slumped beside her. "I do know twins don't like the same things though. Just because Rosemarie ran away doesn't mean Rosie will."

"So you think she'll stay home with us?" Anna ventured.

Marti nodded. "I hope so."

Anna beamed while Junior added. "Yeah, I heard her tell Rosemarie not to go so I think you're right." Junior turned to his sister. "Remember, Rosie was crying but Rosemarie just got mad at her."

"It made me sad too. I didn't want Rosemarie to go. Rosie yelled, *'I'm begging you Rosemarie, don't do this.'* " Anna shook her head. "I think Rosie should have locked her up in their room. Don't you Junior? We could have brought Rosemarie food and read stories with her. It would have been okay."

"The lock on their door doesn't work."

"Oh, that's probably why Rosie didn't do it then. Too bad, that could have worked."

The door down the hall opened. Three pairs of eyes jerked that direction. Rosie had come out. She leaned against the wall, eyes closed, head bowed.

Anna shook her head, "Poor Rosie."

"We should bring her over here," Junior decided.

"Yeah, she can sit here and I'll sit on her lap. She likes that," Anna added for Marti's benefit.

Junior jumped up, went over to his sister then touched her arm. Startled, Rosie's head jerked up and her eyes flew open. Junior grabbed her hand to tug her toward the bench.

With vacant eyes Rosie joined the trio. Junior plopped her down.

Anna scurried onto her lap then threw her arms around her sister. As she nuzzled her head into Rosie's chest she murmured, "Poor Rosie, my poor Rosie."

Tears streamed down Rosie's cheeks as she buried her face in her sister's hair.

"It'll be okay," Junior added as he stroked Rosie's arm. "You still have us."

Touched, Marti silently watched the siblings comfort one another.

After a few minutes Anna squirmed in her sister's arms. "You should say hi to Marti. She's nice. Her daughter's younger than you. She always wanted to be a twin."

"You have twin daughters?" Rosie murmured as she lifted her tear stained face to Marti.

"No, she wanted to be the twin," Anna clarified pointing at Marti.

"She's not though Anna. Her sister and her are a year apart, remember," Junior clarified.

"Oh, I love being a twin, Rosemarie and I are, were..." Rosie's face crumpled as her voice trailed off.

Junior glanced down the hall. "You should tell Marti about your dream before mom and dad come back," he urged.

"Yeah, tell her," Anna added, as she got more comfortable on her sister's lap.

Rosie shook her head, no.

"Come on, she might know something about dreams. Do you?" Junior raised his face to Marti's, urging her to get his sister to share the dream.

"Well," Marti hedged. She wished Marni were here. She was the dream interpreter in the family. "Why don't you tell me the dream and we'll see if we can figure it out together? It can't hurt."

"Yeah, it can't hurt," Anna echoed.

Rosie sighed. She rubbed tears away with the back of one hand then sniffed.

"She needs a Kleenex," Junior noted. "Do you have one in your purse?"

"Oh, of course." Marti rummaged in her purse for a tissue. She passed one to Rosie then brought out mints.

As she passed them around Anna murmured, "Yum, candy, I love candy." She clapped her hands then popped one in her mouth.

"Tell her," Junior urged.

Rosie stared down at the top of Anna's head. "I had this dream, it was more of a nightmare."

Anna nodded. "She cried."

Rosie sighed. "Yeah, I cried." She put the mint in her mouth. "I saw my sister, Rosemarie. It was weeks ago. She was with these two kids, a girl and a boy. They were older than Anna and Junior, about ten or twelve I'd say." She glanced toward Marti quick before her eyes skittered away.

"Tell her about the mom," Anna urged.

"We don't know if it was their mom," Junior corrected.

Anna scoffed. "She weren't nice whatever she was."

"Wasn't," Rosie corrected.

"Weren't nice whatever she wasn't?"

"No, Rosie means she wasn't nice whatever she was." Junior clarified.

"Oh, okay, I'll try to member that."

Rosie sighed but didn't correct Anna's shortening of the word remember.

"Tell her," Anna urged.

"This woman, I don't know who she was had Rosemarie's head in the toilet."

"Pardon?" Marti leaned forward. Had she heard wrong?

"Yeah, I thought it was weird too." Rosie turned toward Marti this time. "Rosemarie sputtered and the woman pushed her head into the toilet water then she screamed and lifted Rosemarie's head again. She pushed her in and out of the toilet water over and over." Rosie lowered her head then closed her eyes. "That's why I cried. Rosemarie cried and gasped for air. The kids cried while the woman screamed. It was horrible."

Marti frowned. "Horrible doesn't begin to describe it. Your poor sister."

Rosie's eyes flashed open. "The woman left a few minutes later so the kids lifted Rosemarie to her feet then dragged her off."

Although she didn't believe in dreams, Marti made a mental note to ask Worthington if Rosemarie had water in her lungs. Had she been tortured repeatedly?

They heard a noise down the hall.

"Quick, tell her the rest," Junior urged.

"Just before I woke up I heard Rosemarie repeat a rhyme we sang when we were young. She added a few lines." Rosie glanced down the hall. When she saw it was empty she murmured, "Quick like ketchup, thick like spam, home schooled, home ruled. It's a woman, not a man."

"That's it?"

Rosie nodded. "She repeated it a few times then her voice drifted away. I never heard or saw Rosemarie again in my dreams after that." She leaned her head on top of Anna's while tears flowed.

The door down the hall opened. Marti repeated the rhyme so she'd remember it later.

Their parents murmured to Worthington in hushed voices. Their dad had his arm around his wife. She slumped against him. The children watched their parents, silent, intent. As they turned to walk towards the bench Marti's eyes were drawn to the mother. Her face was ravaged by grief.

The children jumped up. Anna slid off her sister's lap to run to her mother's side. She grabbed her mom's hand than stared at her brother to convey something. He must have gotten the message as he moved to his dad's side to grab his free hand. Rosie stood there, alone, until her dad glanced her way. He motioned with his chin. Rosie moved into the circle and the family embraced one another.

Marti and Worthington turned away to give them a private moment.

When the father cleared his throat Marti and the detective moved closer to the silent circle.

"Thank you for," the father paused, "For, explaining everything to us." He nodded at Worthington.

As they turned to go Marti found her voice. "I put together a list of people you might be interested in talking to…" Her voice trailed off. Would they want to speak to strangers about their grief? As she noticed the dead eyes of the mother she held the list out to Rosie. "There are support groups, families that have gone through what you're going through."

Rosie frowned but took the list.

"I don't know if you have a computer at home but there are groups of women and families online you can talk to. It won't cost anything if you have Internet."

"We have a computer," Anna confirmed.

"Good, some of the people on the list are here in Saskatchewan while others are spread throughout Canada."

"When your daughter came up on the national missing persons list I called Marti. She's involved with groups dedicated to awareness of missing and murdered Indigenous women and their families," Detective Worthington explained.

The mother closed her eyes then leaned against her husband.

"Is your name on this list?" Rosie whispered.

Marti gulped. She hadn't added her name. Should she? She glanced at Worthington who shrugged.

"No, I can add it though if you'd like."

Rosie thrust the paper back at Marti. "Seems like a dumb list if it's just a bunch of strangers."

Marti bent over to grab her purse off the floor. "I'll give you one of my cards. How's that?" She rummaged for her card case then pulled one out. She passed the card and paper back to Rosie.

Junior grabbed the card from Rosie. "Marti Rose, Author," he read.

"What's an author?" Anna asked.

Marti closed her eyes then flashed them open to meet Anna's gaze. Why was everything so hard when it came to grief? Her motive for involvement had gotten cloudier now that her profession was exposed.

"An author is someone who writes books," Rosie answered as she gazed at Marti. "Why would an author want to talk to us? I don't get it." She crossed her arms then glared at Marti.

Marti's eyes widened. Why indeed?

Worthington saved her. "Marti's involved in another teen murder. That's one of the reasons she's here. As a consultant we call her in now and then.

Marti is also a famous author. Her dedication to the missing and murdered Indigenous women and families support groups has raised their awareness level. I have no doubt funds and resources have increased because of Marti's involvement. She's a valuable addition to their team."

"Is the other murder connected to our daughter?" the father wondered. He turned to Marti. "Is that why you're here?"

Marti shook her head as Worthington murmured, "We can't say at this time." He relented somewhat. "It doesn't seem to be though," he allowed.

Rosie frowned. "You're not going to write about our family are you? Is that why you talked to us?"

"Oh, no," Marti reassured them. "I wanted to tell you about the support groups and other families that are out there. I would never write about your grief."

"We should go," the father said. He steered the group toward the door.

"Bye Marti," Anna called as they were led off.

"Bye Anna."

Marti slumped against the wall. "Remind me to mind my own business next time I want to talk to a grieving family. That was rough."

Worthington nodded. "It always is."

Marti shook her hair then squared her shoulders. "I have to tell you something before I go."

They sat on the bench. Marti told him about Rosie's dream and the children's comments about Rosemarie running away.

"It could be a clue. The killer could be a woman or it's a woman and a man with a family. On the other hand the children could be other victims." Marti shook her head. "So many questions. Oh, can you check to see if Rosemarie had water in her lungs? I hope she wasn't tortured repeatedly." She thought of Anna's earlier comment as she uttered, "Poor Rosemarie."

Marti glanced at her watch. "Whoa, I gotta go. I need to pick up Cindy and Marni for Diane's funeral. I assume you'll be there?"

"Of course. How can I miss the chance to spot our killer?"

They smiled. If only it were that easy…

CHAPTER 14

When she drove up Cindy was in the yard pacing. Intent on private thoughts, shoulders hunched, she was unaware of Marti's presence until Marti was a few feet away. Marti regarded her niece silently as she waited. This murder had taken a toll on Cindy. Her eyes had bluish circles underneath as if she hadn't slept in days, her hair was lifeless and she'd revived her nervous habit of nail biting.

"Oh Auntie."

Cindy threw herself into Marti's arms. "You're here. Mom's inside, I'll get her. Did you need to change or anything?"

Marti glanced down at her clothes. She'd thrown on a dark brown skirt and tan top this morning. It seemed fine.

"I'm good."

Cindy left the shelter of Marti's embrace to get her mom.

⋏

It was worse than Marti had imagined.

The church was filled to capacity with family and friends. Young people lined the walls. Pews overflowed while people crammed into the foyer in an effort to get close to the action. Teens were everywhere. Some were grief stricken while others regarded the occasion as a social event. It was an activity they longed to be part of, onlookers at best, morbid thrill seekers at worst.

Diane had been a popular girl. She had a large family with an abundance of relatives in attendance. Their grief was real and painful to watch. Like spectators at a sport, people glanced in their direction then quickly flicked their eyes elsewhere as if caught in a dirty act.

The priest intoned the virtues of Diane and skirted around the issue of her death. Marti appreciated his need to downplay the sordid details. With skill and compassion he acknowledged the raw grief of her family. His sermon focused on the suddenness of death and the certainty that our dearest know we love them. Mourners broke down when Diane's aunt got up to deliver a stirring, gut wrenching tribute to her niece.

Diane had been a remarkable girl, spiritual, in tune with her inner self. Cindy was fortunate to have known Diane. Friends like her were hard to find. The depth of their feelings was often too cumbersome for the average person to appreciate. Glancing at Cindy, Marti gave her shoulder an affectionate squeeze.

Cindy insisted on paying their respect to the family. Marti knew it was the proper thing to do yet wasn't eager to join the throng headed to the basement for refreshments. It was the inevitability she dreaded, the moment when one encountered the parents, that instant when their eyes met and she'd be presented with the raw pain within.

Marti longed to shirk her duties and slink away into the background. She wanted to avoid the inescapable fact they were about to be introduced to another set of parents of a murder victim. Marti had already met one grieving family, she had seen more anguish and pain today than her mind could comprehend. These cases had become far too real for her comfort level.

She longed for the objectivity of strangers. Marti had anticipated she would have the ability to regard these crimes the way a professional would, with detachment, bound by rules of evidence. Instead, her emotions had gotten in the way. She felt close to the victims, related to them as a mother.

Diane was a friend of Cindy's. Marti had met Diane on a previous occasion. Now she was about to meet Diane's parents. It would further acknowledge Diane as a person.

Meeting Rosemarie's siblings today and talking to them had increased their familiarity. Rosie and Rosemarie were just a few years older than Cindy and Andrea. Marti had encouraged Rosemarie's family to contact her when she handed Rosie her card.

Strictly professional was preferable to what she'd experienced today. Yet how could Marti dismiss the similarities between Cindy, Andrea, Diane and Rosemarie? She'd come to the funeral to be with Cindy and Marni today. Whether she liked it or not, both cases had become personal.

Marti moved forward with the crowd, towards the parents, away from the general detachment she longed for. As they surged onward she yearned to postpone the inevitable, poised to invade a parent's personal hell. Please don't let me become part of their misery she prayed while she swept forward, a reluctant sunbather caught on the incoming tide.

Marti's eyes scanned the crowd as she tried to avoid the onslaught of emotion as it swept through the room. She closed her eyes, intent to place the entire wretched incident in a detached box within her mind. How were others battling their private wars?

⊥

Brad had taken it hard, harder than he'd imagined in his worst nightmare. He'd met Diane's parents more than once so he felt compelled to pay his respects.

How would they greet him? Would they understand his grief was real, feelings genuine? He wanted to say something sincere to convey the depth of his emotions.

Brad avoided the eyes of people who nodded at him across the room. He didn't want to make small talk with friends or listen to hollow words. He needed more than that to get him through today. He needed substance, grief in its entirety to cut through him like a knife. Brad craved it. He wanted absolute pain to course through his mind, body, heart and soul.

He hung onto it, the intense brutality of grief. It was real. By embracing it, Brad maintained an outward façade of serenity. The thread of his sorrow was buried deep within, safe from prying eyes, to be explored later in solitude.

The number of people at the funeral surprised Monica. She recognized classmates from school. There were grieving people with red-rimmed eyes who must be family and other people that had known Diane. Reluctant to come today, Monica had been compelled to attend the funeral. Although Diane hadn't been a close friend they'd known each other all their lives. They'd lived in the same neighbourhood and attended the same school.

As her eyes scanned the crowd, Monica acknowledged she hadn't come for Diane's sake today. She'd come to see Murray, hoping for a moment alone. They had to talk. She knew her timing was off yet it was a conversation they had to have.

As she glanced at her brother, immobile at her side, Monica sighed. She regretted sharing her news. Andy hadn't taken it well. Had blamed Murray. Andy did that a lot, held Murray responsible for what happened to her. Murray did influence her but she had a mind, could take care of herself. Not totally maybe, but with Murray's help she'd be alright. If only she could see him, explain things.

Andy resented the fact Monica had dragged him to this funeral. He didn't know her friends nor did he want to. He'd met that bum Murray once and it had been enough. Andy had been clear about how things stood. If Murray had any brains he'd do the right thing. He'd been warned, now he better do something about it.

Putting his hand inside his collar Andy wished his tie wasn't so tight. His throat felt constricted and it was hard to breathe. The air in here was close, like the stillness you felt before a storm struck. Uncomfortable and thick, the air hung like a fat cloud ready to explode at a moment's notice.

Who were all these people? Did they care about Diane or were they here for another reason like him and Monica? As he caught the eye of one of the boys nearby, Andy stared him down. The guy's appearance was rough. He was either ill or a close friend of the dead girl.

Closing the door on his feelings, Andy coolly regarded the room. People at funerals were a sorry bunch. Some were depressed or pitiful while others pretended to be miserable. It was morbid. Andy hated that state.

Brian had come with a group of classmates. He tried to catch Cindy's eye but family and friends surrounded her. Stacey was zoned out like she'd been since Diane's death. Brian shuddered. It would be rough to have your best friend die like that. He was about to move toward Cindy and her group when one of his buddies grabbed his arm to get his attention.

As Brian had noted Stacey was in a fog. She refused to emerge from the cobwebs that surrounded her, into the reality of this nightmare. If she got through today tomorrow would be better. *"Tomorrow"*, she chanted silently to herself like a mantra, *"Tomorrow"*.

⋏

Marti checked out the people nearby as they moved slowly forward in the crowd. She dreaded their arrival at the front of the line. Watching those close by kept her mind occupied. With hand cupped to her mouth she whispered to her niece. Cindy pointed at a young man named Brad. Clearly grief stricken, Marti was told he'd been a former boyfriend. Judging from his dire state Marti guessed he regretted the break up.

Stacey was in front of them. As she heard Cindy's whispered comments Stacey jerked to attention. She turned around, grabbed Cindy then held her close like a lifeline in a storm. Racking sobs tore through Stacey's slight form. Her mouth jerked, moaning sounds snatched from bloodless lips. Stacey appeared to be lifeless, her skin pale, a living corpse.

Marti shook her head. What a description. The writer in her had taken over. Why was she so morbid? She was caught up in emotions near at hand. That was the problem. She didn't have the luxury of engulfing the grief that coursed around them. She had to concentrate on other matters. Marti turned her back on Stacey and Cindy. She wanted to distance herself from Stacey's naked misery. Now was not the time to get caught up in a maelstrom of pain.

Marti focused on the people behind them. She recognized Marni's neighbours in the crowd. Teens milled about. She noticed a few guys considerably older than Cindy and her crowd. Did Cindy hang out with men that old? They must be in their mid twenties. They could be relatives of Diane, cousins perhaps. Marti hoped that was the case.

One guy caught her attention. He appeared detached, clinically uninvolved. A girl, Cindy's age, stood at his elbow scanning the crowd. It was clear she was watching for someone. Shock coursed through Marti while she observed them. The girl was pregnant. Slight and bony her stomach had a distinctive pouch. Marti was sure the teen was in the early stages of pregnancy. Her heart went out to her. She was so young to be expecting a baby. Was the guy beside her the father or an older brother? Too similar to be a couple Marti concluded they were siblings.

Marti turned back to Cindy, anxious to ask about the couple. She groaned inwardly as she noted it was their turn to offer condolences. Not the time for idle chitchat. Marni, who had wandered off to talk to people, hurried back to join their group.

Diane's father engulfed Stacey and Cindy in a crushing bear hug that left them gasping for breath. They began to cry, unabashedly ignoring the crowd as it surged around them. Diane's mother turned from the person she'd been talking to. She spied the girls, threw her hands up then joined their weeping. Marti turned to Marni, at a loss for words. What did one do in this situation?

As they stood there Marti felt awkward. Marni had joined the mourners to offer her words of comfort. Spent by tears, the group was joined by one more, the teen Cindy had identified as Brad. Welcomed into the grieving cluster like a person rescued from a shipwreck, Brad clung to the unit like a man about to go under.

Forced to watch this grief near at hand Marti attempted to detach herself. The sorrow of Diane's parents and close friends was all encompassing. She brushed a tear away, close to breaking down at the futility of it all. After an eternity, Cindy gathered her tattered shreds of dignity. Turning, she gathered Marti into their circle introducing her to Diane's parents.

Marti shuddered as she was exposed to a brief glimpse of despair before they were forced to move along. Murmuring, she passed on her condolences. Anxious to progress beyond the sphere of mourners she made her way to the other side of the room where platters of food were laid out. Marni followed her. Cindy and her friends wandered over after they'd loaded their plates with refreshments.

"Who's that guy over there by himself?" Marti asked Cindy while they nibbled on finger sandwiches.

"That's Tony, I guess everyone got mad at him at a party yesterday. That's why he's alone. I should call him over here since he was a good friend of Diane's."

"He seems scared," Marti noted.

"Yeah, well Tony's scared of life. He's strange so kids avoid him. Diane was nice to him though. I'll go get him."

A moment later the wiry teenager joined them. His face showed relief at Cindy's kindly intervention but he was still scared, terrified. After she introduced Tony to her aunt, Cindy and Tony leaned their heads together then began to murmur.

Turning to Marni she whispered, "Do you think Cindy will be ready to get out of here soon?" Marti's feet hurt and she longed to leave. Funerals were traumatic, particularly when a young person died. Again, Marti wondered how she'd gotten caught up in this painful case.

As she caught Cindy's troubled expression and Tony's frightened one Marti knew why. Cindy needed this crime to be solved. It would absolve her friend Diane of the horrid rumours circulating. Cindy also needed to feel safe in her neighbourhood again. That was reason enough.

Marti sighed as she tuned in to Cindy and Tony's conversation. Marni had wandered off again. They didn't seem to be leaving anytime soon.

"Why'd they accuse you of being involved in Diane's murder?"

"I don't know. We toasted Diane, talked about how great she was. I told stories about things we used to do. You realize she was special?"

Cindy nodded.

"Yeah, so the next thing I know these girls start yelling. They accused me of being a barbarian. They said I used women then threw them away like a piece of meat. I don't know what they meant.

They pointed at me then whispered things about Diane. Terri, you know how weird she is, stuck her finger in my face then screeched, *"For all we know you did it, you could have murdered her."*

Tony started to shake. "It was horrible, like a nightmare. I prayed I'd wake up from it. It hasn't stopped though. You're the first person that's talked to me today. I never did anything wrong. I loved Diane," Tony whimpered.

Cindy put her arm around him. She whispered in his ear while Tony wept on her shoulder.

"Diane freaked me and Stacey out last night. Did she tell you about it?"

Cindy glanced at Stacey who was bent toward Brad while she watched him eat. Cindy's eyes swiveled back to Tony. She shook her head, no.

"We were at the party, talking. This was just before they accused me of things I never could have done. I loved her."

"I know, I know," Cindy soothed.

Tony hiccupped as he cried softly.

"You said Diane freaked you out."

"Oh, yeah, Stacey and I. We sat there, watched people, talking low. All of a sudden we hear this voice. It was Diane. Sounded just like her and everything."

"What? How could that be?"

"I don't know. It was weird for sure."

They were quiet, thinking heaven knows what.

Marti ground her teeth to keep from interrupting. She sent Cindy thought waves, encouraging her to ask more questions. After eons of waiting while Marti jiggled her sore feet and tried not to draw attention to her presence, Cindy finally asked the question Marti was dying to ask. Weren't teens curious about these things?

"What'd she say?"

"Who?" Tony seemed to have blanked out momentarily.

"Diane, the voice you heard."

"Oh, yeah, she said, '*No, no, stay away.*'"

"That's it."

"Yeah, she said it twice though. I think it was twice. Once when I was with Stacey. Then I thought I heard it again when those girls yelled at me. It floated by on the breeze, '*No, no, stay away.*' Man, it was weird."

Marti turned from Tony's misery. Teens could be cruel. Even though they were friends they treated one another like strangers, or worse yet, an enemy. They were judge and jury rolled into one. When they passed a sentence, they had no mercy. They'd pointed their fingers at Tony, intent on making him a suspect. They wanted someone to pay for the crime committed. It didn't seem to matter if Tony was guilty or not.

Thrown into the mix, Tony was hearing voices. Not in the plural, since he claimed to have heard only one voice, Diane's. Was it possible she'd communicated with him and Stacey? Why them?

It fit with Gwyn's theory Diane hadn't crossed to the other side yet. Did spirits warn people about events? Diane could have cautioned Tony as he ventured near the girls. '*No, no, stay away.*' Taken literally, Diane could have urged Tony not to cross the yard. Bad timing cost Tony. He was now a suspect in the eyes of his classmates. Diane could have meant something totally unrelated though. Spirits were so vague.

Marti started. What if Diane referred to the night of her murder? *'No, no stay away.'* Those could have been the last coherent words Diane muttered to her attacker.

What if Tony had been there that night?

What if he was the murderer?

Narrowing her eyes, suspicious now, Marti stared at Tony. Crime stats stated the victim was often familiar with their attacker. Relaxed, the target was at ease. They never saw what stared them in the face until it was too late. The person responsible for this crime could be the last person you'd suspect.

Tony was weak. He wasn't the sort of person you imagined could kill someone. On the other hand, what if he'd been jealous of Diane's affection for others?

Marti watched Cindy comfort Tony. Cindy's compassion was evident. She wasn't afraid to help her friends in their moment of need. Tony could use a friend. Then again, Marti didn't want Cindy to hang out with Tony if he might turn on her. What if Marti's suspicions proved to be true? Then Cindy and Stacey were in danger.

Something caught her eye when Tony turned towards her.

"Huh," Marti gasped.

Fortunately no one heard her in the crowd.

She gazed with horror at the jewel twinkling in the dim basement light. Tony wore a blue sapphire ring on his right hand. Mesmerized by the gemstone Marti tried not to brand Tony as the killer. It appeared to grow before her gaze. She shook her head. The ring didn't prove anything.

She made a mental note to mention the ring to Detective Worthington. A visit to Tony was in order. Marti gazed around the room. Where was the detective? He'd meant to drop in at the funeral. Something must have detained him.

Cindy's voice interrupted Marti's musings as she heard her niece exclaim, "Brian, I thought you'd be here today."

Marti glanced at the teen as he stood awkwardly beside Tony. It was clear they weren't friends. On the other hand it was obvious Brian adored Cindy. His eyes glowed when he bent nearer to whisper something in her ear.

Marti smiled then narrowed her eyes as she caught Tony's scowl. Was the boy jealous of everyone? She angled her body to keep Tony in her periphery. As Marti turned she caught Marni's eye across the room. Marni motioned for her to join her.

Marti cast a quick glance toward Tony. Although he stood close to Cindy and her friend Brian his eyes darted about. He appeared harmless at the moment. Marti crossed the room to meet her sister.

"What's up?" Marti asked as Marni grabbed her arm.

"Over there, something caught my attention. I saw it out of the corner of my eye."

"What is it?"

"We have to go over there, check it out."

Marni's hold became painful.

"Ouch, no need to clench so hard. Your nails are razor sharp."

Marti rubbed her arm as Marni loosened her grip.

Marni grabbed Marti's hand then moved closer to her sister.

"I don't see anything," Marti whispered.

"We have to go over there."

"Alright."

Marti felt Marni's arm tremble as they walked toward an extra table laden with food. Marni almost dragged Marti as she purposely headed to her target.

Marni stopped abruptly beside one of the tables.

"Now what?"

"We have to search underneath."

"What did you see?"

"Not what, who," Marni corrected.

"Who did you see?"

Marni was slow to turn toward her sister. Her eyes skittered about as she gazed everywhere but at Marti's face. "Wisahkecahk," she whispered.

Marti gasped. "Here, you think the trickster is here."

"I think he's more of a shape shifter today."

"Why?"

"Today, his appearance was laced with evil."

Marti shuddered.

They dragged Cindy away from her friends and the funeral.

They were quiet on the drive home. Drained, the seriousness of the day was impossible to downplay. The funeral had been an ordeal. It had been a sad and depressing event.

Then to top it off, Marni had seen Wisahkecahk. She'd been sure of it. They hadn't found anything under the table. It wasn't as if you could corner Wisahkecahk.

It meant something though. They concluded the killer had been nearby. Had he watched people from outdoors or been inside the room? Wisahkecahk could be many things. Today, he'd been the destroyer. Evil had permeated the event.

It meant no one was safe…

CHAPTER 15

As they walked in the house, Marti's cell phone rang. She'd shut it off for the funeral. As she glanced at it she noted unknown showed up many times. Marti ran her hands through her hair then mouthed, *"Now what?"*

"Got called into the office yesterday and they gave me a warning," he complained, his tone hurt and bewildered. "I've been phoning ya. Where ya been?"

Marti paused to consider who the caller could be, almost placing the voice but not quite.

"Who is this?"

"I was gone too long yesterday. Got hauled into the office. My boss gave me a verbal warning. Said he understood I was confused about rules since I'd just started. If I slip up one more time I'll get a written warning. It'll go in my file. I just started this week. Can't afford to lose this job. Why do these things happen to me?"

It dawned on Marti who the caller was. "Barry?"

"Yeah, who'd ya think it was?"

"I'm sorry, why don't you explain everything from the beginning. Then I'll understand better."

Barry gave Marti his version of the meeting. He'd been reprimanded for being fifteen minutes late after lunch. Barry had skipped his morning coffee break. He thought he could take the extra time at noon. He'd been wrong. Now he'd suffered the consequences of his action.

Soothing Barry took longer than Marti expected. He calmed down when Marti said she'd phone his boss to explain what happened.

"I could mention how you're helping with the murder case," Marti suggested.

"Whattdya mean?"

Barry's tone was suspicious. "I'm not talking to no coppers, ya know. That's the last thing I need now."

"No, this wouldn't have anything to do with the police," Marti assured him.

"You could talk to me and my sister Marni. Like we did the other day. You know the area where Diane was murdered. You might be able to give us some clues. It would help with the case."

Marti held her breath. She didn't want to lose her tie with Barry. She sensed he knew something important. If Marti built up his trust maybe he'd confide in her.

"Yeah, sure ya can tell him that," Barry uttered.

"Oh, by the way, I meant to call today but we had a funeral to attend."

"That's where ya were."

"Yes, I know you can't get off work tomorrow since you've just started your job. I thought your sister-in-law Megan might be interested in attending a live show."

"Why would she want to do that?" Barry sounded suspicious again.

"It's an interview I'm doing at CTV News for their *'Interviews at Noon'* show. It's a discussion about my next novel. I know Megan is a fan. I thought she might like to be in the audience. My sister and niece will be there."

Barry's tone switched from suspicious to excited. "Wow, Marti, that's great. Megan would love that." He lowered his voice. "Thanks for thinking of her. She's gonna be real thrilled. She'll let me stay here longer I bet."

Marti noted the last comment. Where did Barry typically live?

"Should I get her on the phone? She's here. I bet she'd love to talk to ya."

"That sounds wonderful Barry. I'll call your boss in the morning before my interview."

"Thanks Marti, you're the best." The phone crashed down while Barry ran to get Megan.

Marti kicked her shoes off then grabbed a chair. When Megan got to the phone, breathless, Marti repeated her offer. As Barry predicted, Megan was thrilled to be part of the studio audience. She was sure her boss would let her off work for an extended lunch hour.

Marni had put the kettle on for tea. Marti grabbed some mugs and honey out of the cupboard.

How could a man of Barry's age know so little about the work world? He was in his thirties. Shouldn't he know more about how long his lunch hour was and the boundaries of his job? He seemed unaware of the basic rules of employment. He'd recently started this job and could be ignorant of their system but where had he worked before?

Marti made tea then went in search of her sister. She wanted to tell her about her conversation with Barry. She'd decided it was time to give Barry's name to Detective Worthington the next time she saw him.

Would Barry talk to her again after he was called in for questioning? Probably not, but what choice did she have?

⚊⚊⚊⚊ ⬥ ⚊⚊⚊⚊

Barry's thoughts ran parallel to Marti's but for a different reason. He liked how she was gonna mention him helping out with the murder case to his boss. Being an amateur detective would be a real kick.

On the other hand, what if she mentioned his name to the police? If he helped out wouldn't she talk about him to her detective friends? What if they did a search and found out about his past?

It had been an accident. He'd paid dearly for it.

What if they discovered he lived in a car beside the crime scene? Would they believe he'd had nothing to do with that girl's death if they found out about his half sister? It hadn't been his fault.

Barry's head hurt. He needed to talk, get good advice.

He'd have to go back there. They knew what he'd done. No one could tie him to this girl.

He hated that place.

It was the only way he could talk to him though. He shook his head then got up from the couch. Barry headed for the door before he changed his mind.

⁂

It stopped, quit running. No advance warning, no nothing, just stopped.

"Now what?" Don asked.

"I'll fix it, no big deal. We've put a lot of miles on it, that's all. It'll take a bit of tinkering."

"What if you can't fix it?"

"Quit worrying. I said I'd fix it and I will."

Murray was a whiz with cars. His friends knew this but Don was worried. They wanted to cross the border and were so close. It was like a bad omen the car breaking down in the middle of nowhere like this.

Murray pulled his tools from the trunk then hunkered down to see what was wrong. His face tightened as he tried to pull the ring off his finger. Diane had given it to him. He didn't wanna gunk it up with grease. It was on tight and took considerable effort to get off. Gazing at the emerald, Murray recalled how she'd bought it to set off his hazel eyes. Always considerate, she'd gotten it resized to fit his right ring finger. Murray sighed then pocketed the gemstone as he forced his mind from Diane to the matter at hand.

Don and Mark began to pace…

Hours later they'd become a real pain in the ass.

"Leave me alone. How can I fix the car with you two breathing down my neck? Go do something useful."

"Like what?" Mark asked.

"I don't know. Build a fire. It's gonna get dark soon. It'll keep wild animals away."

Murray could have bit his tongue off as he saw the expression of horror cross Don's face.

"Wild animals," he squeaked.

"Yeah, well, I'm exaggerating. Doesn't hurt to have a fire though. Maybe you could catch a rabbit so we have something for supper."

Don blanched.

Jeesh, the guy was squeamish. "Okay, okay, don't worry about it. Build a fire. We don't need to eat tonight."

Murray worked on the car until it was too dark to see.

"Do you think you can fix it?" Don ventured.

"Huh, oh yeah, it'll be ready tomorrow. No problem, just had to clean the plugs and make a few minor repairs. It's no big deal."

Don and Mark visibly relaxed.

Murray stared at the car. Man, he loved his Grand Prix. He could hardly wait to get to Mexico. The car needed a good wash and wax job to get rid of the dust. It had needed a tune up. He should have done it before the car broke down. It was getting on in years but was still mighty fine. His friends said he should buy a new one but he'd rebuilt the engine. He couldn't bear to part with it.

Chicks dug the shiny maroon colour. When he roared up next to them he knew it was a turn on. Wait till he had it spruced up again.

Too bad they hadn't made it to Mexico yet. They should have driven more and drank less. They'd stopped at a lot of bars on the way and met some hot women. Yeah, this trip had been a great idea.

It was unfortunate they'd had to leave for a while, quick like. They hadn't called in to work or anything. Not that he cared if he had a job when he got back. Labour jobs were easy to find.

It would have been more fun if they'd come just for the hell of it. This way it seemed like they'd run from something. They were, but not the way people thought.

They couldn't stay there and show their faces. It was too painful, horrible and degrading. How could anyone understand? They had to have been there.

How could they have done that?

What possessed people to behave like that? It was inhuman, unbelievable. Man, if only…

Nah. It wouldn't have made any difference.

Murray couldn't shake the feeling they should have done something. Thinking back, maybe they'd wimped out. Nah. They'd had no choice.

They had to leave, just had to. They'd been so out of it.

No one would believe what they'd done…

CHAPTER 16

Friday

Barry felt better the next day, able to go to work and function normally. Dr. Werner had put everything in perspective. He'd calmed Barry down, helped him see things clearly.

"Live in the present," Dr. Werner said. "Let the past go. Don't dwell on anything unpleasant."

Barry liked that.

She'd been a horrid person. She'd deserved everything she got in the end. Barry had paid his dues. Now it was time to move on.

⊥

"Who's that guy over there?" Barry asked Greg, one of his co-workers.

"Haven't seen him round the coffee room," Barry added. Although he'd been there less than a week, Barry felt comfortable. He was getting to know the routine.

"Name's Andy. Stay away from him. He's got a bad temper and can be real mean, you know?"

"Yeah."

Barry knew the type. They liked to pick on others weaker than them. Mean for no reason, just because they felt like it.

"He was at some funeral yesterday," Greg noted. "Maybe he took a few days off, cause you're right. I haven't seen him around for awhile."

Greg shrugged then wandered off. It was no business of his.

Barry nodded. "Interesting."

Marti said the girl who'd been murdered was buried yesterday. Wonder if it was the same funeral? Might be a good time to do some investigating.

There was still five minutes left in their break. Barry decided to go introduce himself to Andy. Couldn't hurt. He rubbed his hands in anticipation. They were slightly sweaty.

Barry wandered over to the window. He tried to appear casual as he gazed outside. Hands in pockets he rocked back and forth on the balls of his feet, cool, calm, relaxed.

He glanced over at Andy then said, "Seems kinda nice outside again. Great to get out of here soon, eh?"

"Huh, oh, yeah, right, whatever."

It wasn't much to go on but Barry plunged forward nonetheless. "Started here this week." Barry turned towards Andy. "Name's Barry." He leaned over the table to shake hands.

Andy ignored his outstretched hand but replied, "Name's Andy." With an abrupt movement he turned in the other direction.

Barry knew he'd gotten the cold shoulder. He shrugged then glanced at the clock. It was time to get back to his post before he was late. He didn't want to get in trouble again.

⋏

She couldn't concentrate. Scattered, Sue's mind jumped. How had this happened? Where was Cora? They'd been together an hour ago. People didn't vanish into thin air. After a frantic search, Sue admitted defeat. She couldn't find Cora.

Sue gnawed on her fingernail as she called home. No one had seen nor heard from Cora. Her mom said they'd head to the mall.

Two carloads of relatives arrived. Someone had the idea to share Cora's picture.

"We'll meet every half hour. Show the picture, someone must have seen Cora," Donald said. Donald, Sue's dad, had taken charge of the group.

Everyone nodded then set off.

Two hours later there was no sign of Cora. She'd been missing four and a half hours.

"Okay, the mall is about to close," Donald announced. "There are eleven of us. We'll stand outside as many exits as we can to see if she leaves the mall."

Sue's mom mentioned some of the stores, like the Bay, had two exits.

"We could find a mall sign then count the number of exits," Sue suggested.

Initially, Sue thought it was her fault Cora was gone. No one blamed her though. As the afternoon wore on, the guilt began to lift from her shoulders.

They headed down a corridor to locate a mall sign. Time ticked by, relentless. Twenty minutes until mall closure.

Donald read off the list. "I count fourteen. Anyone see more?"

They agreed there were fourteen exits. "Okay, you young kids can watch more than one exit. Your eyes are better. Everyone know what she's wearing?"

They nodded. Donald assigned exits and they ran to their posts. "Meet inside the theatre entrance after the other doors have been locked," he called.

Sue ran to her post. Eager to be the one to find Cora she hadn't yet admitted defeat. Hope swept through the group.

Sue stood inside the store as rain poured down. She wasn't eager to get wet. It was easy to see each person's face as they walked by. Soon, there were only a few stragglers.

Sue began to lose hope as the clock ticked. It sounded loud in her head, tick, tick, tick, as minutes counted down. Sue dreaded the moment when the store clerk came to kick her out. As the thought entered her mind, an older woman hurried toward her. Sue knew this was it.

"The store is closed. I need to lock the door."

Sue's lower lip trembled.

As she turned away the woman asked, "Are you all right?"

Sue turned. "My sister is lost. I hoped Cora would use this exit." Sue's face crumpled on the last word. Tears flowed. She hadn't allowed herself to break down earlier. Eager to search, her mind had been focused on the task.

The woman touched Sue's arm. "I'm sorry. Are you alone?"

Sue brushed tears away with the sleeve of her sweater. She wished she had a tissue. She opened her purse blindly groping for something to wipe her nose.

The woman produced a clean tissue from her pocket.

Sue reached for it, blew her nose then gulped out a grateful, "Thanks."

The tears wouldn't stop but Sue felt better as she added, "No, I'm not alone. I called my family hours ago." She gulped. "We've searched but nothing." Her voice wobbled. "We hoped to find Cora as she left."

"Someone in the group might have spotted her." The woman's voice was soft, sympathetic.

"Maybe." Sue's voice trembled. "We're supposed to call if we find her though." She waved her phone. "No call." Her face crumpled as big crocodile tears flowed.

Sue was mortified. How embarrassing, crying in front of a stranger. Her tears wouldn't stop.

The woman touched her arm again. "We should find a security guard. We can tell them about your sister."

Sue blew her nose then nodded. With the heels of her palms she vigorously rubbed her face to rid it of tears.

"I need to lock these doors first," the woman said as she pulled out a key ring. "You should call your mom. Tell her what we're up to. We don't want her to worry."

"Good idea." Sue flashed a grateful smile then called her mom as they walked from the exit doors.

"Who are you with?" Her mom's voice rose. "What's her name? Does she seem official? I don't want you with a stranger."

Sue stopped. "Just a sec. I'll ask." She turned to the woman. "My mom wants your name." She noticed a store nametag on the woman's jacket.

"It's Doreen Pendgrass. She has a store nametag on that says Doreen," Sue added with a smile. "Doreen, I mean Mrs. Pendgrass and I are going to find a security guard, to tell him about Cora. Okay, I'll tell her."

Sue pressed end then said, "My mom wants my brother David to come with us. She's stressed since we can't find Cora."

"Of course. I'm a mother and I'd be frantic." Doreen turned back toward the door. "What's your name dear?"

"Sue. My brother will be right here."

"We'll watch for him. I'll unlock the door when you see him."

Doreen chatted about the weather while they waited. "It's pouring out. I'm not eager to walk to my car."

"How old are your kids?"

"My daughter is twenty-two and in university and my son is seventeen. He's in high school. How many siblings do you have?"

"There are four of us. David's twenty, Daniel's eighteen, I'm sixteen and Cora, my sister, is fourteen."

A face appeared at the door.

"That's him," Sue confirmed as Doreen unlocked the door.

David walked in. As he shook his dark hair, droplets flew.

Introductions were made as they set off to find a security guard.

"Do you have a picture of your sister? It would help with the search."

"Yeah, on my cell phone."

"Good. The office is down this hallway." Doreen led them in that direction. As she knocked on the door, Doreen added, "They'll want a report."

A heavyset man answered the door.

"Hank, great, you're here." Doreen bustled through the door. "These two have lost their sister. They want to make an official report."

"Sure, when did this happen?" Hank moved toward a computer then sat down. His hands were poised on top of the keyboard, ready to type.

Sue glanced around the room as she moved forward. Pictures flashed on eight screens.

"Um, I lost her just before four."

Hank raised his eyebrows but didn't comment as he typed. "Name, age, do you have a picture, where was she last seen?" The questions were fast and furious while he recorded their answers.

"This scene was about a moment." Marti gazed at the audience with their expectant faces. She pushed the hair that had tumbled into her face aside as if it would stop the flow of words.

"This was a defining moment. We all love someone. A spouse, parent, sibling, lover, special friend, animal…" Marti waved her hand. "The list is expansive. This description illustrates how Sue felt. She wished time had stopped. Sue mentioned the clock in her head going tick, tick, tick. People continued their actions while Sue watched as if from afar. Her movements were hindered, stilted, frozen." Marti gripped the sides of the chair she was perched on then leaned forward.

"This fictional example described how it felt when Sue realized her loved one was missing." She waited a heartbeat for the crowd to digest her words. "It was an exercise a student wrote in one of my writing classes. She said I could use it however I wish."

Marti's gaze darted toward the studio audience. "The ideas and discussion generated in this particular writing class provided the basis for my upcoming novel *'Stolen Spirits.'* It offers a starting point for discussion of missing and murdered Indigenous women and girls. That's one of the themes in my novel." Marti smiled. "We have time for a Q and A session. Does anyone have a question?"

A hand shot up in the audience. "Did they find Cora?"

Marti smiled. "Yes, they did. She saw a friend then wandered off to shop with her at another mall. Cora thought she sent a text to her sister Sue but hadn't pressed the send button. Then her battery died. She arrived home shortly after her family came home from the mall search."

A collective sigh swept through the audience. Marti grinned. This had happened before. Although she'd announced the example was fictional, people had to know Cora was safe, even if she didn't exist anywhere but in a writer's imagination. Relief brought people closer to one another. Former strangers, currently united, smiled or nodded at their neighbours.

Megan was enthralled. Marti was awesome. Megan flashed a sidelong glance at Marni and Cindy. They were fortunate to be related to a celebrity. Megan puffed her chest out. She'd been invited today as a special guest of Marti Rose, bestselling author. She owed Barry big time for this favour.

CHAPTER 17

When Barry entered the coffee room that afternoon he saw Andy sitting at a table by himself. He should talk to Andy again. He was supposed to be helping Marti with the investigation wasn't he? If this guy had been at a funeral yesterday it was up to Barry to find out more about him. Feeling duty bound, and rather self-important, Barry straightened his back then strode over to the table.

"Hey, you're Andy, aren't ya?"

"Yeah."

Barry racked his brain for something to say. He couldn't blurt out '*Hey who's funeral were ya at yesterday?*' Then again maybe he could, wouldn't hurt.

"Heard ya were at a funeral yesterday." Barry sat down on one of the chairs.

"Yeah, what's it to ya?"

"Nothing, some of my friends were at one yesterday, thought it might be the same one. That's all." Barry gulped. "Big city though, odds are it was a different one."

Andy glanced up from his contemplation of the table. He glared at Barry, mean like.

His eyes were dark green and intense. Barry felt like probes had attached themselves to Andy's eyes to search the depth of Barry's thoughts. It was freaky. It was like a silent interrogation.

Barry gulped. He felt hot and cold at the same time. Sweat freely gathered. Liquid poured out of his underarms, great gobs of it. What if it gushed everywhere? Breaking contact with Andy, Barry checked the side of his shirt but didn't see any telltale stains. With a sigh of relief Barry leaned on the two back legs of his chair, relaxed now, prepared to stare Andy down.

Andy scowled then glanced away. "Yeah, was at some broad's funeral. Friend of my sisters ya know."

"Oh."

Now what was that girl's name? Marti had mentioned it the other day. It started with a D so it had to be Debbie, no, Donna, no, Diane, no. Wait a minute yeah that was it, Diane.

"Yeah, heard Diane had a lot of friends ya know. Did ya ever meet her?"

"Nah, but they're all the same yippety yap, blah, blah, blah, ya know how it is."

"Yeah, don't I know it?"

Glancing at the clock Barry decided he'd better go. Break was almost over. As he made a move to get up Andy started to talk. Ain't he the chatty guy, Barry thought.

"Hate this place, stupid hellhole, nothing ever goes on."

Barry nodded, unsure if Andy meant Sears or the city.

"Seems as if everywhere you turn someone knows ya. Maybe I should move along."

Andy seemed to be talking to himself so Barry kept quiet. Andy's movements mesmerized Barry. He flicked his lighter, open, closed, open, closed. Barry liked the insignia on it, Monte Carlo. Had Andy traveled there or someone brought it back as a souvenir? Maybe he'd ask later, after they got to know one another better.

Barry missed part of Andy's conversation as he envisioned their future discussion. Likely wasn't important what Andy had said. The guy was negative. He interrupted Andy to say, "Hey man, I better get back to work. Break's over."

Barry got up to leave.

"Yeah, me too. Man, I hate this place."

Barry was eager to tell Marti about his conversation with Andy. Maybe it didn't mean much but he'd interrogated Andy and done a pretty good job. The guy had mentioned Diane even though he claimed he didn't know her. Andy could be more familiar with her than he'd let on. Barry nodded. Yup, he'd better call Marti tonight. She'd be pleased, real pleased.

⋏

The moderator, Karen smiled at Marti. "You're doing great Marti. I love working with authors who've done a lot of interviews. You're a pro."

"Thanks," Marti murmured.

"And you're on in three, two, one."

"Welcome back to *'Indigenous Circle*,*'* " Karen chirped. "Today we're honoured to have Marti Rose, famous author join us." She held up a poster advertising Marti's upcoming novel, *'Stolen Spirits.'*

"Tell us Marti, why did you include the topic of missing and murdered Indigenous women and girls in this novel? Isn't that a heavy subject for an author and I mean no offense by this, an author often described as a mystery writer and amateur crime solver?"

Marti grinned. "Thanks for your kind words Karen. That's why I've included the heavy topic of missing and murdered Indigenous women and girls in *'Stolen Spirits.'* Now that I have a number of devoted fans I thought it was time to give back to the community."

Marti contemplated her tented hands then lifted her chin to stare straight into the camera. "As the story unfolds, my hope is readers, especially teen girls, get caught up in this cautionary tale. I've included the usual Marti Rose elements." She flashed a quick smile. "I wouldn't want to disappoint my fans."

Marti addressed Karen. "I went to lunch this week with Barry and his sister-in-law Megan. Megan is an avid fan. She's read all my books. Megan mentioned one of the things she relates to in my novels is the characters are ordinary people. Megan felt a connection to the characters."

Marti turned back to the camera. "That's one of the highest compliments for an author. Writing is solitary. Our characters become real to us. We live, eat, breathe, sleep and dream about them as if they're living entities. When I create individuals they're like an extended family. My characters are everyday people. They have the capacity to do extraordinary things or may have heroic tendencies, just like real people. I want my readers to relate and like them."

Marti pushed the hair back from her temple. "The thing is," she leaned forward in her chair. "None of us are perfect. We all make mistakes."

Karen seemed about to interrupt.

Marti flashed another smile at the camera then turned back to Karen. "Some of the teens in *'Stolen Spirits'* made a grave mistake." She frowned. "I don't want to give the story away. I can say this though." Marti leaned back in her chair. "For some of them, their lapse in judgment," she paused, "Results in death. I don't think that gives anything away since it is a murder mystery."

Karen gave a slight smile then nodded. "Yes, one expects murder in crime fiction. Why do you refer to this novel as a cautionary tale?"

"That's a great question Karen."

Karen beamed at the praise.

Marti leaned forward then pierced the camera with an intent stare. "Many youth don't give a second thought how their actions affect other people. In Canada the stats are disturbing regarding the number of missing and murdered Indigenous women and girls out there. The numbers shocked me." Marti shook her head. "I've read Aboriginal women are seven to eight times more likely to be murdered as a result of violence than non-Aboriginal women."

Karen frowned, glanced at the camera then away.

"I love stats Karen. I hope I don't bore you or the audience but I'm compelled to share these with you."

Marti pulled a piece of paper closer. "I'm going to read from my notes since I don't want to get this wrong." She smiled into the camera then focused on the comments she'd written. "The Native

Women's Association of Canada, Sisters in Spirit Project compiled data until their project funding was cut in 2010. They documented 582 cases of missing and murdered Indigenous women and girls. Aboriginal leaders stated that number was closer to one thousand."

Marti shoved her hair back. "A new study was released at the end of 2013. That public database included three more years of cases and intensive research. It documented 824 cases of missing and murdered Indigenous women and girls. An Ottawa researcher Maryanne Pearce spent seven years on the project. She published her thesis for a doctoral degree in law on the issue of why so many Aboriginal women are vulnerable to violent predators and why disappearances go unsolved. Some cases date back to the 50's while the majority is from 1990 to 2013."

"I know, I've read the articles and followed media reports," Karen murmured.

Marti nodded. "The numbers are out of proportion with the rest of society. Simply being an Aboriginal woman puts us at risk of violence." She sighed. "The numbers are higher than Maryanne Pearce's database indicated."

"Higher," Karen echoed.

"Yes." Marti glanced down again. "The latest numbers were released in May of 2014 when an RCMP cross-Canada review was completed. The police hiked previous estimates and reports to almost 1,200. That's the known number of cases that date back 30 years. Information was compiled from 300 police detachments across Canada."

Karen shuddered.

"I know. I was shocked too when those numbers were released. The Aboriginal leaders were right. There are almost 1,200

Indigenous women and girls missing or slain in Canada. The percent of Aboriginal female homicides are higher than original estimates and greater than what police disclosed in the past." Marti shook her head, pushed her notes aside then leaned toward Karen. "I don't want to lose our viewers by quoting too many stats." She smiled into the camera. "I believe you mentioned we'll discuss where people can get more information at the end of this segment."

"Yes, we provide references and links on our website. We'll have a list of statistics and details onscreen before the final credits."

"Great, thanks Karen. There's another point I'd like to raise. Media sensationalize murders or focus on the conditions of Aboriginal women as opposed to the gravity of these crimes. Society ignores or dismisses the subject. There are key factors in the victim's lives that contribute to a significant number of the cases including homelessness, addiction, mental illness, and involvement in the child-welfare system or the sex trade."

Marti frowned. "The perception is most of these cases involve prostitutes or women in high-risk behavior. That's not true though. Maryanne Pearce's findings show 80% of missing or murdered Indigenous women were not in the sex trade. That's why I wrote about this issue. I want young girls and women to know about the dangers out there. This topic needs to be discussed."

She pointed at the camera. "We tell our children never to talk to strangers or get in a car with them. Yet they hit the teen years and throw all caution aside. As a First Nations woman I worry about my daughter and all the daughters, sisters, mothers and women out there who could become a victim of racial and sexist violence. Hence the cautionary tale."

"You mention racial and sexist violence. Why is that Marti?"

"This is a national human rights tragedy Karen. I consider it an epidemic. Some men feel they're justified in committing violent acts against women, in particular Aboriginal women. These are acts of hatred. I've researched and written enough about violence and murder to make that statement. People who commit murder are not kind, caring, compassionate or loving. They're the opposite."

Marti sighed. "We need to address the root causes of violence. Racism and sexism come into play when one considers the frequency of violent crimes against Aboriginal women. Sexual assault is common for female victims of crime. The girls in *'Stolen Spirits'* could be one of our daughters or sisters. Do you have a daughter Karen?"

Karen flinched then whispered, "Yes, she's seven."

"Mine is fourteen. My mind refuses to entertain the notion anyone could ever harm her."

Karen's eyes widened as Marti added, "I can't begin to imagine the grief and emotion a family experience as they wait to hear from a loved one who's gone missing." Her voice caught. "The not knowing, constant worry, ache in your heart, the agony, it would never go away." She closed her eyes. "For a family, the worst news possible is to be presented with the grim reality of death." Marti's eyes flashed open. "Is knowledge worse than uncertainty?"

She shook her head then rubbed her forehead. "I feel fortunate, blessed not to know that answer. Hope springs eternal, that's a famous quote by Alexander Pope, an 18th century English poet. If a loved one has been missing for many years hope is all one has. Even if evidence says our loved one will never return to us we have to think they will." Marti's eyes filled with tears. "That's all we have is hope." Her voice shook on the last word.

Karen reached over to lay her hand on top of Marti's. With her other hand she made a cutting motion across her throat. The cameraman turned the camera off.

⊥

After Marti composed herself they resumed their interview. "I'm glad this one is taped and not live, that would have been embarrassing," Marti confessed.

"Don't worry about it," Karen soothed. "I was ready to take a break as well." She blew her breath out. "As you said I can't and don't want to imagine this ever happening to anyone I love. Can we start there? Are you good to go again?"

Marti nodded. "Sure, let's do this."

"I can't comprehend the level of pain and grief a family goes through. To lose a loved one in the senseless manner these lost and murdered Indigenous girls and women are exposed to. As a mother, my mind refuses to imagine the *'what if.'*" Marti bowed her head. She closed her eyes then sat with clasped hands as if in prayer.

The silence was powerful and absolute.

As Karen watched Marti take a deep breath her eyes darted here and there. She fidgeted in her seat, readjusted the microphone on her collar, mopped her forehead with her hand, rubbed her neck then ran her hands through her hair. Karen's relief was palpable when Marti flashed her eyes open. In a low voice Karen murmured, "Thank you for that Marti."

Marti nodded.

"This is not an easy topic to talk about," Karen continued. She sighed then stared straight into the camera. "Death and murder is not something to take lightly. If you've just joined us I'm pleased to have Marti Rose, famous author with us today. We're discussing the reality and potential of brutality and abuse for many Aboriginal girls and women." Karen tore her eyes from the camera to focus on Marti.

"Marti's current novel, *'Stolen Spirits,'* focuses on the topic of missing and murdered Indigenous girls and women." Karen reached over to the table beside her. She lifted a large illustration. Artwork, Stolen Spirits and Marti Rose were splashed across it. "This is the front cover of *'Stolen Spirits.'* The release date is sometime this fall isn't it Marti?"

Marti appeared relaxed beside Karen whose tone was rushed. "Yes, it will be out by the end of September, beginning of October. I'm not supposed to give the exact date since my publicist likes to keep that hush hush." Marti grinned as she leaned forward. "She loves to keep my fans on edge."

"From what I understand Marti your fans are in for another treat with this novel. We discussed earlier how this is a heavy topic." Karen smiled. "I'm sure you've managed to weave your brand of Marti Rose favourites throughout to keep readers engaged."

Marti nodded. "Yes, my focus group had a few surprises this time. There's the usual recipe for disaster but I've cooked up some unknowns that should keep people on their toes."

Karen nodded then leaned forward. "Tell me Marti, how do you write the scenes from the viewpoint of the victim and family when you mentioned earlier you can't fathom this level of brutality as a mother?"

Marti shuddered. "I knew you were going to ask that question Karen. It's a hard one to answer." She massaged her cheeks then temple. "As I said when one writes, our characters become real to us. When a tragedy occurs it hurts deeply. These characters are like my family. I'm the mother to these teen girls."

She sighed. "People responsible for these types of crimes need to be held accountable. If someone witnesses something out of the ordinary they need to report it to the police. There's often insufficient evidence to convict those responsible for heinous crimes."

Marti turned to the camera. "People relate to the need to find these immoral, wicked individuals guilty of unimaginable horrors. As a mother I don't want to acknowledge their existence. It's preferable to live our lives in ignorance. Otherwise we might be too scared to let our children outdoors." She shook her head. "We can't imagine the worst. It's too scary."

Karen nodded. "You're right Marti. As you said earlier I can't go there as a mother. Yet as a moderator I discuss heavy topics on a regular basis. We do compartmentalize various aspects of our lives. I guess that's how we cope."

"I agree Karen. I'm working on an outline for my next novel. It's not a sequel to *'Stolen Spirits'* yet will have some similarities. As a novelist I feel it's important to address the injustices of our society even if I do write fiction. Hope will be a sub-theme of my next novel, hope and the future of our next generation."

Marti turned back to Karen. "On that note, I'd like to mention there are community and advocacy groups for families of a victim of violence. I understand a list will be provided onscreen at the end of this segment and on your station's website."

"Yes Marti, as we mentioned earlier stats and links will be available for further information."

CHAPTER 18

Marti sighed as she watched the teakettle. Her second interview had been intense. It was rare for her to lose control in a question and answer session. She appreciated Karen's compassion. They'd taken a number of breaks, as the topic was heavy. They'd provided a list of community and advocacy groups to list onscreen and on the station's website. If they reached one family of a victim of violence and provided a link for them to access, the interview was a success in Marti's mind.

The list filled pages. Marti was sure she'd missed groups. She thought it more important to mention the ones she knew rather than be caught up with the ones she'd forgotten. Facebook alone had sites for Families of Sisters in Spirit, Missing and Murdered Aboriginal Women in Canada, Missing Manitoba Women, Saskatchewan Missing Women & Children and the National Inquiry into Missing and Murdered Women in Canada. Amnesty International Canada highlighted Canada: No More Stolen Sisters, there was the Native Women's Association of Canada, the database from Maryanne Pearce's thesis *'An Awkward Silence: Missing and Murdered Vulnerable Women and the Canadian Justice System,'* the RCMP cross-Canada review *Missing and Murdered Aboriginal Women: A National Operational Overview*, reports from committees, media articles and much more.

The teakettle boiled as Marti glanced out the window. Karen had bought tickets for an entire table for tomorrow evening's fundraiser. Marti turned off the kettle then grabbed her phone. She sent a text to the organizer of the event for the last minute tickets.

The door slammed as Marti made tea. She wandered into the living room to find Cindy's friends gathered there. The teens glanced her way as Marti entered the room.

"Auntie, come sit by me," Cindy encouraged with a motion of her hand.

Marti slapped a smile on her face. She didn't feel up to an intense teen session yet didn't want to disappoint her niece.

The door slammed again, louder this time. Tony strode into the room. Clearly agitated, Tony paced as he launched into what happened to him earlier that day.

"I knew something bad was going down when I saw the squad car pull in front of our house." Tony's voice shook.

"Oh no, what happened?" Cindy asked.

"The police took me downtown. They asked me a bunch of questions. They weren't mean but I felt like a criminal. The room they took me in smelled bad, like dirty people had been there before."

Tony shuddered.

"How long were you there?"

"I don't know it seemed like hours. I just got home. Hey do you have anything to eat, I'm starved."

"Yeah, let's go in the kitchen."

Cindy led the way while Tony trailed behind.

Marti sipped her tea. Either Tony would tell them more or she'd ask the detective about him. She was curious to know what Worthington had found out. Was Tony as innocent as he claimed?

Marti turned to Stacey who'd remained quietly seated on the sofa throughout the exchange. As they spoke it became apparent Stacey was still in shock. She couldn't admit Diane was dead. She mixed up tenses, talking about Diane in present time. Her stories were about what her and Diane liked to do while her general comments implied Diane had gone on vacation and would be back shortly.

Unwilling to shake her out of her reverie Marti played along. She asked who they'd talked to the other night when they went to the exhibition. Stacey mentioned the same people she'd talked about to Detective Worthington.

"Was Diane close to Tony and Brad?"

Stacey scrunched up her face.

"I guess she was. Brad and her went out for a while earlier in the year, we all thought they'd get back together eventually, maybe they still will."

She glanced at Marti then her eyes slithered away. Marti let the statement pass without comment.

"Diane understood people. She saw beyond your exterior and got right inside your soul. She's spiritual, especially for someone our age. We're only fifteen you know."

Marti nodded as she sipped tea, content to let Stacey talk about whatever she chose.

"Tony's weird," Stacey whispered. She glanced toward the living room door then shuddered. "He gives us the creeps. He can be normal and then bam goes off the deep end and freaks everybody out. It never bothered Diane though. She said there was more to him than meets the eye." Stacey frowned. "Diane said they understood one another."

Stacey leaned forward. "I think Tony's in love with Diane. He follows her around, like a puppy dog."

"Do you think he could hurt Diane?"

Marti was conscious of how she'd slipped into the present tense as she mimicked Stacey.

Stacey stared into the distance. Brow furrowed, she gave the question considerable merit.

Stacey might regret those intense frowns. Wrinkles could plague her later in life. Marti shrugged. The moment didn't lend itself to that suggestion.

"It's hard to say. Like I mentioned before Tony's strange so you never know when he's going to fly off in a weird direction. He seems like the jealous type. He might hurt Diane but then again he likes her. They talk a lot so I don't think he'd want to destroy the bond they share. Tony doesn't have a lot of close friends."

Stacey frowned again. "Diane talked to Tony the other day. I heard her. I think…" As she trailed off, her voice wobbled.

Marti watched her, interested to see what would happen next.

"Do you believe in ghosts?"

Marti hesitated. "My sister calls them spirits."

Stacey nodded, apparently satisfied with her answer.

"It sounded like Diane. Do you think it was her?" Pale blue eyes stared into Marti's, crystal clear.

Marti gulped. "It could have been," she whispered.

Marti had eavesdropped at the funeral as Cindy and Tony discussed hearing Diane's voice. She was grateful as it helped her grasp Stacey's meandering thoughts.

"It was mean of Terri and those girls to accuse Tony of hurting Diane. Everyone's talking about what happened at the party. How could they suspect one of Diane's friends of murdering her? Tony liked Diane, he couldn't harm her."

Stacey shook her head. "Do you know who Wishkecak is?"

Marti had leaned forward to retrieve a book under the coffee table when Stacey asked her question. Startled, her eyes flew to Stacey's as she automatically corrected her pronunciation.

"Wisahkecahk, yes I do? Why do you ask?"

Marti glanced at the book then laid it on the table.

"Diane mentioned him the night she was murdered. She called him a trickster. Diane said a bunch of things about him. I think she was frightened because of Wisahkecahk."

Stacey filled Marti in on the conversation. "We should never have gone out that evening," she concluded.

What did it mean? Diane saw Wisahkecahk the night she was murdered. Then Marni saw him at Diane's funeral. It had to be Wisahkecahk the destroyer.

Evil was at the heart of this mystery. Marti would have to keep her wits about her. Wisahkecahk could reappear at any time.

"Aren't most people murdered by strangers?" Stacey asked breaking into Marti's thoughts.

Marti wished it were in her power to alleviate Stacey's fears. Unfortunately facts didn't lend themselves to that theory. How could she tell Stacey police regarded people close to Diane as suspects? Those connected with Diane, family, current boyfriend, past boyfriends, friends, potential enemies. They were the ones questioned first.

Marti longed to ease Stacey's doubts. To tell her Diane's stolen spirit had been the result of a random stranger. Rosemarie's murder, the one Worthington had familiarized Marti with yesterday, could have been committed by a stranger.

This murder wasn't similar to Rosemarie's though or other cases Marti had been involved with. It didn't follow the pattern of many Aboriginal girls and women who were victims of violent crimes. It was likely someone within Stacey and Diane's circle had been responsible for the horrendous crime.

How could she tell Stacey that? Marti wished the crime had been random. She knew longing for something didn't make it real though.

"If I were to write a novel about Diane's murder I think I'd make the murderer someone people knew." Marti shrugged. "Then again, I might make it a random murder. Many Aboriginal girls and women are victims of violent crime so one could consider that avenue."

Stacey flinched. "Violent crime," she whispered, eyes wide.

Marti almost slapped herself in the forehead. Why had she mentioned the words violent crime? As she gazed at Stacey, Marti noted her pain. Her eyes were haunted. There were dark circles rimmed beneath them. A veil of doom hovered around Stacey like a black cloud.

Marti shook her head. Thoughts like that mirrored those of her sister and Gwyn. This wasn't the time to think of doom, evil or hauntings.

Stacey needed more help than Marti was capable of. Diane's friends needed support. She'd bring it up with Worthington. He should know the name of a counselor in the area. They needed to talk to someone who dealt with violent death and grieving.

Brad wandered into the room interrupting the moment. The conversation switched tacks. Brad had come to terms with Diane's death so he didn't bounce back and forth from present to past tense.

"I made more tea," Marni announced as she strode into the room with a tray.

Brad leaned forward. "Yum, I smell peppermint. Can I have some? I love peppermint. My mom gives it to me when I have a stomach ache." He glanced at Stacey. "You should drink some. It will make you feel better. Peppermint is soothing."

They helped themselves to tea and cookies then settled back in their seats.

As they spoke, it became apparent Brad had shared a great deal with Diane and they'd been close. There was no doubt in Marti's mind Brad had loved Diane. If she'd returned those feelings the two of them could have had something special. They might have been soul mates.

Marni talked about how we bond with certain people in our lives and have special feelings for them. She mentioned words like spiritual and well-being then threw in divinity and mystical for good measure. Brad nodded while Marni talked, content to sit back and listen. Stacey stared into space.

"What sort of relationship did you have with Diane?" Marti asked when her sister paused.

"It's interesting you mentioned spirituality." Brad nodded at Marni. "Diane was spiritual. She believed in God and went to church on a regular basis. Diane prayed and talked to God all the time. She had premonitions and felt vibrations. She said they came from the earth." Brad grabbed his peppermint tea, took a sip then continued.

"Diane was superstitious when the moon was full. That's when she thought something bad would happen. Diane said evil had more strength at certain times of the moon's cycle. During a full moon people are the most dangerous. She was cautious when the moon was full and reluctant to be around strangers. Was there a full moon the other night?"

"Yes there was."

Brad sighed. "She shouldn't have been out then. Had I known the moon was full I would have made sure Diane got home." Brad's mouth quivered. He glanced away. A moment passed while he regained control.

"We talked that night at the exhibition. She was edgy but I never guessed it would be the last time I'd see her. I would have chosen my words, said much more." Brad broke off, barely choking back a sob.

Stacey jumped up then headed to the kitchen.

"Can you think of anyone who might have wanted to harm Diane?" Marti whispered.

Brad turned away. Was he loath to answer the question or unable to imagine someone had hated Diane that much?

In a low voice he answered. Marti and Marni leaned forward to hear his words.

"How could anyone harm her? I can't believe this is happening…"

Tony bounded back into the living room.

Marti sighed. She should question Tony while he was here.

Tony didn't wait for questions though. He answered them before they were asked. Since he'd been interrogated that morning Tony anticipated what Marti wanted to know. He was free and easy with information.

Marti watched Tony as he bounced around the room. Nervous and agitated, the boy couldn't sit still. Fascinated with the way his mind worked Marti didn't learn anything new until the end of the conversation.

Tony turned toward her then blurted. "Can I ask you something?"

"Sure Tony, ask away."

Tony's eyes darted to the living room entrance. His friends had departed to the family room to play video games. Marni had taken the tea tray back to the kitchen. "It's about my real dad."

"Mm hmm."

"I wonder if the police will think I have something to do with Diane's death because my dad's in jail for…"

Tony's voice dropped off at the crucial moment.

"Yes," Marti encouraged.

Tony's eyes flitted around the room as if he were guilty of something. Marti couldn't believe he was about to confess to Diane's death though.

She leaned forward just in case.

"My dad's been in jail for the last ten years. He, well, he, murdered someone," Tony whispered.

His eyes met Marti's for a brief instance. Her amazement must have shown since his glance slithered away.

Marti sat back. With heavy limbs, voice silent, Marti acknowledged the emotions of the day had taken a toll. Not for the first time

Marti wished she weren't so close to the players in Diane's death. She was at a loss for words. How do you comfort someone close to the victim when he confesses to having a murderer for a father? Were murderous tendencies hereditary?

Marti shook herself. How ludicrous. Why had her mind wandered that direction? Of course it wasn't hereditary to have murderous impulses. If Tony had grown up with his father and been involved in murder then he would have learned about violence firsthand. That wasn't the case though.

In a quiet voice Marti asked. "Why do you think what your father did long ago has anything to do with Diane's death?"

Tony jerked his right leg. He licked his lips, rocked to and fro then stared at something over Marti's forehead.

Was this a nervous mannerism or was he thinking?

"Don't know, thought the cops might think Diane's murder was similar that's all."

He slumped down on the couch as he rocked to and fro.

Marti scrunched up her face. "How do you know the details are the same?"

The question caught Tony off guard. He stopped rocking, shook himself like a wet dog then frowned at Marti.

"Well, well I don't," he admitted.

"Then I wouldn't worry about it. What your father did in the past has nothing to do with Diane's death. No one will blame you for something you had no control over. Do your friends know about your dad?"

"No, you're the first I've told."

"Do you want to talk about it?"

Tony narrowed his eyes then nodded.

Marti watched him. She longed to read his mind. If she were a psychic like Gwyn she could receive impressions from Tony. She thought his body language conveyed guilt and secrecy. She couldn't shake the feeling Tony wasn't an innocent bystander. On the other hand, his friends described him as weird so his actions could indicate typical nervousness on his part. Marti frowned. There wasn't time for doubt. Tony required her total attention.

"We moved here when my mom remarried. She changed my name. It's the same as my stepfathers' so no one knows who my real father is."

He stopped. When he spoke again his words were jerky. "I looked it up in the library. The murder I mean. My mom won't talk about it and I wanted to know the details. I had to know."

He put his chin in his hands, leaning elbows on knees. "There were three of them. They took a woman they worked with out of town. They were partying. I guess things got out of hand." Tony sighed. "One thing led to another and before they knew it they'd raped the girl."

Tony's head jerked up, gauging her reaction.

Marti kept her face impassive, willing herself not to show shock or revulsion. She was surprised at the cavalier attitude Tony presented while he told the disturbing tale. Had Tony faked detachment or did his indifference signify coldness, an inability to relate to the victim?

She shook her head to erase the doubt. "Go on."

"One of them killed her by mistake. The article said she wouldn't stop screaming. One of the guys panicked. They were drunk. He strangled her to death. It wasn't my dad though."

Marti stared at Tony, shocked by the story.

The significance of what Tony related dawned on her.

It sounded like... a copycat murder.

It was an effort not to stand and point at Tony in an accusatory manner. "*Killer, killer, the spawn of a madman. You're evil, no good,*" Marti longed to say. If this was a novel, at this point she'd shout, "*Did you kill Diane? Are you a heartless murderer?*"

Instead, Marti's mind spun as she tried to be logical. It wasn't fair to blame Tony because his father had committed a heinous crime. Or was it? It was hard to be rational in light of this new information.

The scene of the crime differed but the circumstances were similar. Diane's death paralleled Tony's father's crime to a large extent. If one assumed Diane had been screaming, strangling had brought silence. A lethal option but it kept her quiet.

"Are you going to tell the police?"

Marti nodded her head. She couldn't ignore this. What if evidence from that crime helped with this one? What if Tony experimented and killed Diane by mistake? What if he was a madman like his father?

"Yes Tony, I have to," Marti uttered.

Tony bowed his head. His shoulders slumped.

"Tony this could help the police with Diane's murder. You did a good thing telling me about your dad. I'll make sure no one besides the police know. Don't worry. You won't be a suspect because your father's in jail. One has nothing to do with the other."

Marti watched Tony's nervous hand movements. His wiry frame reminded her of a rodent, a longish rat with a toothy grin that contorted into a grimace.

"Why did I mention anything?" Tony moaned. "They'll think I had something to do with Diane's murder. It's not fair. We were soul mates."

Tony rocked back and forth. "We had something and now it's gone. It's not my fault. How could I know what would happen that night? I'm not psychic."

Tony's whiny voice grated on Marti's nerves. She felt like the girls at the party yesterday. It wasn't fair to blame Tony. She shouldn't be suspicious. It was coincidental his father was in jail.

First Tony mentioned Diane's spirituality. Then he claimed no knowledge about the other evening. Now he dropped info about his father's copycat murder. Did one have bearing on the other? What if Tony knew more than he claimed? What if he'd had something to do with that fatal evening?

After all, he was a suspect. She'd encourage Worthington to keep an eye on Tony.

Just in case…

⁂

"I'm glad to see you Andrea. I've missed you," Marti gushed as she crushed Andrea in a bear hug.

"Mom, what's up? We saw each other a few days ago." Andrea gently pushed her mom away. "Are you okay? Did something happen?"

Andrea's face scrunched up as she flashed her mom a puzzled frown.

"Of course nothing's happened darling. Can't a mom hug her daughter?" Marti's laugh was a little too shrill as she reassured Andrea.

Marni moved forward to sidestep the awkward moment. "Andrea, I haven't seen you in far too long."

Andrea tossed another frown her mother's way before she embraced her aunt. "What's with mom?" she whispered in Marni's ear.

"Nothing, just a mom that misses her daughter, perfectly normal," Marni soothed.

"Hmm," Andrea murmured. As she turned she caught sight of her cousin. "Cindy," Andrea enthused as they threw themselves at one another. "It's been ages. Wait til you see what I brought."

The girls chattered away excitedly while Marti and Marni beamed at them.

"They're like sisters, I love that," Marti noted as Marni leaned over to plant a kiss on Marti's cheek.

"Always have been, always will be," Marni agreed. "The next best thing to a sister is a favourite cousin."

"Yeah." Marti sighed. "I guess this case has affected me more than I'd like to admit. That hug was fierce."

"Hey, it's allowed. Moms worry, it's no biggie."

"Thanks."

Marti reached over to grab her daughter's carry-on from the floor. "Everyone ready to go?" she asked brightly.

"Yeah, hey is that a new statue?" Andrea asked as they passed one of the airport tourist attractions.

"You're right, I didn't notice it there last time. Let's get a picture Andrea, we'll post it and pretend its cool."

Andrea hooted, "Wicked idea, Cindy."

They passed cell phones to their mothers then preened and posed to their hearts' content. Marti and Marni took pictures while

Marni called, "Work it girls, work it." Laughter peeled down the airport corridor while onlookers smiled at their antics. The girls were back in town…

⋏

Barry phoned later that evening, jubilant at his first taste of being an amateur sleuth, Marti's words, not his. As Barry talked Marti longed to warn him about tomorrow. It was time to mention Barry to Worthington.

Marti sighed then turned to Marni who'd overheard the conversation.

"I'm sorry sis. I know you don't want to do it but the detective needs to know about Barry."

"Yeah," Marti admitted. "I know. I have to tell him about Tony too." She shook her head. "I can't elaborate but Tony told me details today I have to share with Worthington."

Marni leaned over to give her a hug. "You can't protect everyone. Not when there's a killer out there."

"Don't I know it," Marti agreed.

CHAPTER 19

SATURDAY

Marti's meeting the next morning with Worthington was productive in more ways than one. She gave information she'd gleaned over the past days while he highlighted pertinent areas of the case for her. The detective also gave Marti the name of a counselor. She wanted to pass it on to Cindy and her friends.

Marti mentioned Barry to Worthington. In what she hoped was a casual manner she outlined her conversations with Barry.

"Why didn't you bring up this guy earlier?"

Marti shrugged. "It didn't seem important but I thought one should never leave a stone unturned in a murder investigation."

"Hmm," was the only comment Worthington made as he took notes. "I'll have my partner bring him in for questioning."

Marti blanched. "Couldn't you go to his place? Make it more casual?"

"No time for pleasantries. Tick tock we gotta solve this thing. As you pointed out he might know something."

Marti bit her lip. "I guess."

Worthington leaned closer. "Take my advice. Don't get too close to these people Marti. One of them could be the killer." He shook his head. "One of them is the killer. We might have met he or she already. Keep your distance."

Marti sighed. "I need to tell you about my conversation with Tony."

Worthington was quiet as she finished her story. Then he put down his notes, leaned his chair back and said, "On the surface this murder could be a copy cat of Tony's father. I'm sure as we delved further we'd find more differences than similarities. Every crime is unique unless we're talking serial killers who like to make their crimes similar. This isn't one of those. Even though you think checking into that crime would help us out, the likelihood is slim to none there'd be any bearing. Thanks for the information but I'm afraid it won't help with this case."

He paused. "On the other hand, it doesn't hurt to bring Tony in for questioning again. We can make further inquiries about that evening. He could know something he's not telling us. Can you drop by tomorrow? We'll have talked to Barry and Tony by then. We'll check them out, see what their stories are."

She nodded, leaving shortly after that.

Marti glanced at her watch as she left the building. Great, she still had time to meet the girls for their shopping trip. She grabbed her cell to call Marni. Better make sure the girls were up and ready to head over to the mall.

▲

He worked on his car again, always with the car his friends told him. He didn't care what they thought. Cars never talked back or cared if you said stupid things. They shone bright and bold. Chicks dug you when you drove a stylish car.

He heard a sound like air slowly leaking out of a tire.

Circling his black beauty he gazed around, nothing was nearby.

With a shrug he went back under the raised hood then heard the pitter patter of footsteps. Faint, somewhere far off in the distance, remote and indistinct. He swore then moved away from the car, reluctant to stop what he was doing. Strangely spooked, he heard an indefinite humming that rose through the electrified air. The hair on the back of his neck lifted. Air chilled as something eerie drifted by. Unnerved, he rolled his shoulders, eager to shake the feeling off.

He circled the car warily then wiped his hands on an old grease rag. Raising his arm he rubbed the back of his neck, impatient and annoyed at the interruption. He came upon her standing near the driver's side, nose raised, stance sure footed.

He almost laughed. It was a mutt, nothing to get worried about. He turned to go back to what he'd been doing when she barked. Pausing, he glanced her way again, banging his shin on the tire in his haste to back up.

It was that bitch. Her eyes burned, boring into his skull, shiny, diabolical with evil intent. Gaze locked, she judged him, forced him to hold her critical, unwavering stare.

Scorched, he was branded by the hatred.

He'd been judged and found wanting. There was no doubt. She'd come back to get him.

He retreated, hands held above, surrendering to her foul glare, eager to put distance between them.

He wished she'd vanish into thin air, disappear in a puff of smoke like the apparition she had to be.

She couldn't be real.

It was that bitch from the railroad tracks.

And she was dead...

He knew. He'd squeezed the life out of her, felt her heartbeat flutter before it became unresponsive. The frozen gaze told its' own story. These eyes were alive, horribly intent, furious, feverish, laced with contempt...

⋏

Hours later he tried to convince himself it couldn't have happened.

How could that mutt be her?

She was dead.

He'd read about the murder in the newspaper, gone to the funeral, watched them cover her with dirt, seen her parents and friends grieve.

It was over. She was gone.

Could the dead come back to seek revenge?

First the strange dream the other night, nightmare really, and now this. What did it mean?

He thought she'd gone, left to do whatever spirits did.

Had she been present all along? Was it the dead girl, watching, biding her time, waiting for her chance?

Could ghosts harm you from beyond?

He tossed and turned the night away.

What if?
No, it couldn't be her.
She was dead, gone.

⋏

He woke abruptly, shook his head, desperate to clear images as they coursed through his mind. Caught in the midst of a nightmare he'd walked through the flames of hell.

He lifted his hands. Moist with sweat he noted intense heat as it coursed through his body. The room was unbearably hot. He threw off the covers then lay there while imagery persisted. Like a movie scene caught in a loop it played forward then backward, an endless performance for his sole benefit.

Flames licked toward him while he tried to walk forward. Unsure where he was headed he sensed movement was key to his safety. Red-hot heat, a raging inferno whipped past his face. He was pushed further from an unknown destination.

He stood on the edge of a pit as it yawned toward him. It pulsed and throbbed with scalding intensity. He gazed down, horror struck by the bodies that thrashed about. Boiled beyond recognition, covered in thick goo they'd been scorched and seared in a diabolic barbeque.

He forced reluctant limbs to move forward then cautiously edged around the struggling mass. Arms reached for him, poised to pull him down into the violent hellhole that moaned beneath him. He shuddered as he recognized the disguise beneath the friendly demeanor of a local butcher. The bodies morphed to slaughtered cattle destined to meet their maker.

The earth beneath his feet tilted dangerously. Frequent tremors erupted, caught then trembled and shook while quivering moans groaned beneath. Like a bough caught in a storm he was immobilized, unable to break free. He clung blindly, eyes unseeing, frantic to break through the cloud of confusion.

If he believed in God and sin this would be a passage from the bible thumpers who preached of fire and brimstone. Distant voices called. They urged and cajoled him. He heard their echo. "*Renounce your sins or your soul will be tossed into the fiery oven, thrown into the furnace of torment. Fearsome and terrible consequence ensue to those who embrace sin,*" they ranted.

A relentless chant and litany of fates were shouted. He covered his ears while they quoted scriptures rich in detail of fire and smoke. They raged of temptation, the common man, ruin, and misery of his soul. Their mantra repeated like a broken record, of sin and the destructiveness of its nature. He was in the mouth of hell. With one fell swoop he'd be tossed into the never-ending firestorm laid before him, a tableau of eternal misery and pain.

Laughing, he jeered at the unknown speakers touting gloom and doom.

"Do you think I have a conscience?" he raged. "What do I care of your hackneyed principles and far-flung beliefs? They're nothing to me," his crazed mind chorused.

"God won't strike me down with his mighty sword for justice doled out to mere mortals unworthy of mercy. Swathed in vice, women stand before me. They are there for my entertainment, to be used and abused." He shook his fist at their stupidity. "Their true nature and vulgarity were exposed in the face of goodness. For I am good."

The righteousness of his deeds were touted forward before his maker. He found nothing wanting in his actions.

His contempt and hatred for the lesser species of women was flaunted. His distorted faith was bent to satisfy his misguided deeds. The flames of hell were not for him. Vengeance was his blade of truth. In the name of God his deeds would be carried forth.

He fell asleep. Not with blazing thoughts of agony and despair licking at his heels but with the righteousness of his conduct. It fluttered forth, a white flag, valiant as it waved in the summer breeze.

⋏

Hours later he woke again, this time in a cold sweat. Moaning, he shook uncontrollably then slowly calmed as reality set in.

He'd been caught in the deadly grip of another nightmare. Opening his eyes he caught sight of the gemstone glowing eerily in the radiance of early dawn. The jewel beckoned him like a neon light, throbbing with wickedness. It embodied evil.

He'd tossed the ring onto his dresser that night. He'd backhanded her hard then watched, as the ring etched itself onto her skin. At the time, the impression unnerved him. Now it melded with the images of hell he'd experienced in his earlier nightmare.

Closing his eyes he refused to succumb to the torment his nightmare presented. Too late he sunk deeper into the second outlandish delusion he'd been fleeing from.

Worse than the first, this vignette had the slut as the main character. Instead of doling out punishment he was her slave. The brazen hussy bossed him, whipping him into submission.

He had to get her out of his mind. The bizarre images were out of control. With his internal sense of right and wrong in turmoil he leaned naturally toward the pursuit of evil and immorality.

Tomorrow he'd get even with her.

Show her so-called good for nothing spirit who was boss, get back at her for messing with him.

A wicked smile graced his lips. He replayed vivid images in his mind. To torment her, he dared the spirit. He'd show her, the tart had challenged him. It was time to carry out his plans. Thoughts that simmered slowly were at a low boil, ready for action.

His smile turned to an evil grin. A visit to one of her friends was in order. It was time to show the slut who was in charge. Then he'd branch out, take others of her kind. Punish those who provoked him or flaunted their vulgarity.

"I'll take care of those whores. Like Jezebel, the wicked women will pay for their shameful influence."

He liked the resonance of the words.

Justified by the soundness of forthcoming action he fell asleep lulled by violent imagery bent to his twisted way of thinking.

They'd pay. It was time for the sluts to pay...

CHAPTER 20

"*You asked about my sisters and brothers. I, hhh, hhh.*"
"*Okay, it's all right, let it out, that's fine.*"

Gut wrenching sobs filled the room. Gwyn bowed her head. A shudder coursed down her spine as pain throbbed through the confined space.

"*Take it easy. How about if I tell you a story about my family? Then if you're up for it you can tell me about yours.*"

Sniffles and hiccups reverberated around the room.

"*I'll take that as a yes. Hey, you still haven't told me your name. I'd like to hear it. Would seem like we're kind of friends or something instead of strangers.*"

Gwyn heard a shuffling noise then something whispered.

"*Rosemarie, that's a pretty name. It's nice to meet you Rosemarie. As I said earlier, my name's Diane.*"

Gwyn smiled. Diane had returned. She'd gotten the name of the other girl with her…Rosemarie.

"I never knew a tree trunk was so comfortable. It feels like a fluffy pillow here. Why don't you come out from behind that bush? You can lean against the tree trunk beside me or if that's too close you could sit over there on that rock. You could just lie on the grass too. I did that for ages the other day while I checked out the clouds." Diane sighed.

"After awhile I got bored though. I felt lonely since I had no one to talk to. That's when you showed up. Hey, hi, good to see you Rosemarie. I like your long hair. I was going to tell you a story about my family." Diane sighed then took a deep breath. "This is harder than I thought. To begin I mean. I want to say something meaningful about them. That sounds dorky though."

A harsh laugh echoed. Gwyn winced as the sound bounced around the room. Jarred, Gwyn shook her head. Diane had forgotten how to laugh naturally.

"Sorry, I'm not sure what that horrid noise was. Did I sound as ghastly as I thought? Man, now I can't laugh anymore. What's up with that?"

Diane swore. "Oh yeah, I can still swear. Guess that's something."

Gwyn heard a giggle.

"Hey, did you hear that Rosemarie? I giggled like some little girly girl. That sounded better than the laugh though, don't you think?"

"Yeah."

"She speaks. Sorry, that was rude. I'm normally not rude. This whole death thing seems to have affected my personality. Hope I don't turn into some evil witch here. Not that witches are bad or anything. Well, they are when they're evil. Everyone knows that."

Diane put her hands behind her head. "I know I'm rambling. It must be the lack of company. I'm real glad you're here Rosemarie. Even if I have been doing all the talking, it's great to have someone to talk to. Maybe we'll move up to conversations soon."

"That would be nice," Rosemarie whispered. "I'd like that."

"I'd like that too. So my mom and dad split up again a few months ago. She leaves him lots, my mom. They argue all the time over money, well more like lack of money. I don't understand why she leaves though. Then we have less money. It doesn't make sense to me."

Diane shook her head then lifted her arms up towards the sky. "Ah, stretching still feels good. It's weird how things are the same here. Well, except for my laugh of course. I'm gonna have to work on that one. So, like I said my mom moved out and took us to this divey end of the city. She rented a tiny house. It barely fits all of us. There are only two bedrooms."

Diane swore again. "I complained every day about sharing a room with my sister. She's the thirteen year old I mentioned before. I hated her being around me all the time." Diane sighed. "Now, I, well…" Her voice trailed off.

Gwyn heard sniffling.

"I promised myself I wouldn't cry. It seems that's all I've done since I got here." Diane stared at Rosemarie. "Yeah, I know, I bugged you before about crying and carrying on. I admit it. I did my fair share already. I won't hassle you if you need to cry again. I understand."

"Thank you Diane."

"You're welcome. I'm the oldest. How about you, are you the oldest?"

Rosemarie nodded. "Yeah, well, sort of." She bowed her head while tears coursed down her cheeks. "I'm a twin," she whispered.

"Whoa, brutal, a twin. So you've left behind a part of yourself. That's how I always thought it would be as a twin. Is that true?"

"Yes, except I think Rosie is the better part. I'm the one that's never satisfied." Rosemarie gulped. "That's why I took off. I wanted more." She shook her head. "Rosie was right, I never should have left."

Rosemarie wiped tears away then glared at Diane. "I'd be alive if I'd listened to my sister. But no, I knew better, thought I was so smart. Well, I'm not. That's what I'd tell Rosie right now. I never should have gotten into that van with those strangers. How stupid is that?"

"Yeah, that's pretty stupid all right. I can't brag though. My friend Stacey and I got into a car with two guys who were strangers the last night I was alive."

"Are they the ones that killed you?"

Gwyn held her breath as she waited for Diane's answer.

"Nah, they were jerks. Harmless though. How about you? Were the strangers in the van good people or bad?"

Rosemarie shuddered. "They were bad, worse than that, an evil family. I never understood how the mom could do so many horrible things to me. It never seemed to bother her. She, she," Rosemarie gulped. "She tortured me."

Rosemarie pushed her shirt back from her shoulder.

"Whoa, those are wicked welts. What are those from?"

"A belt," Rosemarie whispered. She raised her head. "She wasn't like a real mother to her kids. I think she stole them a long time ago. Her and her husband made them watch as they did, as they..." Rosemarie's voice trailed off.

"It's okay Rosemarie, you don't have to tell me more unless you want to. I understand. There are tons of evil people out there. I hope my sister and brothers never cross paths with wickedness. You know what I mean. Bad enough you and I got caught up with the depraved, less than desirable trash that populates this city. If there's any justice in this world, our siblings should be safe. That's fate right? We got the bad, they should get the good."

"Do you think that's true Diane? Do you really? If we had to die and go through all that pain and torture do you believe our families will be safe now?"

"Yeah, I gotta believe that."

"I have two sisters and a brother."

"Hmm?"

"You asked before, how many sisters and brothers I have."

"Oh right, yeah that was awhile ago. So one's a twin and her name is Rosie. The other two are younger than you since Rosie and you are the oldest. That's like me except I have one sister and two brothers. See Rosemarie, we already have things in common."

"Three siblings, what are the other things?"

"We're teenage girls who are stuck here, wherever this is." Diane sighed. *"And we both died violent deaths."*

"Aiee!"

"Ah, the ears, ouch. Come on Rosemarie do you have to do that high-pitched scream? That couldn't have been a surprise to you since you mentioned pain and torture."

Rosemarie wailed.

"Would you like a hug? We could try that. I'd feel better with a hug," Diane whispered.

There was silence while Gwyn imagined the girls hugging. She smiled as tears coursed down her cheeks. If they found comfort in one another's company it would make their misery more bearable. Gwyn found no pleasure in Rosemarie's tragic fate. Yet she was relieved Diane had stumbled upon a friend in the place they were trapped in.

As the minutes ticked by Gwyn stood up, stretched then reached for her cell. The girls had disappeared again. It was time to phone Marni and relay the latest connection.

⚔

"Stop it, stop it," he cried out, covering his ears to silence the din.

Why was her scream constant, never letting up?

The noise deafened him. Frightening and intense it was more pronounced than usual, desperate somehow.

Barry woke from a fitful slumber, damp and perspiring. He couldn't remember the last time he'd had the nightmare. It was different somehow.

Was it her screaming or someone else? The voice was less shrill. Terrifying in strength she'd sounded deathly afraid. If it wasn't her, who was it?

Barry glanced at the alarm clock by his bed, 3:00am, too early to rise. Could he shake the image of her screaming and get back to sleep? He needed to think about something else. That's what the doctor told him to do.

It was worth a try.

He drifted off to enter a dark and treacherous nightmare. As Barry thrashed about, details poured forth. Startling images coursed past. Barry felt like a kid on a roller coaster ride. He rose up then down, flinging in one direction then the next before he could think things through.

Incoherent, fragmented imagery raced across like a movie on fast forward.

Barry woke dazed and confused. Pictures tore through his mind. Unable to focus, he couldn't shake the feeling these dreadful scenes were significant.

It wasn't his stepsister screaming. It was another girl. He remembered long hair, raven black. Her face and arms were tanned, skin bronzed by the sun. She reminded him of a Native princess he'd seen in a book once. She didn't have bracelets or fancy clothes on like the one in the picture book though.

The girl was familiar. Had he known her? He shook his head then headed to the kitchen for coffee.

Fragmented information thrust itself at Barry. Bits of a story plunged past, in and out of sequence. It was dark but the girl was clear. Barry witnessed her terror, as if on exhibit. Open to interpretation yet stark and raw. It was real, not contrived for an audience.

How could he see her when it was so dark?

Then Barry noticed the headlights…

They raced towards her. Caught in their glare her features were vivid. Stark, alone, like an actor in the spotlight she stood there legs planted. Immobile she watched something out of range, black eyes focused on a spot far away.

The dream took place outside the fence of the auto wreckers where Barry lived. Why was a girl out there in the middle of the night?

Coffee swooshed over the edge of his mug when Barry laid it down too fast. He absentmindedly wiped it with a cloth. His eyes darted around the room unable to settle. Anyone watching would have thought Barry guilty of something, a crime perhaps?

That wasn't it though…

He'd figured it out.

The girl in his dream was the one murdered then dumped nearby early Monday morning. The one Marti's niece had known. He was sure it was Diane. Were the bizarre events her last moments alive? Had the car run her down?

Barry rubbed his forehead. He should tell someone about this. First he should go over everything in his mind though. See if anything else jogged his memory. Barry brushed the hair out of his eyes while he struggled to focus. Logic and attention to detail weren't natural for him.

While he debated what to do his sister-in-law Megan entered the kitchen. She poured herself a cup of coffee then sat down across from him.

Staring at her, Barry toyed with the idea of telling Megan what he knew, to get another opinion.

Sensing eyes upon her Megan glanced up then smiled. She was easy going in the morning, not uptight like later in the day. She was mellow, fresh from a good night's sleep, ready to face the day.

The smile made Barry decide in her favour.

Barry cleared his throat then shrugged as he uttered, "Need your opinion about something."

"Sure, shoot." Megan picked up her mug then blew on her coffee.

"I had a dream last night, more like a nightmare. This girl was screaming and she wouldn't stop."

He glanced at Megan, caught her raised eyebrows.

"Couldn't place her at first, ya know how dreams are, kind of disjointed?"

Megan nodded.

"I think it could have been that girl murdered the other night."

Megan stared, mouth open. "Go on," she commanded.

Barry told her everything. This time he remembered the car with the headlights had been a dark green Grand Prix.

"She ran away and the car chased her toward the houses. Then she disappeared. I must have fallen asleep after that."

"Do you remember anything else?"

"No, I don't think so. There's screaming in my head though. It's weird how I hear her screaming again don't ya think?"

"Yeah."

"It stops, sudden like. Reminds me of a sound that goes on and on then gets snuffed out quick."

Turning at the same time Megan voiced the thought Barry had out loud.

"That's when it happened."

"Yeah."

They sat still for a long while, staring at one another, not sure what to do.

Megan broke the silence.

"You've got to tell someone."

"Yeah."

"What about Marti?"

"Yeah, I'll call Marti. Great, thanks Megan."

As he lifted the receiver Barry saw a second car. It drove slowly past the car wreckers then turned onto a side street. Barry didn't recognize the make but it was a dark colour, maroon, black or dark blue.

Poised to dial Marti's number Barry sighed when the doorbell rang. He put down the phone then shuffled off to answer the door. Little did he suspect who was on the other side.

CHAPTER 21

It was worse than Barry could have imagined.

Barry was confused by the ordeal. About to call Marti, the police had shown up then dragged him into the squad car like a petty criminal.

"Let's go over this one more time," the detective said.

Barry shook his head hoping to clear it. He imagined being somewhere else, anywhere besides this bleak, smelly room. He was surprised and skeptical about the man who called himself Detective Worthington.

This serious, middle-aged guy with a slight paunch didn't seem like the type of fella Marti would help out. His eyes were pale and sunken. With eyebrows too thick like a child had taken a marker then drawn on his face to emphasize his features, the detective didn't instill trust.

Barry didn't want to go over his statement again. Eager to hear about the case, Barry longed to be involved. He wanted to figure out the puzzle. He couldn't understand the detective's desire to question him further.

He'd gone over the dream a few times already. Now Barry wanted to swap information, not rehash boring details. He sighed as he caught sight of the rigid set of the detective's face then grudgingly launched into his story once more.

The detective was no more impressed with the story the second time around.

"Where'd you get that?" he asked, indicating the ring on Barry's finger.

"This, from my brother Mark."

Barry proudly held out his finger twisting it as he watched the red garnet blaze. It reminded him of fire licking greedily from the edge of a bonfire he'd been to once.

"Can I borrow it awhile?"

"What for?" Barry asked, his tone suspicious.

"Just to run a few tests, nothing special."

Shrugging, Barry handed the ring over.

"We both got the same one," he said offhandedly.

"What?"

"Me and Mark, we got the same ring."

"Oh, really."

Barry noticed the detective sat up real straight, paying more attention to what he said.

"Yeah, Mark bought them for us a few years back. One of them blood brother things, ya know."

Abruptly, the detective got up and left the room, just like that. Barry thought it was rude not even saying "*See ya later,*" or "*I'll be right back,*" but the detective left without a backward glance.

He should mention this to Marti. She'd have no qualms discussing manners with the detective, or his lack of manners. Nodding to himself, Barry decided that was the way to handle it. Marti would be good at that sort of thing.

A few minutes later the detective returned his face grimmer than before.

"We found out about your past."

Barry went cold all over, like he'd been doused by frigid water.

Barry never suspected what else happened when the detective left the room. He would have been devastated to learn a squad car was headed over to Mark's house to bring him in for questioning. Mark had gone out early that morning so it would be hours before they tracked him down.

"Whattya mean?" Barry managed to stammer.

"We know about your stepsister."

"Oh."

Barry could think of nothing to say in his defense. He'd tried before but no one ever wanted to listen to his side of the story. This guy wouldn't be any different. Turning his chair away from the detective, Barry drew into himself like a turtle hiding in its shell.

Detective Worthington watched Barry dispassionately.

Wasn't so eager to talk now it seemed? All these guys were the same, find information and confront them with it and they clammed right up, quiet as a mouse. Shrugging, he decided for Marti's sake to delve further into this one, see what he could dig up. First he'd see if the guy talked.

"Seems you have a prior record for beating up your stepsister. Nearly killed her the last time."

"Yeah, well that wasn't my fault. Ask the doctor he'll tell ya," Barry whined, his manner halting. Waving his arms in the air, he punctuated the words as if in a weird primal dance.

Nervous, Barry licked his lips while he waited for the damning remarks. They liked to condemn you without knowing the whole story. He knew the drill.

"Why don't you tell me?"

Barry jerked his head up. Disbelief caused his mouth to open in an unbecoming manner. He closed then opened it again, like a fish exposed to air craving the security of water.

"Yeah, yeah sure."

Barry turned his chair so he faced the detective square on again. This guy was all right he decided. May as well lay the truth on him. See if he could understand what it was like back there in hell.

"She was always screaming," Barry began.

"Ya know how some girls are. They don't talk, just yell and boss ya around. She was like that, my sister. She's my half-sister. We have different mothers. My dad liked to sleep around a lot when he was younger. My brother Mark and I have the same mom though. Now Mark he's a nice guy..."

Barry trailed off. Where should he go with the conversation? It was important to give this guy a picture of what it had been like.

"Guess I should tell ya what it was like there."

"Sure, why not?"

"Pa was a hitter, beat me and Mark all the time. Killed my mom when I was young, hit her one too many." Barry shuddered then shook his head. "He never hit my sister though. It was the strangest thing. She'd barely glance his way and he'd be off in the other direction or take it out on Mark and me. Seemed afraid of my sister for some reason."

Barry was off in the past, almost talking to himself.

"He drank all the time, was always outta work. He had no education to speak of and hated everyone in authority. Taught us to be wary of people, never trust strangers he said, or do-gooders. They'd come to the house a lot, to check up on us. I guess they wanted to make sure he didn't get outta control again."

Barry paused to inspect his hands. He noted sweat on them. Talking about his past always made him nervous and edgy. He wiped his palms on his pants.

"My sister ruled the roost, we did her bidding no matter how unreasonable it was. If we didn't do as she said he'd beat us. Sometimes he locked us up for days with no food or water. Til she said we could come out again."

Barry shook his head. "It was the screaming that got to me. Day or night, it didn't matter, she'd scream, never let up." Barry shuddered. "I couldn't understand it. Still don't. Even after they locked me up for good. In that hospital," he admitted, meeting the detective's eyes for the first time.

Worthington examined Barry closely, searching his soul. There was a genuine note of sadness in the tale, an honest rawness portrayed emotions hard to fake. Simplicity made the story real. He nodded, urging Barry to continue.

"Sometimes I thought she was a witch. Ya know one of them people with special powers. She had some control over the old man. He did her bidding no matter how unreasonable it was. Couldn't figure it out, was weird. When she watched ya, it was like she seen straight through ya, to the other side. Gave me the heebie geebies it did."

Barry's voice trembled.

"Hit her once. She yelled in my face, poking me with that finger of hers. She poked and screamed again and again. I couldn't take it so I plowed her. Saw surprise on her face. Then she gave me this evil smile like she was pleased about something. I couldn't understand it at the time. When I told the doctor years later it hit me why she'd been happy about what I'd done. She made sure I'd suffer in a different way."

Barry stopped to lick lips that had gone dry.

"Do ya think I could have some water?"

The detective got up, returning a moment later with a glass of ice-cold water.

Sipping it, Barry gave an appreciative nod.

"This from one of them coolers?"

"Yeah."

"Thought so. Like I said I never would have figured it could have gotten worse. But, it did. She started doing things to me." Barry's gaze slid away. "I never would have imagined she'd do such weird stuff."

His eyes met the detective's. "She'd undress in her doorway so I could see her from the living room. It made me hot and heavy even though she was my sister. I couldn't help it. She'd lick her lips inviting-like then swish past me real close. It made me nervous. I tried not to watch but I couldn't help it."

Barry shook his head.

"She burnt all my food. I could barely eat any of it. Then she'd come into my room in the middle of the night, screaming and moaning like someone possessed. It damn near drove me insane waking up night after night. I hit her again one night. It must have been months after she began doing the moaning and screaming thing. I snapped, lack of sleep I guess. I know I shouldn't have hit her but it just happened. I'm not making excuses for it. I'm just trying to explain."

He glanced up for silent confirmation. Seeing the detective's nod Barry continued.

"Pa threatened me all the time. He began to pick on me for every little thing. Left Mark alone so that was good. He's younger than me ya know and was a scrawny kid. I tried to protect him when I could. Mark slept downstairs when she started coming to my room every night. That way he wouldn't hear the screaming so much. We knew it was no use me going down there cause she'd just follow me."

"Did you ever touch her besides those two times you hit her?"

"Nope. I just lay there with my hands over my ears praying she'd leave. Took her time about it but she'd go eventually. This went on for years. The whole time I was growing up. Then one day, she stopped."

Barry furrowed his brow as he thought about what happened next. It was like a puzzle he longed to place in order. It was impossible though since it still didn't make sense. Even though he'd told it so many times, to so many people…

Barry shook his head. "I thought it might get better after that. She was quiet for weeks, no screaming, moaning or teasing. She was almost like a normal person. Pa still drank and beat on us." Barry shuddered. "One day she lost it for good. Don't know what set her off, Pa maybe.

Mark and me had just got home. I'd been at work and he was at school. I dropped out but made sure he stayed because he could read and write. I knew he'd make something of himself. So long as I quit and went out to make money, I pumped gas, Pa let Mark stay in school. We always came home together. It was safer. That day we should have both stayed away."

Barry began to shake. He closed his eyes then made a conscious effort to breathe normal. It was at this point of his story that he often couldn't go on. Words got stuck in his throat and he couldn't think clear. Things got fuzzy and jumbled.

"She was screaming when we walked in, yelling something but it didn't make sense. It was mumbo jumbo, like curses and spells. She waved her arms around. She was dancing but not like to music, more like a mad dance." Barry shook his head. "I don't know how to describe it other than that. Pa sat there watching her like he was in a trance. She raised her arm up, stared at the ceiling then keeled over."

Detective Worthington couldn't help it. He interrupted Barry, something you never did when suspects were on a roll.

"What? Did you say she keeled over?"

"Yeah, straight over on the ground. Like one of those boards ya have leaning against something that tumbles over. Boom right on the ground. It was the strangest thing." Barry glanced at the floor as if his sister might be there.

"Yeah," the detective agreed. After a moment of silence curiosity got the better of him. He leaned toward Barry. "So, what happened next?"

"We ran over there to help her. When we bent over she opened her eyes. She held our gaze, never blinked. This went on for a long time. I couldn't tear myself away. My eyes started to water. I got stiff from staying in the same position. Mark said the same thing happened to him. It was weird man."

Barry shook his head then flexed his fingers, pulling on them one by one til they popped.

Worthington gave an involuntary shudder. He sensed Barry's next words would be implausible, similar to the rest of the tale.

"We were mesmerized when she stood up, couldn't take our eyes off her. She began to dance to some inner sound only she heard. Then she threw her clothes off and stood in front of us naked as a blue jay. We stared at her. Didn't know what to do. Now this is the part nobody believes but I swear to God it happened. Mark knows. He was there."

Barry paused to gather his thoughts. Had he been an actor his hesitation would have been deliberate, to prolong the anticipation of his listener. The detective doubted Barry capable of that ploy though.

"She danced, swayed and chanted. Then these things popped out of her head." Barry shuddered. "We couldn't figure out if they were real at first but they were. They were all over her skull. Bunched up together, writhing and squirming in time to the music. I swear there was a weird sound that came from her, or them, like music." Barry passed his hand over his brow. "It was the most bizarre thing ya could imagine. Mark and me saw it. Pa admitted nothing. Mark said it was etched in his mind like a bad dream that comes out every now and then."

Barry stopped, wiped more sweat from his brow. His hands shook.

It appeared dredging up the tale had cost him a great deal.

Worthington couldn't help himself. The oddity of the tale got the better of him. He had to know the rest.

"What did she have on her head?"

Barry glanced up. Eyes drawn, a frown marred his forehead. He appeared deep in thought, immersed in the hell he'd been caught up in.

"Snakes," he stated, in a flat, emotionless voice.

"Snakes?" Worthington clarified, disbelief evident.

"Yeah. I heard them described once in this play my sister-in-law Megan saw. She read this line out loud to Mark and me. It described what we seen that day. It was about this woman who controlled snakes while they danced and squirmed above her. Megan called it a macabre celebration of life, a massive cortex of illusion. This woman in the play was a sorcerer or conjurer and she had a way with them. Just like our sister. Man it was something out of this world her and them snakes. Weirdest thing I've ever seen. Don't even know where the snakes came from."

"How long did this go on?"

"Don't know, hard to say. We were mesmerized like in a trance so time could have flowed by fast or been dragging along. Mark and me were real quiet. Tried not to draw attention to us cause the next thing ya knew she went berserk. That's when she started screaming again and hitting us with heavy stuff she dragged from the kitchen." Barry shuddered. "She had pots and pans, an iron and her rolling pin. That's what she broke my fingers with."

Barry pointed to his right hand. The fingers had never healed properly and were bent at an odd angle.

"We couldn't move to defend ourselves, none of us. Powerless, that's what we were. We just sat there while she beat on us. Then she plugged in the iron."

Barry stopped. Eyes wide he stared inward, watching some horror forever etched in his mind.

"When it was hot, she began to iron us, starting with me." Barry licked dry lips then closed his eyes. "She never got to Mark or Pa though. That's when I came to from that trance she'd put us in." He opened his eyes to stare into Worthington's. "The heat must have got to me. Dazed, my skin throbbing, I attacked, nearly killed her."

Barry covered his eyes with his right hand, his fingers bent at an awkward angle. "I was in pain and everything was red hot. That's all I could see and feel, like it licked my skin. She screamed again, wouldn't stop, always with the screaming…"

After moments of shocked silence, the detective found his voice.

"Where did she burn you?"

"On my back and legs." Barry moved his hand from his eyes. "Do you wanna see it?"

It was proof of his sister's insanity. That had been the deciding factor for the jury when they'd deliberated then given their verdict. They'd decided Barry should go to the hospital instead of jail since he'd been forced past the edge of reason by pain.

"If you want to show me you can."

Barry shrugged then undid his shirt buttons. He turned slowly toward Worthington. The red welts were vivid, the sketch of an iron blazed fiercely on his back. The painful tableau was laid out for Worthington, testifying the validity of Barry's story.

The detective cleared his throat. The scars provided a dramatic illustration, truth of the bizarre tale.

If Barry had been honest about this, could his dream on the night of the murder be accurate? Worthington gazed fixedly at the scars while his mind skittered back to Diane's murder. It was hard to ignore facts when they stared you in the face.

It was time to talk to Barry more about his dream.

CHAPTER 22

"It's gorgeous, can I get it mom, huh, can I?" Andrea twirled in her dress. "Will there be dancing?"

Marti laughed. "I doubt it hon, it's a fundraiser." She grabbed her purse from the floor. "I guess I should check the invitation. See what's scheduled."

"Cindy, come out, show us," Andrea urged.

"No, it's terrible. I want to go somewhere else."

Marni frowned then caught Marti's eye and mouthed, "Oh no."

"I'm sure it's not that bad Cindy. Why don't you show us," Marni uttered. She was torn. If the outfit was dreadful it was best to move along. Then again, Cindy often exaggerated when it came to what was fashionable.

Cindy grumbled as she threw the curtain aside. "Check it out, it's all wrong. It's too tight, the colour sucks, the length is ick, take your pick."

Marni's eyes widened as she took in the dress.

Andrea laughed. "Did you just rhyme? Length is ick, take your pick, that's hilarious. You're like Dr. Seuss or something."

It was just what they needed. As Cindy stared morosely into the mirror and heard her cousin play back her rhyme she saw the hilarity of the situation.

"Mfk," Cindy uttered as she covered her mouth with her hand to stifle her giggles. "It is ick. What a pick. Eew."

Cindy spied Andrea in the mirror. She turned to check out the dress. "Wow, awesome, it's so you. Are you going to buy it? Say yes, you have to."

Andrea tossed her hair back. "Mom, can I?"

Marti glanced up from the invitation she'd unearthed from the bottom of her purse. "Of course darling that's why we're here. New outfits all around."

"You're getting one too mom. Even though you hate shopping."

"Yeah, that's why I need something new. You're right Andrea there is music. Check it out." She thrust the invitation at her daughter.

Andrea's eyes scanned the contents. "At least we get a choice for supper. Chicken or beef, yuck I hate red meat. Lucky they have chicken. I hope it doesn't have any junk stuffed inside it. Whoa, Cindy, get a load of this, is this who I think it is?"

Cindy grabbed the invitation. "Whoa, yeah, awesome. We'll dance the night away. I love her songs. I definitely need a new dress for tonight." She thrust the invite back at Andrea then raced back to the change room. "We gotta get to the next store."

"Wow mom, I'm impressed. You never mentioned you were sharing the stage with this group. How much were these tickets anyway, like a million bucks or what?"

Andrea held the invitation out to her mom. As she took it Marti glanced down. She didn't recognize the name of the group. Nor did she want to seem too old to appreciate who they were. She shrugged instead.

"I'm not sharing the stage. I'm the keynote. Totally different," she muttered.

Andrea stared at her mother. "You need something bright or flashy for tonight, an outfit for a star. I'll get out of this so we can move along." She bounded back to her change room. "We'll need new shoes," she added over her shoulder. "Aunt Marni, how many fancy clutches do you and Cindy have?"

Marni raised her eyebrows at Marti. "Guess we'll be here awhile."

Marti shook her head. "I love to shop, I love to shop," she chanted. "Bring me your outfit when you've changed Andrea," she called as she went to stand in line at the till. "One down, three to go."

⋏

Barry liked how Worthington treated him after their conversation. With respect, like he thought Barry had something important to say.

This time when they went over Barry's dream the night of the murder the detective nodded a lot. He wrote things down in his notebook, interested in what Barry saw that evening.

It made Barry feel like his dream was pivotal to the case. Yeah, he liked that word. He'd seen it on one of those cop shows once and that's how they'd solved everything. An informant had given valuable information pivotal to the case.

Barry was better than an informant. He was an important eyewitness. They'd probably need to put him on the stand. He smiled and nodded while they discussed the car. Barry imagined the amazing things he'd say on the stand and maybe even on TV. Yeah, this was more like it.

The best part was when he mentioned the second car to Worthington. Barry knew it was a new clue, most likely would break open the case. The detective couldn't help it. He got excited when Barry revealed the second car. It had been after the first car, quite a while later, after the screaming.

If only he knew the make of that car...

Barry spent hours poring over magazines searching for the second car. He narrowed it down to three or four vehicles that were pretty much the same. At least it wasn't one of those foreign cars. It was a GM. Barry had never liked those foreign jobs.

Barry pointed out the dark colour to Worthington. It was black, maroon or navy blue. More likely black though. He also recalled it was a two door.

When Barry showed the cars to Worthington they discussed which one it might have been. The detective leaned towards the Alero since it was new and sleek. Barry preferred the Monte Carlo, Grand Prix and Buick Regal. Barry commented how it would be cool to have a car named after a place.

While they chatted about different makes and models someone came to get Worthington. They talked low then the detective left, excited like.

Barry was dying to know what it was about. He figured it must be another break in the case. Every time he heard a noise in the hall he glanced up with a ready smile, eager for the detective's return. Time passed. Another cop came in.

"Where's Detective Worthington?"

"He's on the phone with fellow officers. Said I should drive you home. I'm his partner Pitt. I gotta check something out so I can take you now if you're ready."

"Yeah, sure, why not."

Barry would have loved to be a fly on the wall to hear the phone conversation.

⋏

The conversation Barry missed was about Murray and his two friends caught near the Mexican border.

"Are you on your way?" Worthington asked.

"Yeah, picked them up late last night. We've been driving since. Should be back sometime tomorrow, probably late. Sorry I didn't call earlier but this was our first stop today."

"That's all right. I'm glad you got them. They talkative?"

"Nah, one guy's whining. Doesn't want his car abandoned on the road. I said we'd get it hauled to one of the nearby stations so he finally shut up. When'd you put that APB out?"

"Wednesday."

"Yeah, that's what I thought. You owe us one Worthington."

"Don't I know it?"

"They killers?"

"Can't say. That's why I need them here. If they're not killers they know something. They ran far and fast for innocent guys."

"Yeah, see you when we get there."

"Can hardly wait. Thanks."

Worthington couldn't wipe the smile from his face. Things were coming together. When they found Barry's brother Mark, more pieces could fall into place.

⋏

Stacey was going to be late for work.

She'd missed a few shifts already this week. If she kept this up they'd fire her. Her employers understood this was a difficult time because of Diane's death. They'd lost Diane though too and were short staffed now.

A black car pulled up slow beside her.

Stacey didn't recognize it but when the passenger window slid down she scurried over to see who beckoned. It was one of the neighbourhood guys. He was older. She'd seen him somewhere lately. What was his name?

"Want a ride?"

Stacey flinched. Eyes wide, she shook her head. She wasn't supposed to accept rides from strangers. Her mom and dad harped about the danger of hitching rides. The other night she'd gotten in a strange car with Diane and now Diane was dead.

Stacey stumbled from the car door. Her legs wobbled as she rushed to get away. She caught her foot on the edge of the sidewalk then tumbled to the ground.

"Ow," she complained as she felt her ankle turn. "Man, this sucks," she griped.

The guy jumped out of the car and was at her side in an instant.

"Hey, are you okay? I stopped to offer you a ride. I've seen you with my sister. You're shaking. Can you stand?"

He helped her up.

Stacey tried to stand then groaned as her ankle throbbed. She burst into tears. "This isn't fair. Now I'll never get to work."

The guy picked her up, opened his car door then shoved her inside.

"Guess you need that ride now," he grumbled as he slammed the door. He strode to the driver's side, jumped in then revved the engine. The locks snapped shut.

Stacey whimpered as he pulled into traffic.

"Where were ya headed?"

Stacey fumbled in her purse for a tissue. Her nose was running. "Oh, to work. You know the family restaurant on Fleury Street and Victoria."

"Yeah, I know it."

Stacey didn't know what to do. Should she head to work, explain what happened, call her mom and head home? Or should she ask this guy to turn around and take her home? She leaned down to inspect her ankle. "Ouch," she complained as she touched it. The ankle had already swelled.

They passed the Leader Post building. Stacey glanced across the road as they drove past Subway and KFC. "Wish I could work there. My dad likes this restaurant though. He doesn't want me to work at a teen hangout. What's the difference?" Stacey turned to watch Subway and KFC in the rear window. "I'd rather be around teens than families. It's not as if I get tips here anyway."

The guy grunted.

Gloomy now, Stacey slumped in her seat as they turned onto Fleury. Still unsure what to do Stacey was startled when the guy drove past the restaurant and parked down the block.

She turned to protest but thought better of it when she caught his eye. He seemed pissed off, not friendly like when he'd helped her into the car. She scrunched further down in the seat, hoping whatever he wanted wouldn't take long.

He turned toward her, put his arm along the back of the seat then stroked Stacey's hair with a distracted air.

Stacey held her breath and tried not to squirm.

"I heard you've been talking to the cops about your friend's murder."

"Yeah," Stacey whispered. She let her breath out in a whoosh.

He sneered. "What are the cops trying to prove?"

"I don't know. They're searching for Diane's murderer. Thank you for the ride but I should go," Stacey murmured. She tried to pull away from him without appearing obvious.

"Not so fast, we've got unfinished business."

"We do?" she asked in bewilderment.

Clueless as to what he wanted Stacey's stare was frantic. She clasped her shaking hands. She dreaded his next words when she caught his evil, unforgiving gleam.

"Yeah, consider this a warning."

His voice was steely, eyes boring into hers.

"What kind of warning?" she whimpered.

"I want you and your friends to quit answering questions." He shoved his finger in her face. "If ya don't stop, next time I'll finish what I started."

Stacey stared at him, perplexed. Mouth open she was about to ask what he meant. Her eyes widened as she caught his gaze and her hand fluttered up to cover her cry.

His eyes flashed pure hatred, venomous and deadly. The guy seemed capable of... murder.

It was Stacey's last conscious thought before he attacked her.

After he knocked Stacey out he systematically beat her. He knew what organs to avoid and how to produce the most bruises. He wanted it to appear as if she'd been hit by a truck and barely survived.

He admired the ring he'd donned that morning. As he pummeled her, he smiled as the skin on her face tore. He chuckled as veins were pierced by metal, ripped from the flesh brutally. He broke one of her fingers for good measure. Then, with a malicious kick he booted her out of the vehicle. He grabbed her bag, threw it out and left her lying there on the road. He snickered as he closed the door on her crumpled heap. He drove off slow so as not to draw attention.

Alone in the street, Stacey was now dependent on the kindness of strangers. He'd parked beside an abandoned house to eliminate prying eyes. It was awhile before Stacey was found.

Two young boys walked down the street after a snack at Subway. They laughed at a joke one had told then pointed at the bundle ahead of them. "What's that?"

"I don't know. It's kind of bulky. We should check it out."

"Is it some kind of doll? It's really big."

The braver one leaned over to inspect it closer. His eyes widened as he shrieked, "Blood, there's so much blood."

His friend peeked around him. "Is it a person? It could be a girl, she has long hair."

With a gulp his friend agreed.

"What should we do?"

His friend shrugged.

"I know. I could run home and tell my mom. We should maybe call the hospital or something."

"Yeah, great idea. Get your mom to call 911. They'll know what to do." He moved away from the body and turned his back to it. "I'll wait here." He straightened his spine, duty bound to do the right thing.

An ambulance and the police arrived shortly after.

Stacey was rushed to Regina General Hospital where they whisked her into Emergency. When Stacey's parents arrived she was unconscious. They were told Stacey had a concussion but no internal injuries and minor broken bones. She'd been lucky, the police officer told them. It could have been worse.

CHAPTER 23

Barry approached his place with caution in case the cops were still around. He needed more clothes out of his trunk. He'd only had one pair of pants and a couple of shirts with him.

He was surprised by a lone figure that stood nearby. The guy stared toward the railroad track. Curiosity got the better of Barry. He advanced soundlessly toward the guy who started guiltily when Barry called out. "Hey man, how's it goin?"

"Huh, what, who are you?"

Barry narrowed his eyes. The guy was nervous.

"Name's Barry, I live nearby. Was out for a walk and noticed you here. I thought I'd say hi." Barry put his hands in his pockets like he had all the time in the world.

"Yeah, oh right, okay."

Barry frowned with concentration. Why was this guy here, staring at the tracks? "What's your name?"

"Huh, oh it's Tony."

"Pleased to meet ya Tony." Barry held out his hand. After a brief hesitation Tony shook it. His grasp was limp and clammy like a dead fish.

Barry was about to walk away since the guy seemed to be in a trance when Tony began to talk.

"My friend died here the other night."

"Yeah, whoa."

Barry was excited at this piece of news. It had to be Diane. He leaned toward Tony. It was time to get some detective work done.

"Yeah, she was special, you know."

"Wow man, that's rough."

"I just wish…"

The guy trailed off. He sounded pathetic, kind of lost.

"If only I'd…"

He stopped again.

Man, didn't the guy ever finish a sentence?

"When I saw her the other night I wish I would have, you know."

"What night?"

"Huh, oh, on the night of her murder."

"Ya saw her the night she was murdered?" Wow, sounded like he might know something. Barry rubbed his hands.

"Yeah, a bunch of us saw her earlier at the exhibition."

"Oh, like ya mean before she was murdered."

"Well of course I mean before. How could I have seen her after when she was dead?"

Tony's eyes flashed.

"I meant I wish things could have been different between us. She would have been with me. Then she'd be alive today instead of dead."

"Oh."

Barry scratched his head. He was at a loss as to what Tony meant.

Tony glanced at his watch.

"Gotta go, got something happening tonight. Important, you know."

"Uh yeah, right, sure."

"It's funny how you regret something that only took place in your mind. I should have been more persuasive, made her see my side of things. Forced the issue."

Barry thought Tony was like a lost puppy except his face was longish. His appearance resembled a rat more than a cute dog.

"Yeah, I should have done it. Put a stop to it. Made Diane see my way of thinking. She would have come around eventually."

"Uh huh."

"Women, they're all the same. Need someone to take charge."

"Yeah, right."

"Well nice talking to you. I better go. I've got things to do."

"Bye."

Barry watched Tony wander away. The conversation had confused him. Barry wasn't sure what Tony meant by most of his comments. He'd have to tell Marti. She might figure it out.

He shook his head as he walked purposely toward the locked gate. He had to get his stuff before it got dark. Barry paused as he noticed where Tony had gone.

Tony was getting into a black car. It appeared to be a Buick Regal, like the car from his dream.

Barry hurriedly got his gear together, eager to call Marti and share his news.

⚜

Whistling, he went to the car wash to clean the inside of his vehicle. He wanted to erase any sign of Stacey from the car, like he'd done for the other one.

Man she'd been scared, gotten what she deserved though. Her and those friends better stay away from the cops. Otherwise, he'd do more than threaten them. They'd regret coming up against him.

Besides, it wasn't as if he'd done it on purpose. It had been an accident. They couldn't pin anything serious on him just because the harlot wouldn't quit screaming, could they? He'd had to kill her.

He went over what happened that night in his mind again.

He'd been doing that a lot lately. Couldn't seem to shake the feeling something had gone wrong or was gonna go wrong. It was Diane's friends who worried him. Why were they helping the cops? Everyone asked too many questions, he'd heard names bandied about as they tried to pin this on someone.

He'd dropped the guys off after they'd done the dirty deed. She'd passed out. She couldn't stand the heat or they'd been too much for her. With an evil grimace he thought that was it. How much lovin' could one woman stand, especially one so small and loud?

Man, she'd been a noisy chick. She wouldn't stop screaming and crying. It sounded like they'd butchered her or something. They'd finally knocked her out. None of them could stand her wailing.

She'd been unconscious in the back seat when he'd taken the other guys home. He'd headed to the train yard alone to dump her off. He'd meant to roll her out and leave her there. She'd wake up eventually. When he touched her though she'd screamed again then hit him. For Christ sakes you'd think the bitch would have known better.

No, just like the slut she was, she couldn't leave it alone. She had to egg him on, drive him over the edge. He realized she had to be a Jezebel, a whore to corrupt him. She made him mad enough to see red.

She'd brought it on herself.

What could he do?

He'd had to shut her up. A man could only take so much. It had been an accident. It could have happened to anyone.

No jury would convict him. They'd likely had the same thing happen to them before. Sometime you just got so bloody angry you didn't know what came over you. They'd understand.

He'd backhanded her expecting her to leave him alone. But she'd turned into a she-devil. When she'd scratched and clawed at him he'd grabbed her by the neck, pushing her away. He started to squeeze. Her eyes bulged and she'd hung onto his shirt. He was gonna stop but he couldn't. He didn't know why. His fingers wouldn't loosen up.

Not till she was gone…

Then he'd dropped her, like a bucket of slime. He didn't want the body to touch him. He felt soiled.

He'd had to pry the fingers from his shirt.

He shuddered at the memory.

Dead people didn't look good. He'd been revolted by her. If he'd known her appearance could change so drastically there's no way he would have had her earlier. Slut or not, if he'd known her body would turn like that he'd never have done it with her.

How did guys nail broads when they were dead? Man, there were real sickos out there.

He shook his head then smiled. He'd kicked her to make sure she was dead. Yup, she had been. Oh well, he'd thought, another dead Indian slut. Who'd care anyhow? She was a whore. She deserved it.

He paused when he recalled how she'd screamed "*No, no, don't kill me.*" He laughed out loud at that one.

They'd had no intention of killing her. They just wanted to use her then toss her out like yesterday's leftovers. As they'd passed her around the circle it had been fun at first. They'd gotten tired of the game though when she collapsed halfway through. His face darkened as he thought how it had gone downhill after that with all her screaming.

Now she'd come back to try to frighten the hell out of him. Who'd she think she was, an avenging angel?

"You don't scare me ya bitch. Stupid squaw."

He laughed then shook his fist in the air. Imagine a spirit that wandered around intent on revenge. Yeah right, that was rich.

He bent down to focus on cleaning out his car with the vacuum. He got down close to make sure there was no trace of Stacey on the front seat. Wouldn't do to leave evidence, would it?

In the light of day his nightmare from the evening before receded into meaningless clutter. It meant nothing. The bitch was dead and gone.

While he cleaned, another brain wave entered his mind, unbidden yet foremost, it clamored for attention. It was about that slut of course. That's all he thought of lately.

The idea had merit. This thought didn't make him uncomfortable or scare him like last night. He shook the frightened images off as unimportant. He started as he checked guiltily over his shoulder. What if someone read the unmanly thoughts on his face? That wasn't the real him.

He shouldn't care about that bitch, no one else did. Well maybe her sappy friends and family, crying about her life being snuffed out. They were all a useless waste of skin anyway, who cared what they thought.

As he licked dry lips he scanned the area to see if anyone paid attention to him. He hated when others watched him, made him nervous.

No one was in sight and the car wash was empty. He leaned against the hood of the car then lit a cigarette. As he blew smoke upwards he watched it snake towards the sky in a lazy spiral.

The scheme he contemplated had his undivided attention. Details needed to be worked out. If he were successful they'd never track him down. He'd be free to conduct his affairs how he saw fit.

He had plans, man he had plans. He grinned as he thought of the smorgasbord before him. After that first taste he craved more. Today had been an appetizer. Not enough to satisfy him. He'd have to go out tomorrow, see who he could find. Those whore-some Jezebels were everywhere.

Lucky he'd kept it after all. It would come in useful. The cops would be confused. Those fools would never figure this one out.

His grin turned to pure evil as he ground the cigarette under his shoe.

Yeah, this was gonna be sweet. He could hardly wait…

⁂

Marti checked her outfit in the mirror. Was it too much? As she stretched her arms to admire the flowing sleeves Andrea bounded into the room.

"You're gorgeous mom. I love it. You should get more tops and dresses in that style. I think it adds to your storytelling."

Marti smiled. "I wouldn't call what I do storytelling Andrea. I think that refers to authors who write children's books."

Andrea grinned. "Come on mom, murder and mayhem lend themselves to storytelling. People love guts and gore. You just have to work it more."

Marti laughed. "The next time I do a reading with teens I'll remember that." She leaned over to grab her purse. "I'm not sure how I'll fit everything in this clutch," she muttered as she transferred items from one purse to another. "Where are my notes?"

Andrea groaned. "You don't have a bunch of boring stats written down do you mom?"

Marti ignored her.

"Mom, seriously." Andrea jumped up to search the room. "Aha, here they are." She grabbed them off the dresser then returned to her spot on the bed. As her eyes scanned the page she groaned again. "No way, mom, you're not going to do this speech are you?" she wailed. "It's terrible, boring, boring."

"Andrea, really, that's rude."

Andrea hung her head. "I'm sorry," she mumbled. "You're right, I didn't mean to offend you."

"Apology accepted. Thank you." Marti bent over to kiss Andrea on the cheek. "Let's see, what part do you think is boring?" she asked as she moved to sit beside her daughter on the bed.

"The stats, no one wants to hear stats. You should talk about your book. That's what people want to hear."

"I don't know." Marti skimmed the page. "It could be a serious event, since it's a fundraiser. People paid a good deal of money for tickets. They might expect more than a book reading."

"So don't do your typical book reading. Do some of the speech, we could mark a few paragraphs. Then you could launch into a story about your latest book, how it's a cautionary tale for teenagers. That ties together doesn't it? Where's the invitation? How does it describe you?"

Marti fished the invite out of her purse then passed it to Andrea. She grabbed a pen then bent over her notes to slash the boring parts. Andrea was right. Someone else might mention stats. She'd write down the link she'd gotten the stats from and refer to that instead if no one else mentioned the data.

"Hah, they describe you as Marti Rose, international author. See mom, they want you to talk about your books. That's what people come to hear. I bet they sold tons of tickets since you're the keynote. You don't need a boring speech. Jot down a few notes like you do for an outline. Storytelling, that's what people love."

Marti glanced at her daughter then smiled. "You're right Andrea. Shall I do murder and mayhem or blood and guts?"

CHAPTER 24

Saturday Night

Marti glanced at the table as she paused in her narrative. Andrea gave her the thumbs up. Marti grinned as she nodded toward her daughter. Andrea was right. Someone else had done boring stats. People were relaxed and wanted stories. Her job as the keynote was to entertain. It was time for her '*A*' game.

"That was awesome mom, you nailed it," Andrea praised as Marti returned to the table.

Marti bent down to hug Andrea. "Thank you darling. I owe you one. Thanks for reading the invitation and steering me straight."

Andrea flashed her a smile then turned to whisper to her cousin as Marti sat down. As Marti scanned their flushed faces and watched Andrea squirm in her seat she realized they were pumped about the next act. Like most teens they wanted to dance, sing, and make noise while music pounded. She rubbed her temple. "I hope the music isn't too loud," she whispered to Marni.

"Tell me about it. The girls can hardly wait. They know all her songs." Marni laughed. "Of course even I know the chorus to most of them. I must be a groupie too."

Marti frowned. She was just about to admit she didn't have a clue who the group was, when someone tapped her on the shoulder. Marti turned to find one of the organizers at her elbow.

"Ms. Rose, I wonder if we might ask a favour of you?" The woman gripped her necklace then began to twirl it as she fidgeted in front of Marti.

"Call me Marti, please."

"Oh, could I? Thank you, what an honour," the woman gushed.

Marti smiled. "I'm sorry, I've forgotten your name."

"Oh, no you haven't." The woman bobbed her head then jiggled from one foot to the other. "I never introduced myself." She laughed. The sound came out high pitched and shrill. She clamped her hand over her mouth then uttered, "I'm sorry Ms. Rose, I mean Marti," she stammered. "I don't laugh like that." She leaned forward. "I'm just nervous. This isn't me. I," she pushed her hair back.

Marti put her hand on the woman's arm. "Relax, I don't bite."

"Sara."

"Pardon."

"My name. It's Sara."

"Oh, great, nice to meet you Sara." Marti turned to include the others at the table. "This is my sister Marni, my daughter Andrea and my niece Cindy. This is Sara. She's on the committee that organized this evening." She pointed at the other two chairs. "I'm not sure where our other tablemates have wandered. I imagine they'll be back in time for the music."

Sara flashed the girls a smile. "They'll be on shortly," she promised. "In the meantime, as I mentioned, I have a favour to ask you."

"Oh, right, go ahead Sara, ask away."

"We meant to request this in advance but I guess our wires got crossed. Each of us thought someone else asked you, meanwhile, none of us had. It's so awkward when that happens. We dropped the ball." Sara fiddled with her necklace again then took a deep breath. "Anyhow, Ms. Rose, I mean Marti, would you mind signing some autographs? I know it's a lot to ask at the last minute."

Marti smiled. "Of course Sara. I don't mind at all. Would you like me to set up in the lobby? It will be quieter when the music starts."

"Oh Marti, we'd love that. I appreciate this so," Sara gushed as she gripped her hands.

Marti turned to tell Marni where she was headed, as Andrea and Cindy were deep in conversation. As she stood up Sara added, "I have all your novels. I brought a few with me. I was hoping…"

Marti chuckled as Sara trailed off. "Of course I'll sign them for you Sara."

"Oh thank you. I know quite a few people brought books. They've asked if you could sign them. Your publicist sent postcards advertising your novel *'Stolen Spirits'*. I'm sure people would love you to autograph those."

"I know. People love postcards and bookmarks."

Marti barely had time to add her comment as Sara launched into another story. Marti smiled. It was fascinating when anxious fans tended to talk rather than ask her questions. Once they got comfortable they moved to standard subjects. Then as they got to know her, they'd ask more personal information. Based on Sara's comments, fidgeting, and nervous mannerisms, she'd chatter for the rest of the evening.

As they approached the lobby Marti raised her eyebrows at the crowd gathered. It appeared her fans were anxious to meet her. Sara drew her forward then announced in a loud voice, "Marti Rose has graciously agreed to sign autographs and books if you've brought them. Please don't crowd her. Would you prefer to sit or stand Marti?"

Marti grinned. It was show time.

⁂

Time passed quick as Marti chatted with fans, signed books and autographed postcards. Sara had organized everyone and proved to be a helpful assistant. As music thronged inside, people wandered in and out of the lobby. It was a lively atmosphere.

"Your keynote was outstanding," a fan gushed. "We were so glad you talked about your book." She leaned forward to confide. "We attend a number of fundraisers annually. I hate when the keynote quotes facts and figures. That's such a bore. I can read that in pamphlets and on the website online. I don't need someone to recite that to me at an event like this." She stood back. "It's been a pleasure to meet you. It's not everyday a famous author graces our city with their presence."

She nodded at Marti then turned to go.

Marti grinned as she thought of Andrea. Score one for the persuasive teen as she'd encouraged Marti to tell stories. Andrea had the instincts of a publicist.

As the next person strode forward to talk to Marti, Andrea hurried to her side. "Mom, mom," she interrupted. "Sorry," she apologized to the fan. "I have to talk to my mom. It's important."

Marti smiled at the woman then turned toward Andrea. "Hey, I was just thinking of you. What's up?"

Andrea frowned. "It's horrible mom. We have to go to the hospital right now. One of Cindy's friends got hurt, real bad. Someone beat her up."

"Oh no, which friend?"

"Stacey."

Marti's hand flew to her mouth. She groaned. "Poor Stacey." Her eyes flew to the small crowd still gathered. "Where's Sara?" she wondered. "I need her to sort this out."

Marti stood then turned to Andrea. "Can you get my coat please?" She bent to retrieve her purse from under the table.

"Cindy and Auntie Marni are getting our coats. I said we'd meet them by the door."

People started to murmur as they realized Marti was about to leave. Catching sight of activity, Sara scurried toward them from across the lobby.

"Sara, I have to go. One of my niece's friends is in the hospital. We just got the call." Marti raised her voice slightly, "Sorry to rush off. I have to get to the hospital. It's an emergency."

People nodded and exchanged sympathetic glances.

"Thank you Ms. Rose, we appreciate the time you were able to give," Sara gushed. "I'm sorry about your friend," she murmured to Andrea.

Marti shook hands with the remaining group, nodded at their polite remarks then strode across the lobby with Andrea.

"I'm sure she'll wake up soon." Marni rushed to soothe Marissa, Stacey's mom, who was clearly in shock. Marissa was afraid Stacey would remain in a coma indefinitely.

"How could this happen? What sort of monster would do this to her?"

"I don't know. Did the police have any ideas?"

"No, they didn't say anything."

"I'll talk to Detective Worthington tomorrow, see if he knows something," Marti offered.

"Thanks, we'd appreciate it," Stacey's dad Jim uttered as he stared at his daughter.

Cindy and Andrea sat silent by the foot of the bed. After they'd whispered remarks of sympathy to Stacey's parents they'd clutched hands then fallen into gloomy silence.

Marti speculated who had done this to Stacey. What if a friend picked her up on the way to work? Someone she'd never suspect of foul play? Tony perhaps? She wouldn't have gotten into the car of a stranger would she? It seemed far-fetched after what happened to Diane.

Stacey slept on, oblivious to Marti's theories and her parents' worries.

Funny how you didn't have trouble staying up late when you were revved about something.

He checked his watch again then glanced up and down the street. Should be late enough now, it was 3:00am. The houses were dark and he hadn't seen a car near the area. He'd been parked for the last few hours. It should be safe.

He longed to whistle while he crossed the street but controlled the urge. He needed to be quiet and blend into the night. He glanced up at the clouds that had moved in over the last hour covering the damn moon. With an eerie glow, it had illuminated the entire block. Like a light switched to low, clouds dimmed its radiance. Luck was on his side.

Stealthily he moved towards the back door. His eyes darted to the far corners of the yard then skimmed the entire area to confirm it was empty. Idly he stroked the cold steel of his tools then checked the door. It shouldn't be too hard to get in. First he'd check the windows though, often one was left ajar. Then you'd get in real fast.

He grinned as he thought about his teen years when he and a cousin had been in the habit of breaking and entering. They'd never been caught and had fenced some pricey items. They'd gotten a lot of cash and liquor so it had been a profitable venture. It gave him skills he never bragged about. They came in handy though.

He found pay dirt with the third window he tried. It was open a few inches. He moved the wooden box he found near the garage closer to the wall. People always left junk around their house. It was perfect to stand on and pry open windows.

That's something they'd noticed when they broke into places. People left useless items around outside. They were more likely to leave windows ajar in the spring, summer and fall. Damn cold prairie winters didn't lend themselves to open windows.

Grunting from the effort, he pried the screen off then tossed it into the bushes. He'd put it back after he planted the evidence. He pushed the window open the rest of the way then hoisted himself up and in. He was working out these days so his upper arms were like steel.

He banged his shin on the way in. "Damn, that hurts," he whispered as he rubbed the delicate spot.

He turned on his pencil light to check out the room. It was a bedroom. No one was in the unmade bed and clothes were strewn everywhere. Either the occupant was in a hurry to leave or a slob, more likely both.

He closed the window all the way then quietly moved to inspect each room in the house. It was important to make sure no one was there.

He and his cousin had found old folks snoring in their bedroom once. They'd closed the door then tiptoed around giggling as they filled their loot bag with household items. They'd scored a new TV and computer but found no cash or liquor. It was likely hidden in the bedroom.

No one was in Murray's house though so he brought out his full size flashlight. As he shone it around he saw crap everywhere.

"Man this guy is more than a slob, place is a pigsty."

He wrinkled his nose at the smell in the living room while he scanned the area for a spot to plant the evidence. Not the coffee table. It was piled high with ashtrays overflowing, beer bottles empty and half empty, pizza boxes, chips, cards, paper, matches and drug paraphernalia.

"Hmm, interesting. Guy could get nailed for possession as well as murder. It doesn't hurt to jack up those charges."

He leaned closer and spied a few roaches in the ashtray but there was no sign of drugs. "Better make a little trip out to the car."

He opened the front door then stepped outside. Cautious, he scanned the area. No one was in sight. Moving soundlessly, he was at his car in moments. He had some stash hidden in the spare tire, to sell on the side. When he entered the house again he placed the bag of goodies under one of the pizza boxes. No need to make it too obvious.

"She wouldn't have put it there, too much crap," he muttered.

While his eyes scanned he recalled where she'd been when they'd slammed through the door early Monday morning. He imagined her on the couch dozing. "Yeah, perfect."

He placed her rabbit's foot partway between the cushions, like it had fallen out of her pocket. "Didn't bring her much luck did it?" he sneered. He tossed the lip-gloss beside it.

He was tempted to take the stereo then thought better of it. That might raise a few eyebrows if the cops decided the room was too empty. Obviously a party house, the place screamed loud music.

He locked the front door behind him, went out back to replace the screen then put the wooden box back where he'd found it. His grin widened as he returned to his car then drove off without a backward glance. It had been a fine evening's work. Tomorrow he'd focus on the next part of his plan.

CHAPTER 25

SUNDAY

"*Why do you* think they picked me?"

"I have no idea. You might have seemed lost or alone. What did you do when you got to the bus depot?"

"I followed everyone off the bus. Then I stared down the street for a few minutes. It's a big, busy street. I wandered inside to Robin's Donuts, went to the bathroom. Then I went outside again. I wasn't sure what direction to go."

"Yeah I get that. So what was your plan when you got here?"

Rosemarie ducked her head then began to play with a piece of hair. As she wove hair through her fingers she stared into space. "My plan?" she whispered, "I didn't have one."

"Seriously, no plan." Diane lowered her voice as Rosemarie flinched. "How much money did you have with you?"

Diane barely heard the answer as Rosemarie mumbled, "$47.00."

Rosemarie jiggled her leg then peeked at Diane from behind her hair. "Pretty dumb, huh?"

Diane put her hands behind her head then leaned further back against the tree. "I'm not going to lie to you Rosemarie. Yeah, it sounds pretty dumb." *She shook her head,* "No money or plan and you seemed lost. When you walked outside were there people around?"

Rosemarie shook her head. "No, everyone had left by then. I stood by the front door a few minutes then hoisted my backpack onto my shoulder and walked across the parking lot. I had no idea where I was headed."

"Directionless and alone, let's add that to the list."

"What?"

"You asked why they picked you. So far we have directionless, alone, you seemed lost, had no plan, or money. Of course they didn't know you had no money but they might have guessed. Did you wear those clothes?"

Rosemarie glanced down. "The jeans and runners are the same, different t-shirt."

Diane nodded. "So nothing flashy or stylish. Let me guess, your backpack is navy or black, isn't it?"

"Black and cheap."

"When did they approach you?"

"I was halfway across the parking lot when this van rolled up beside me. I glanced inside and saw this woman in the driver's seat, a girl in the passenger's seat and a boy in the back. They waved at me and I waved back." *She shook her head.* *"They were friendly. I can't believe they turned out to be so horrid."* *She shuddered.*

"Shirley, that's her name, rolled down her window and asked if I needed a ride." *Rosemarie bit her lip.* *"I got in, just like that. I can't believe I was so stupid. Who does that?"*

Gwyn's eyes flashed open. The woman's first name was Shirley. They'd gotten another clue. Now if only Diane asked about the van or Rosemarie offered up a colour. She leaned forward.

"Well, since you had no plan it seemed like a great idea. I understand why you did it."

"You do? Thanks Diane."

"Yeah, it was stupid but it's not as if you thought they'd be evil. You were naïve and trusting, that's not a crime."

"I'd never met anyone like them." Rosemarie began to play with her hair again. *"I don't think I would have gotten in the van if the dad had been along. He was a creep. I could barely glance his direction."* She shivered. *"His hair was long and greasy, I don't think he ever washed, eew."*

Gwyn leaped up to grab a pen and paper then wrote down the description of the man. She held her breath as silence filled the room. Had she severed the connection when she jumped up?

"Gross, did the guy work?"

Gwyn grinned, relieved to hear Diane's voice.

"Yeah, I think so. He left more than Shirley did. She called him a loser all the time." Rosemarie raised her voice, *"Darryl, you're such a loser, you'll never amount to anything."* She shook her head. *"She was mean and abusive."*

Gwyn's smile broadened. Shirley and Darryl, she had first names now.

"Their van broke down, it was old. Shirley went berserk when that happened." Rosemarie cackled. *"Guess she couldn't pick up girls to murder without a van."*

"What'd they drive after that?"

Rosemarie shrugged. *"I don't know. Shirley complained about walking to Safeway so it might still be in their driveway. Ugly green thing, it reminded me of a tank."* She grinned. *"The kids called it their armoured vehicle. I think they said it was bought at some army auction or something. I don't know. Have you heard of those?"*

Gwyn grabbed her pen and paper then scribbled madly. These clues might track the killers down.

"Nah, I'm not into that kind of stuff. Hey, did you see that Rosemarie?"

"What?" Rosemarie craned her neck in the direction Diane pointed.

"I don't know. It could have been a person. Something moved over there. Should we check it out?"

Rosemarie jumped up. "Yeah, definitely. It'll keep my mind off Shirley and the gang of creeps." She grabbed Diane's hand. "Hurry."

Gwyn waited a few minutes. Silence greeted her as she called out, "Diane, Rosemarie, are you still there?" When there was no answer she dashed out of the room to call Marni.

⋏

Barry called early to report his strange conversation with Tony. Marti mentioned it to Marni as they discussed their plans for the day.

"Any idea what Tony meant?"

"I don't know. He was confused when I talked to him the other day. It's not fair to suspect him of anything without evidence but the dark car, and his ring." Marti shook her head. "It's not enough to go on but I hope the detective brings him in again. You're headed to Gwyn's today?"

"Yes, I told you about the communication she had this morning with Diane and Rosemarie. She wrote down names and facts to pass on to the detective. They're on the pad by the phone. Gwyn hoped they'd help with Rosemarie's case. Do you have time to come with me?"

"No, I better skip it. I need to phone Worthington. Then I want to update my notes. I can't shake the sense I've missed something significant. You know the feeling?"

"Yeah, the little voice?"

"That's the one. A visit to Gwyn sounds great though. While you're there can you pick up a crystal for Stacey?" Marti sighed. "I never thought of her when we bought one for the girls. Stacey needed one to protect her from evil and destructive spirits."

"It wasn't a spirit that put Stacey in the coma Marti."

"Yeah, I know. I just wish we could have done something."

"Remember the stories grandma told us about nature and harmony?"

"Are you trying to distract me Marni?"

"Yeah."

"Fair enough." Marti grinned. "Yeah, I remember her stories. She talked of nature, energy and the universe. Grandma was balanced and serene. She knew the importance of harmony. You remind me of her Marni. The abundance of flowers and herbs in your garden, when I watch you work out there, you're one with nature, like grandma."

"Thanks Marti. I loved to listen to grandma, the stories about our roots and ancestors. She stressed the importance of being close to family. I'm sure she appreciated every living thing, even bugs."

Marti laughed. "Right, remember the stories about dad and his siblings? I'm not sure grandma appreciated her kids when they played tricks on her and grandpa. Remember the bread story or the rotten eggs?"

"Yeah." Marni giggled. "I love those. Tell me one now, you're the storyteller."

Marti's grin broadened. "Sure, when it came to chores, dad's sisters liked to bake, cook and gather eggs. One sister always volunteered to bake bread. She made it so heavy the boys would take it outside then cannonball one another with it."

"Hah, that story is priceless. Imagine the mischief they got into."

"Yeah, this one's epic, the relatives love to tell it. Dad and his siblings would lay flat on the roof of the barn when they were in trouble. Our grandparents would check everywhere for them. When they heard giggling they'd figure out the hiding spot. When they tried to come near though, the kids threw rotten eggs they'd collected and kept for that purpose."

Marni sputtered. "It doesn't sound like dad and his siblings cared about balance and harmony with nature. They were into mayhem and hijinks."

"I'll say, meanwhile grandma had practical ideas for old food and scraps."

"Yeah, she'd focus on compost and fertilizer for her herb and flower garden. Not getting splattered with rotten eggs. She preferred to tell us those tales instead of dad's impish memories."

"That's why grandma liked stories about herbs, spirituality and living in harmony with nature. It's a serene subject, more in tune with maintaining one's peace of mind. With eleven kids, nature and grandma's garden were infinitely more tranquil than the spirited ways of her offspring."

Marti rubbed her chin. "I'd take a calm, peaceful environment anytime. It beats focusing on the evils of this world like we've been involved in. It's draining to dwell on the motives of a killer. The hilarity of dad's stories brings a smile to my face even though good behavior wasn't their goal. They weren't evil though."

"Yeah, I know what you mean. The antics of dad and his siblings mirrored more positive energy than negative. I'd think evil people are negative in the extreme, wouldn't you Marti?"

"Definitely. I've done research and discovered evil people respond with hatred when they're around wholesome, decent individuals. Their purpose is to destroy goodness. Many books and movies have good-versus-evil in the plot. It's common because it's real. Evil is at the root of murder."

Marti laughed. "Of course as an author I'm not above writing about wicked people. They're infinitely more interesting than boring, everyday folk. It's easier to create conflict when you tap into malevolence."

"Yeah, well you are known as the queen of murder and mayhem. Isn't that the nickname Andrea gave you?"

Marti grinned. "We've added blood and guts to my repertoire as well."

"How fitting for a crime novelist." Marni leaned toward Marti, her tone earnest. "Do you think our close proximity to the murder investigation and the wickedness that surrounds it, will have a long-lasting, negative impact on our lives?"

Marti grabbed Marni's hand then squeezed it. "Our intentions were good. We need to protect Cindy and Andrea. Cindy has been on the fringe of danger because of her friendship with Diane and Stacey. Was Stacey beaten up as a result of Diane's murder or was this a random act of violence? We won't find out until Stacey regains consciousness and describes her attacker." Marti shook her head. "Our personal involvement could help us grow as we fight these criminals. Our family could get closer."

"You're right Marti. I never thought about it that way before. We need to take ownership to fight evil. It'll make us stronger. As for crystals, I've worn mine for a long time. I'm glad you and the girls have one as well. They'll protect us."

Marti nodded. "That's why we need a crystal for Stacey, to keep her safe and help her heal. As you've said, part of the power of crystals is your belief in them. Could you ask Stacey's mom if the crystal can be near her bed? I'm not sure if Stacey will be allowed to wear it in the hospital."

"I'll ask Marissa. The power of belief is what works for these objects. Crystals are a natural energy source. Remember the crystals around grandma's house?"

Marti smiled. "We loved to watch the sunlight reflect off them onto the walls. They made rainbows everywhere. They helped grandma maintain positive energy. Her house was cheerful, warm and sunny. It reminds me of your home with your splash of colour, flowers and crystal display."

"Yeah, thanks for the reminder, I should water my indoor plants this morning." Marni stood up then stretched. "Too bad Stacey's room doesn't have a window. We could have put the crystal there." She glanced toward her window where crystals bobbed. "Would you like tea before we start our day's activities?"

Marti stood up. "I'd love some. I bought scones to warm up. I noticed you have blueberry jam."

"Yum, tea, warm scones and jam. That's a positive force for sure."

They linked arms then headed to the kitchen for breakfast.

He sat outside Cindy's place, eager to see who came and went. He sensed the people in her house knew something. He'd heard the aunt was some famous amateur crime fighter. That bothered him. The last thing he needed was an avenging angel meddling in his affairs.

While he waited his mind wandered.

Had he made a mistake letting that trollop Stacey live? What if she fingered him? The cops could arrest him.

What if the trail he'd left, the well planned out frame, backfired? He was smarter than them, no doubt. Things could go wrong though. Then where would he be?

Brooding, he admitted the stupidity of his actions. He drummed his fingers on the steering wheel.

He should have killed her while he'd had the chance. He'd heard Stacey was in a coma. He'd have to finish her off in the hospital before she talked.

"Man that was stupid. I must have been soft in the head letting her go." He banged his fist against the dash. "Ow, damn."

Red dots swam before his eyes. He needed an outlet. He started the car then revved the engine. Time to set in motion the rest of his plan.

Later that day, the full force of his rage would be released.

▲

Tony paced back and forth. "I can't believe they hauled me in again for questions. Now they're focused on my ring and car. What's up with these cops? Why don't they search for the killer instead of picking on Diane's friends?"

Cindy ignored his rant. "Tony, what do you think about evil?"

Cindy shivered. Why had she asked that question? Had she glanced outside she might have glimpsed the face of evil parked across the street. Was that why her thoughts leaned that direction?

"What?" Tony stopped pacing then ran his fingers through his hair.

"The killer, he must be evil. Normal people aren't murderers."

Tony plunked down on the couch beside Cindy.

"Yeah, tell that to the cops. Maybe they'll get my number off speed dial."

"My mom and aunt talked about evil this morning with Andrea and I."

"Yeah, what'd they say?"

"They said it's everywhere. It surrounds us, tries to encircle us with its stench. When you're young, like us, evil lurks in the strangest places. It hovers, corrupts then captures you in its clutches. That's how my aunt put it. Of course she is a writer." Cindy rubbed her face. "Maybe that's what happened to Diane. She knew evil was there, poised to catch her yet was powerless to stop it. That's what she could have felt that evening."

"Yeah, that makes sense. That's why Diane was on edge. She knew it was inevitable but couldn't admit it, even to herself. Deep down though, Diane knew, she knew…" Tony trailed off, whispering the last words.

Cindy stared at him. She hated when Tony talked like that. As if he knew facts no one else had discovered. Why imply he'd seen something or sensed it?

Unaware Cindy's train of thought had taken a sudden turn Tony believed they were on the same wavelength. Joined in awareness, intuitively alert, tuned in to Diane's pain and the onslaught of evil.

"Do you think it's arbitrary or intentional?"

"Hmm, what?" Cindy rubbed her temple to shake off her doubts.

"Evil, do you think it's arbitrary or intentional?"

Cindy shuddered as a shiver ran down her spine. "You mean was Diane the intended victim or was she in the wrong place at the wrong time?"

"Yeah kind of, but even more than that. If evil is out there waiting for us, can we stumble on it anytime or does it single out certain people? Do you think people can be evil one day then normal the next? Has everyone got the potential to be evil? What do you think?"

Cindy sucked in her breath. How had they gotten on this topic? Oh yeah, she'd started it.

"I don't know. I guess it's out there. Maybe it knocks at your door to see if you're home." She shrugged then scrunched her face up. "If you answer then it makes a move. If you peep out at it through your window but don't respond, it moves along, to grab someone else."

Tony bobbed his head. "Yeah, yeah, that's good."

"Think of the daily temptations we're faced with. There's drugs, sex, booze, cigarettes, dating strangers, stealing, lying, cheating… the list goes on and on. It comes down to choices."

"Yeah, choices."

Cindy shook her hair back. "If we don't have enough common sense to distinguish between right and wrong, good and bad, than evil can get a grip on you pretty easy."

"Do you think Diane chose to die or Stacey wanted to get beaten up? What alternative did they have? What if it was more than that? Something beyond their control or even the killer's control?"

Cindy stared at him. A lump formed in her throat. She rubbed her neck then closed her eyes. Tony was right. What choice did they have? Cindy whimpered softly.

It had happened to her friends. What if she was next? Arbitrary or intentional, what did it matter? Evil was everywhere. Cindy felt it in the air.

What choice would she have? What if the killer was a madman, out of control? Cindy's sobs increased as Tony moved closer to console her.

⚘

Marni's skin crawled. The sensation increased as she walked to her car. Something was off. She stifled the urge to brush imaginary grime away then shivered as fear coursed down her spine. She rubbed her arm then glanced down. She expected her skin to be bright red, as if she'd developed a sudden rash. It was clean though. There was no trace of the foulness she sensed.

It was something deeper then, not surface filth. Had evil filtered through, flooding the area with the stench of immorality?

Marni couldn't shake the uneasy feeling. Her senses were on high alert. Something horrible and wrong was about to happen. She closed her eyes as she leaned against the car. "Please don't involve anyone near and dear to me," she uttered.

Her eyes flashed open. It was stronger here, near the street. Marni walked to the end of the driveway then searched up and down the road. There were no strange cars parked nearby, nor anyone walking in the neighbourhood. As she combed the street, she heard a noise near the intersection down the block. She squinted in time to see a dark car turn the corner.

Marni's breath caught in her throat. Wisahkecahk the destroyer lurked down the street. She gasped then covered her mouth. With Wisahkecahk it was important not to draw attention to oneself. She backed up toward her car, her footsteps slow and measured. Wisahkecahk darted out to follow the dark car.

The killer was nearby. Evil had followed them home…

CHAPTER 26

"I saw him, I know I did. I've seen Wisahkecahk twice now Gwyn."

"When was the first time?"

Marni raised tired eyes to Gwyn's. "At Diane's funeral."

"What do you think it means?"

Marni shuddered. "Evil has closed in. Something sinister is out there, waiting, watching, biding its time."

"The killer could be close."

"Maybe," Marni rubbed her eyes. "I don't know why I'm denying it. Yes, the killer is nearby."

"Do you think he feels threatened by your family?"

"Yes. He must know about Marti's involvement with the case. Cindy talks to her friends a lot too. They've bounced around a number of theories. Then with Stacey's beating last night, well, that's too coincidental to ignore."

"Have you noticed anyone following you or skulking around? A stranger I mean?"

Marni's breath quickened. "Yeah, this morning, that's when I saw the dark car drive around the corner at the end of the block. Wisahkecahk followed it."

"It could be the killer. It explains your uneasy feeling, being on edge. You're surrounded by the stench of evil. It's moved into your personal realm. You should ask the detective to have a car posted outside your house until this case is solved. Where are Cindy, Andrea and Marti?"

"They're at home. Marti had to call the detective and Cindy had friends over."

"Good, there's safety in numbers. I think you should travel in pairs and never be alone. What kind of protection does Stacey have at the hospital?"

"Marissa and Jim have been with her since she was admitted."

"They have to sleep. You better make sure someone's with Stacey when they leave. What if the creep that did this to her comes back to finish her off?"

Marni's voice rose. "Oh Gwyn, you don't think that could happen do you?"

"Why not, anything's possible. As you mentioned, Stacey's beating is too coincidental."

"Yes, it could be tied to this case." Marni pushed her hair back. "On the other hand, it could be a random act of violence. There's no way of knowing until Stacey regains consciousness."

"Then she could be in danger if the person who beat her comes to the same conclusion. What if it's Diane's murderer? He won't want Stacey alive to identify him."

Marni stared at Gwyn, thunderstruck.

"You're right. Where's my phone? We thought a crystal would keep her safe. A madman is on the loose."

Marni called her sister who relayed Worthington had already posted a policeman outside Stacey's room for protection. Marni urged Marti not to let the girls out of her sight. As she disconnected she turned to pass on the good news to Gwyn.

"You wanted another crystal?" Gwyn led Marni over to her display case where they pored over gems. As they searched, Marni brought up the subject of evil. She couldn't help it. She was transfixed on the theme.

"I'd feel better if Stacey had one. Evil is nearby."

"Yes, it floats out there eager to grab an unsuspecting soul."

"Do you think it hangs around us in the air?"

"No, that was a figure of speech. I think evil surrounds us though. There are billions of people in the world and a percentage of them are bad. Hence good-versus-evil."

"You sound like Marti with her good-versus-evil theory. Of course that's bread and butter for a crime novelist."

"Yeah, well I've heard you mention there's always one bad apple in the bunch."

"True, I hope that's what the ratio is when it comes to evil, one bad apple in the entire bunch. That's why we need comic figure heroes to conquer evil." Marni grinned. "We just watched one of those shows the other night on Netflix."

She shook her head. "I have to admit, before this week I never gave evil a second thought. It was there but never touched my family. It's nebulous, vague, just a word you hear in books and movies. It has no impact on one's life until it reaches out and grabs you. Then it becomes real, and scary."

"Yeah, being close to a murder case would change your outlook."

Marni stroked a crystal. "I'm not sure how Marti does it. She's exposed to people she normally wouldn't meet. One of them could be a murderer and represents ultimate evil. Talk about getting close to a research subject."

"I know. One of you could have crossed paths with the murderer already. Odds are against one meeting a killer, yet you're personally involved this time."

"Yeah, Marti's bent on assisting the police with murder cases. She faces evil on a regular basis. I'm not used to it though. It feels alien. Like a lioness, I want to protect my cubs and loved ones from harm."

"That's a normal reaction Marni."

Marni's eyes flicked over her shoulder. "That could be why my senses are on high alert and I'm anxious. I'm hyper-aware of those around me."

Gwyn touched Marni's arm. "You're a sensitive woman Marni. You're not used to cruelty and the implications associated with that lifestyle."

"Yes, my life has been blessed." Marni gripped her hands as if in prayer. "I have a mate who's good and pure of heart. I've found a friend in you Gwyn. You've helped me figure out who I am and ask profound questions. I feel in tune at a deeper level of consciousness and appreciate all I've been given.

I treasure my close friends. Meeting wonderful people has been one of the things I've cherished over the years. I have a loving, caring family. I've experienced untold marvels and I thank Creator for them daily."

Marni sighed. "Up to now I've felt safe and secure. I've found this week stressful. Everything has been out of kilter. My equilibrium is off. I'm suspicious of everyone. My world has tilted. Like a kaleidoscope it's been slanted toward the wrong side of morality. I've been given a glimpse at the rougher side of life."

Marni folded her hands under her armpits. "I'm unprepared for the front row seat I've been given. I think I've risen to the challenge though. I wonder, when one is exposed to the seamy side of life do you get accustomed to it? Is Detective Worthington used to evil and its destructive forces? Does he accept evil as a negative part of his job? What do you think?"

"That's a hard question. I've never been in the detective's shoes so I can't say. I guess it's important to maintain your own sense of right and wrong. I'd feel good about apprehending criminals. The detective must feel he provides a worthwhile service by doing his job. He could be jaded compared to you or I but he must maintain some sense of self. Otherwise, how could he expose himself to evil daily?"

Marni nodded then leaned her elbows on the display case. "That's what I need to do, get my sense of self back. I should meditate. I need to get in touch with my subconscious. I crave tranquility."

"We can meditate right now if you have time."

Marni flashed Gwyn a smile. "That sounds perfect, thanks."

⸸

"Yes, I agree with you Marti, Stacey's beating is not coincidental. That's why we posted someone outside her hospital room." He chuckled. "If this was a TV show or one of your books the killer would brazenly try to attack our guy. He'd be overpowered, we'd slap the handcuffs on him and call it a day."

"Why Detective, are you proposing a scene for one of my books?"

Worthington grunted. "It's hardly noteworthy of a scene. I think that one's been done before, don't you?"

"Hah, like a million times. By the way, Tony's here, he complained to Cindy about being hauled in again for questioning. I take it nothing came of his car?"

"We got a warrant and searched the vehicle. No trace of anything to tie him to Diane's murder or Stacey's attack. It's his mom's car so neither girl was ever in it. We had to cut him loose."

Marti was about to ask about Barry when Worthington continued.

"Tony had an alibi for last night anyway. So did your buddy Barry. They're both off the hook for Stacey's beating." The detective chuckled. "They passed their rings over to me willingly. We're checking them for DNA now. I brought the brother in and got his ring too."

"What brother?"

"Barry's. I hauled him in after my little chat with Barry. His name is Mark. I had to let him go though. He had an alibi for the night of Diane's death and Stacey's attack."

Marti fidgeted in her chair. The ring bothered her. Someone else had a ring. She'd noticed it this week. It wasn't Tony though. An image floated out there, hazy and indistinct. Where had she seen the ring?

Worthington broke into her thoughts.

"My partner Pitt has been working on the other girl's case."

Marti shook her head. "What other girl?"

"Rosemarie, you asked about water in her lungs."

"Oh, right." Marti rubbed her eyes. "What did Pitt say?"

"She was drowned, definitely water in her lungs."

Marti shuddered. Death by drowning, it was her worst-case scenario since she'd never been a fan of water.

"Quick like ketchup, thick like spam, home schooled, home ruled. It's a woman, not a man."

"Pardon?"

"Oh, I just repeated the phrase Rosie mentioned to me from her dream. Rosie said a woman, not a man, tortured Rosemarie. It sounds like the woman was responsible for drowning Rosemarie."

"Yeah, well we'll need more to bring someone in for questioning than a dream from the deceased girl's twin sister."

"Gwyn called this morning. She had another communication with Diane and Rosemarie."

"Great, a dream and a vision; the case is more solid by the minute."

Marti ignored the sarcasm as she filled Worthington in on the details Gwyn had recorded.

Worthington sighed. "Well, I hate to admit it but Pitt has no leads on the case. He may as well start searching for the van, those are solid clues if they're real."

Marti chuckled. "Come on, spirits, visions and twins communicating are the stuff of bestsellers. Now that's a worthy scene for a novel."

He couldn't believe they were being hauled in like this. The cops had left his car abandoned on the side of the road. Claimed they'd get it towed to the nearest police station. He shook his head. Yeah, that was likely to happen. The car was a classic. Slim chance no one would steal that baby.

Gloomily he tried to stretch but there wasn't room in the back seat. The three of them were jammed in like sardines in a tin. The way the cops talked this was their last bit of freedom for a long, long time. Sounded like they were going to toss them in the tank then throw away the key. They'd rot in jail until their teeth fell out and limbs grew useless from inactivity. Man, what an ignoble way to return back to Regina, stuffed into the back of a cop car like common criminals.

Murray wondered what they'd charge them with. Not murder, that was beyond his imaginings. No way they'd make something like that stick. Negligence maybe, he thought that was the term. When you knew something bad was going down but you let it happen.

Not that they'd known murder was on the mind of those psychos. They'd broken into the house, gone berserk and kidnapped Diane. Unbelievable. Who did that? It sounded like something in a cop show or one of those crime thrillers. He shook his head. Unreal. They'd gotten caught up in it. Now they had to explain themselves.

Resigned to the worst, Murray glanced at Don and Mark. They were in a deep mess. Bummed, barely alert, Murray didn't think their pea brains were capable of figuring how much trouble they were in.

Should they finger those guys as the killers?

It had to be them. Who else could have done it?

"*Why'd you run?*" was the question Murray dreaded.

⋏

"I feel restored after meditating, balanced and relaxed."

"Yes, more grounded, calm. It's like I, ow," Marni grabbed her head then dropped to her knees.

Gwyn rushed to her side. "Marni, are you all right? What happened?"

Marni waved her hand but didn't answer. Eyes closed, she rubbed her temple with the fingers of one hand, intent on slowing her breathing.

Gwyn lowered herself beside Marni, reached for her other hand, gripped it loosely then mimicked her pose.

"In, out, in, out," Gwyn whispered. "Relax, breath, in, out."

They were quiet again, focused on inhaling and exhaling.

Long moments passed.

Gwyn's eyes flashed open as Marni gripped her hand tighter. Marni began to shake as cold filtered through her bones.

Chilled to her core, Marni shuddered. She pulled her hand from Gwyn's, crossed her arms then pressed them tightly against her chest and rocked forward, backward, forward, backward.

Alarmed, Gwyn called out, "Marni, Marni, come back, I'm here, talk to me." She jumped up then ran to get a blanket. She tossed it over Marni's shoulders then began to rub her arms fast and furious.

"So cold, numb, frozen," Marni murmured.

"What's happening Marni, talk to me," Gwyn urged.

"Terrible pain, intense, brutal."

"You're in pain, where?"

Marni's eyes opened. "Not me, someone else," she whispered. "They're in distress. Unpardonable evil." Her hand flew to her mouth. With wide eyes she uttered, "We can't stop it, not yet, we're powerless."

As Marni wept Gwyn gathered her into her arms. Marni folded her body around Gwyn desperate for warmth. Her frame heavy, she dropped her head to Gwyn's shoulder.

"I think it was the killer," Marni whispered.

"That's who you felt?"

Marni shook her head. "No, I think I felt his next victim," she uttered as her eyes fluttered closed.

Gwyn smothered her gasp in Marni's hair as they rocked together.

⁂

He'd noticed her last week while driving home from work. "Damn bitch," he muttered. He hated girls who hitched rides, it wasn't right.

He saw her, in the same place when he drove by. After work, suppertime, on the weekend, she was always in the same spot.

The bitch was asking for it.

That's the site he chose Sunday night.

The temptation was too great. He had to do it, no choice. Fate wasn't shining on her that evening.

He pulled up at the corner then ordered, "Get in, I'll give ya a ride."

While she chattered non-stop he watched her black clad shoe tap in time to the music. He decided it was a nervous twitch.

Black was a fitting colour for her kind. Did she have red underneath those clothes? Weren't black and red the colours of whores?

He grinned. He'd find out soon enough.

She had no inkling of his thoughts. He smirked as he watched her. She didn't suspect a thing.

She never knew it was coming…stupid bitch.

Pretty up close, her face was brutally waxen in death. Her make-up stood out starkly, arm raised in appeal. She reminded him of a mannequin from the store. Preserved, yet lifeless, round circles drawn on each cheek.

He raped her first on a back road far from prying eyes. Brutal, he worked his anger out on her slight frame. Innumerable bruises and welts rose to the surface of her skin before the final moment.

While he did it to her he turned to look down at the black clad foot, mesmerized by the increasing intensity of the tapping.

Tap, tap, tap…

It stopped abruptly. No more nervous twitch.

His face spread in a relaxed grin after he strangled her.

He'd done it, gotten rid of one more slut.

"Jezebal, I commit you to whence you came," he murmured reverently as he gently laid her down on the front seat.

Whistling, he drove back to the city at a leisurely pace. As he cruised down familiar streets he drummed in time to the music. He headed for the same area he'd dumped the first body. Careful, he drove slowly in case cops were nearby.

It was light, early evening. People were in the area yet he didn't care. Driving over a grassy field past an old building he checked neither right nor left. He maneuvered his vehicle behind the shed secure in the knowledge his actions were justified. He casually opened the door then shoved her out. He barely slowed down.

The sole witness to his triumphant laugh was the victim who was beyond caring.

He drove to his favourite car wash where he spent more time than usual cleaning his pride and joy. Other customers waiting in line muttered about time wasters. He hummed under his breath, ignoring protests and dirty looks. He didn't give a damn what others thought.

He took a few hairs from the passenger seat then carefully laid them aside for later. He kept her purse, aware of the risk. People who committed crimes were dumb. Not like him, smart and thorough. Everything he did had purpose.

The elderly man behind him who'd waited patiently for the last half hour was surprised by the abruptness of the guy's laugh. It sounded off, like the fella wasn't quite right in the head.

The crazed guy at the car wash was the key piece to an increasingly complex puzzle. Greasy dark hair fell over his brow. He reminded the elderly man of an Italian guy, from the Sicilian mafia favoured on TV shows. Lanky and long he was the type who worked out and never put pounds on. Hatred emanated from his body like an electric current. On the edge, poised and ready, he could go off at a moment's notice.

"I'm not going to hurry the guy now", the elderly man uttered. People like that could go off their rocker for no reason. He didn't want to be on the wrong end of that stick of dynamite. If it got too dark to wash his car he'd come back tomorrow. No need to antagonize the guy.

The man at the car wash could have provided valuable insight to the police. His analysis was accurate. He never suspected the fellow in front of him was something more though. He just shrugged the Italian guy's behaviour off as strange.

It would have been a valuable lead for the police, the description of the guy and the car. Especially the car since Barry had identified the same model at the station. Like a tidal wave slowed down, water momentarily halted, time ticked on.

CHAPTER 27

Monday

Marni's eyes flashed open as the phone beside her bed rang. She groped for the receiver as she glanced at the clock. It was early for a Monday morning call.

"Marni, Diane came to me again this morning when I was meditating."

Awake now, Marni gripped the phone tighter. "What did she say?"

"Another girl was killed last night. The body is a few blocks from where Diane was found."

Marni drew in a shaky breath. "That's what I felt."

"Yes, it must have been the victim's last moments."

Marni sighed. "Was there anything else?"

"Yes, but I can tell you the rest when you get here. I want to come with you to the site."

"Sure. I'll wake up Marti and get her to call the detective."

"Thanks. See you soon."

Marni woke Marti up, threw some clothes on then headed down to plug the kettle in. It would be a tea and toast morning.

"Convenient Diane told Gwyn about this new body. She's like a spirit crime fighter," Marti remarked as she strode into the kitchen. "If this were a novel I'd hesitate to use this angle."

"Why's that?"

"It could be interpreted as blatant manipulation by the author."

"What's that mean?"

"Well, as an author we manipulate our characters to some degree." Marti chuckled. "Sometimes the characters manipulate us though so it's only fair." She tossed her hair back as she leaned over her tea. "Blatant manipulation happens when there's an unbelievable coincidence. If Diane helps us solve her crime in spirit form she'll achieve something the police are unable to accomplish with clues, hard work, digging and regular detective work. Readers don't like to be deliberately manipulated. I'd dial the scene back if I were the author of this story."

"Do you think Diane stayed to tell Gwyn this news? Gwyn thinks she's been trapped here since her spirit was stolen when she was murdered. If she helps with the case she could leave and cross to the other side after this."

Marti shrugged. "I have no idea. I have a hard time believing ghosts stay around to help police find dead bodies." She shook her head. "Definitely borders on blatant manipulation."

"I don't know Marti. If this victim has something to do with Diane's murder it could be a karma thing."

"A karma thing?"

"Yeah, destiny, what goes around comes around, fate, chance."

"I know the definition of karma Marni."

Marni grinned. "Then you won't be surprised when we catch the bad guys and they get sent to jail. Good-versus-evil, it's the bread and butter of best sellers. You've said it yourself. It's a favourite fan ending."

Marti sighed then rolled her eyes. "Indeed, it is."

⊥

Marti and Marni rushed to pick up Gwyn then headed to the crime scene.

The area was roped off with tape and police bustled about. Worthington waved them over.

"At first glance this one is similar to Diane's murder. Could be the same person. We'll need damning evidence though to get a conviction. There might be nothing more to go on here than at the last site. We'll be no further ahead." Worthington turned to Marti. "Is this your friend and sister?"

"Oh, yes, how rude of me." Marti introduced him to Marni and Gwyn.

"Marti said you've heard Diane a few times in a dream or something?"

Marti heard Gwyn explain Diane's communications. As her voice provided background Marti's mind wandered. Why had Diane led them here? It had to be connected to her murder. Would evidence from this crime solve Diane's murder? What had they missed?

⊥

"Why am I doing this?"

He'd agreed to meet Barry in the Sears parking lot after work to show his car off. The dork likely wouldn't even appreciate what a fine automobile it was.

Barry was taking forever. Man, where was the guy?

About to leave, he saw Barry across the lot. He jumped out of his car, waving Barry over.

Barry approached, a big smile on his face.

"Yeah, this is my beauty." He waved toward his car with a flourish.

"Oh my God." Barry cried. He turned then ran back in the direction he'd come from. Barry shouted over his shoulder, "Gotta go, I just remembered something important. See ya tomorrow."

Narrowing his eyes at Barry's rapid departure he scowled. Man what a weirdo. The guy deserved to be taught a lesson with that attitude. It was time for Barry to get a wake up call. With a wicked grin he thought of options to put Barry in his place. "Hah, a visit from the cops should do it."

Barry was the perfect patsy. Imagine his involvement in a murder with his loser friend Murray. That would be divine justice. He didn't know if Barry and Murray were friends though. He shrugged, "Doesn't matter, the cops can sort that out. Sweet," he hooted.

Cackling at his creativity, he googled Barry's brother's address online. The lowlife mentioned he lived with his brother Mark these days. He stopped by his house to grab Jezebel's purse on the way to Mark's. It had been her last earthly possession, the perfect piece of evidence.

He'd stashed it in the garage last night with the intent of planting it at Murray's house. This was better though. He'd get to watch Barry squirm firsthand when the cops arrested him at work.

"Great, I'll call it in tomorrow as an anonymous tip." He turned the music up then sang loudly, drumming along as he drove to Mark's house.

⁂

Later, he thought how great it would be to share the news of what he'd achieved with his friends. They'd be impressed with the effort and details. Planning and figuring were a lot of work. You had to make sure everything was done right, think ahead, always be one step in front of the cops.

If he could pin suspicion of the first kill on Murray and the second on Barry the cops would be confused. They might never crack these crimes. He'd heard about things like that before. On TV they said lots of crimes were never solved. Wouldn't that be cool if these turned out like that?

What was stopping him from doing more? He'd gotten good at it. Those stupid cops would never find him.

The thought excited him.

Yeah, it was like he was helping society out. The girls were useless. They'd never amount to anything. Probably go on welfare or marry some jerk and have a pile of kids the government would have to take care of. Stupid sluts weren't worth anything.

The cops would thank him if they could. He was like a modern day superhero. He helped the good guys, got rid of garbage on the streets.

Of course they'd never track him down so he assumed they'd thank him. No use waving favours in their face.

His face darkened. You couldn't trust cops though. They could turn on you any time. They loved to bolt the door behind you and throw away the key when you'd supported them all along. Think of all the criminals locked up for no reason. They'd helped society out. They hadn't gotten praise for doing it. Man, the world was screwed up.

Hungry, as he passed a 7-Eleven he pulled in to pick up cigarettes before heading home to eat. That's where he met her. Well, met would be an exaggeration, they both happened to be there at the same time. He knew when he spotted her she was the one, the chosen one. She'd be next.

He parked down the street since he hated the parking lot. Anyone could ding his fresh paint job, bunch of lowlifes. He scowled as he entered the store. That's when he noticed a girl near the counter, picking out candy.

Her innocence grabbed his attention. She appeared sweet in contrast to the clerk serving her. The clerk was hard. She had the air of someone who'd seen it all. The girl on the other hand appeared childlike in her mannerisms. Picking out candy was likely part of it. Deep down though he knew she was a slut like the rest of them. They were all the same.

He paid for his cigarettes, careful not to be caught staring. He didn't want to appear over eager. He watched her out of the corner of his eye as she paid for the candy. She left the store then sauntered across the parking lot. She was on foot. Good, it'd be easier that way.

Hurrying, he slowed his pace when he got near. As he came abreast of the girl he paused mid-stride to light his cigarette. With a casual glance in his direction, her eyes widened as she hungrily eyed his smoke. It was the lead he'd hoped for.

"Want one?"

"No thanks, I gave them up over a week ago."

She greedily watched him inhale.

"How come?"

"I don't know. Just thought I should. I can't afford them. I've been eating these instead." She indicated the bag of sweets in her hand.

"Not the same though." He nodded, trying to appear understanding.

It was easy after that, oh so easy.

He drove with the stink of her on him. It inflamed his senses, made him bolder. Little did he suspect his overconfidence would be his undoing…

CHAPTER 28

Worthington and his partner Pitt were at Murray's house with a search warrant. The paperwork had gone through approving the search and he'd gotten the call while they examined the latest crime scene. One of the guys brought him the authorization. Since the place was nearby they headed straight there.

The place was a pigsty. Murray was a slob.

"What did Diane see in Murray?"

Pitt shrugged. "Seems like a loser."

"Yeah, why do girls hook up with guys like these?"

Worthington didn't expect an answer. He was just talking aloud while they riffled through the mess.

"We'll get the lab guys to come in. They can sift through this garbage. Hope it's not another dead end." He picked up a pipe. "Likely we can charge the guy with possession but I'd love to get him on more."

"Yeah, like a clue to solve the murder," Pitt agreed. "So, I gotta tell you Worthington it was awesome. Great piece of detective work," Pitt boasted as he picked his way past the garbage and filth.

Worthington grunted.

"So, we had these clues and I thought, yeah, right, they're from the dead girl, happens every day." Pitt shrugged. "But you know what, she deserved a chance. At justice, you know."

"Yeah, I know."

"These girls, they don't know any better, trusting, young, naïve. It's sad." Pitt shook himself as if dispelling negative thoughts. "So, I say to the guys, let's check the computer, see if anyone pops out with these first names. I don't tell them where we got the information from though."

"Good call."

"Yeah, I thought so. We checked the last few years to see if any old vans got pulled over for violations. Couldn't believe when Ray shouted out bingo, I got one that fits that description." Pitt grinned. "It was registered to Shirley Mund. Address checked out and everything. Van was in the driveway just like Rosemarie remembered."

"When you're on the witness stand you might want to dial back the awe in your voice," Worthington noted.

"Are you kidding? Jurors love ghost stories. They'll lap this one up."

Worthington raised his brows.

"Anyway, I convinced a judge to give us a warrant."

"Let me guess, Harrington."

"How'd you know?"

"Seems the type to believe in spirits, communication and such."

Pitt chuckled. "I took a few guys with me. Scored the jackpot. Two kids answered the door. I showed them the warrant and asked where their mom and dad were. Guess what they said?"

"What's it to you?"

"Good one, no, they asked if we were the police. I showed them my badge and they just stared at it, real quiet." Pitt's face clouded over. "The girl grabbed the boys hand, leaned forward then commanded her brother to tell us."

Worthington stopped poking around, straightened up then gave his partner a sharp look. "Where were they?"

"In the basement, torturing another girl."

"What? Seriously, with you right on their doorstep. Didn't they hear you arrive?"

"Nah, they've got the basement decked out with heavy duty insulation, to hide the screams I imagine."

"So you rescued another girl?"

"Not just one. They had one more locked in a bedroom, chained to a bed. They were both in rough shape."

"Talk about catching them in the act. The case should be airtight with the girls' statements. Even if we did get the initial clue from a spirit."

"There's more."

"What?"

"The two kids, those aren't their real parents."

"They're not?"

"Nope, the girl talked right away. Got real chatty when we caught the adults downstairs. The woman almost drowned one of the girls. Had her head in the toilet." Pitt shook his head.

"Anyway, the younger girl led us to the area they had decked out as a torture chamber. Then she gave us a tour of all their rooms. They were locked downstairs, at night, when they went to bed. The girl pointed out tapes they hid. These are real sickos.

They stole the two kids when they were young. I don't want to know what they've done to them all these years. We have no idea how many kids they've stolen or killed."

"Are they on the missing persons list?"

"Oh yeah, they've been on it for six years. They were nabbed outside a grocery store. They were on a bench while their mom ran inside for milk. Just a few minutes, that's all it took."

"Whoa, brutal."

"Yeah, I couldn't wait to call their parents, give them the good news. They're headed to Regina now." He glanced at his watch. "I'm meeting them at the station in a few hours to re-unite them with their kids. Ray and Smithy are contacting the other two sets of parents. Those girls are still at the hospital since they've got nasty burns and abrasions."

"A happy ending for three families."

"Yeah, it feels good to get creeps like that off the street."

Worthington agreed, reaching for his cell phone when it rang. He paced around the room saying, "Uh huh, yeah, yeah, great." He pulled his notebook out of his pocket, wrote something down then wrapped the conversation up.

"We're out of here. Barry Moore's at the station. He identified the killer's car. He knows his name, where he works, the make, model and colour of the car and get this, the license plate."

"Bingo." Pitt fist pumped the air. "We're on a roll now."

"Yeah. Cruisers spotted the car in the vicinity a few minutes ago. There's an all points bulletin out. We might catch this sucker today."

They ran out to their car jumping into an unmarked Buick. They were about to pull into the street when Worthington swiftly killed the motor. "Quick, get down," he bellowed.

Pitt obeyed.

"What's up?" he whispered out of the side of his mouth.

"I saw a car in my rearview pull into the street. It's the same colour Barry Moore identified so we'll wait for it to go by, just in case."

They inched up to watch the car in question.

Passing slowly, the driver was focused on Murray's house, oblivious to their car.

Worthington pulled out his notebook to check the license plate number he'd written down. "Yup, that's him alright."

They watched him park down the street, three houses in front of them.

Worthington grabbed the radio. He instructed all cars to proceed to the area but avoid their street and Dewdney Avenue. Officers were to stay out of sight and await further instructions. He didn't want the guy spooked.

They sat and watched an older couple walk their dog down the street. There was no movement from the killer's car. Another vehicle cruised by.

"Lot of civilians in the area," Pitt commented.

"Yeah, we're going to have to be careful. This guy could be a loose cannon waiting to go off."

Worthington's phone rang. He snapped it closed moments later.

"Who was that?"

"Ralby. Turns out the closer they get to Regina, the more Murray Wall remembers about Diane and her killer. He's singing like a jaybird. Ready to strike a deal he claims."

"Was he in on the murder?"

"Nah, turns out him and his buddies were pansies. He told Ralby they passed out. Woke up when the front door was kicked in. The guy here, name's Andy Golder, and his pals burst into the house with guns, startling everyone. Murray and his friends cried like babies, begged for their lives. To hear it now Ralby said they think they're heroes. They want a medal for relaying the story."

Worthington raised his eyebrows at Pitt. They'd seen it all.

"Okay, so I made up the crying like babies part. Ralby said they whined so I drew a few conclusions. Andy and his friends hauled Diane away and none of the guys put up a fuss about it."

"Why'd they take her?"

"I don't know. Nearest Ralby can figure is revenge. Murray dated Andy's sister so Andy dropped by to beat on him. Murray suggested the sister might be hooked on cocaine but he had nothing to do with it. Andy blamed Murray for getting her on drugs. It's a tragic tale."

Pitt snorted.

"It gets better."

"Do tell."

"The sister is pregnant and claims the father is Murray. So she's a pregnant cokehead. Her brother isn't as understanding as Murray thought he should have been about the whole thing."

"So Murray cheated on Diane with Andy's sister?"

"Sounds like it."

"Man, what a jerk."

"Yeah, seems Diane was in the wrong place at the wrong time. Andy took her for retribution then raped her to get back at Murray. Had his friends rape her for good measure." He shook his head. "I wonder if he meant to kill her or if something went wrong?"

"Maybe we should ask him."

"Yeah, good idea." Worthington wiped his brow. "I gotta say I'll be relieved when we haul in this Andy Golder." He grinned at Pitt. "You won't have to check out Marti's sister or her friend Gwyn now. I wasn't looking forward to pissing off Marti. When she called this morning with another ghost story then told us where to find that girl's body, well…"

"There have been a lot of ghosts and spirits interfering in this case. I would have liked to meet this Gwyn woman. She could come in handy in the future if we're at a dead end."

Worthington frowned. "I told you to scale back the awe, Pitt."

Pitt grinned, "Gotcha." He laughed. "You should have seen your face. Imagine putting someone like Gwyn on the payroll as an informer. The chief would go nuts. Then again…"

"Hardy, har, you're hilarious. Let's catch this guy while we have the chance. He appears to be flesh and blood, not some fanciful spirit." Worthington reached into the back seat then pulled out a gym bag.

"Been working out lately?"

"Nah, it's my son's. I drop him off at the gym and he keeps his bag in here."

"Whew, are you going to wear that?"

Pitt wrinkled his nose as Worthington pulled out a t-shirt.

"Yeah, I thought I should. It's better than these dress clothes."

He pulled off his shirt and tie then struggled into the close-fitting T-shirt. "Kinda tight," he grunted. He pulled off his dress shoes then bent over to tie a pair of runners.

"Why would Murray and his friends abandon Diane? Why didn't they call us?"

"I don't know. Guess we'll have to ask when we question them. They bailed on her then took off for Mexico when they heard she was dead. They would have made our jobs easier if they'd called. Not to mention the girl he likely murdered yesterday. Hope there's no other dead bodies out there we haven't found yet."

Worthington told Pitt what to do, slowly opened the car door then dropped to the ground. Inching around to the back he threw open the trunk. Standing, he rummaged around, made a bunch of noise then pulled something out. He slammed the trunk loudly then walked toward the house he'd parked in front of. He carried a bag and loose piece of plywood.

Calm and cool he strode to the back where he threw his props aside. He raced down the alley, three houses forward, even with the killer's car. As he edged towards the bushes Worthington watched for any movement.

Andy sat in his car, drumming his fingers on the steering wheel in time to the music. Every so often he'd glance at Murray's place. He seemed to be staking the house out.

Worthington edged back to the alley then walked one house over. He hid in the front yard, craning his neck to see if Pitt was in position down the street. Fortunately no one had noticed him lurking in the vicinity, like a peeping tom.

He watched Pitt slide out the car door. He headed to the back of the vehicle where he grabbed the tools Worthington had left on the ground.

Worthington smiled at Pitt's attempt to look tousled. He'd taken his tie off, a dress shirt hung out of his pants and his hair was mussed yet he was still neat. Pitt was always tidy.

Worthington inched forward so he was closer to the sidewalk. He was now in position to get behind the suspect's car when Pitt passed. Peering between the leaves, he watched Pitt walk down the sidewalk, toward Andy's car.

Pitt jockeyed the tools he hauled, pretending he had trouble carrying them. He wasn't doing a bad job of it. He managed to make it past the front of the car then dropped them on the sidewalk. There was a loud clanging noise when the toolbox opened. Everything flew to the ground. Pitt cursed extra loud as he bent down to retrieve the tools.

Worthington made it to the back of Andy's car and inched around to the driver's side. He watched Andy lean over to watch Pitt out his passenger window. Worthington whipped the driver's door open. He was gratified to witness Andy's shock as a gun was shoved in his face.

Pitt joined him to read Andy his rights.

When they hauled him in they found a plastic bag on the front seat with fresh evidence from his latest kill. Andy sported claw marks on his face. His last victim hadn't gone down without a fight.

Worthington sent out teams to comb the area where Andy had dumped the last two bodies. They found a third girl. They couldn't believe their luck when they found a weak pulse. Andy had botched the strangulation.

It would be easy to pin the attempted murder on Andy since he hadn't showered after he'd raped her. She'd prove a valuable witness if she lived. The evidence in Andy's car would be vital at the trial to obtain a guilty verdict. When questioned as to why he'd kept the plastic bag with the victim's personal effects, Andy admitted he'd been about to plant evidence at Murray's place.

"Overconfidence was Andy's undoing. Cocky killers make mistakes when they think they're smarter than the police," Worthington noted.

"Ain't that the truth," Pitt agreed.

Marni smiled as she hung up the phone. "Marissa said Stacey came out of her coma. She identified Andy as her assailant." She shook her head. "I still don't understand why Andy beat Stacey up. He didn't have a reason."

"Yeah, I know. Lucky he didn't kill her. The guy's a psycho."

"It's not over yet for Stacey. She'll have to go to court when Andy Golder's trial comes up."

Marti poured tea into their mugs. "Yeah, he's in custody though and can't harm any more innocent girls. I can't believe I couldn't remember Andy's ring. I hate when something flits on the edge of your mind and you can't recall what it is. I noticed his ring at the funeral but wasn't able to figure it out until Worthington called."

"You've always been partial to red garnet rings. That could be why you noticed it at Diane's funeral. Interesting Andy had it on when they arrested him. Guess he isn't the smartest criminal. You'd think the guy would have chucked the ring somewhere."

Marti took a sip of tea. "True enough. Worthington said it had minute traces of Diane and Stacey's skin on it. No other girls though."

"I hope they find evidence for that second murder." Marni shook her head. "It's too coincidental not to have been Andy."

Marti's cell rang interrupting their discussion. She grinned as she hung up.

"They found that evidence."

"What do you mean?"

"That was Barry. His nephews were horsing around in their garage today. They found something half burnt in an old garbage can. They poked it with a stick, pulled out a black purse then ran into the house to tell their mom what they'd found.

Barry called Worthington. He was careful not to let the kids go out again. He told them about clues, evidence and prints. Barry wouldn't let anyone touch anything. They found ID and a picture of the second victim in the purse. Andy tried to plant evidence at Barry's brother's place for some twisted reason. He confessed to the killing when Worthington confronted him with the purse."

"Barry must have felt special. He helped solve two murders."

Marti grinned as she sipped more tea. "Yeah, he does. He's going to take adult literacy courses so he can learn to read and write better. He wants to help Worthington with cases."

Marni smiled then touched Marti's arm. "They must be gone now."

"Who?"

"Diane and Rosemarie."

"How do you know?"

"Justice will be served. Andy has been caught and can't kill again. Diane helped find the body of the second victim and now she can rest in peace. Rosemarie's killers are in custody and the victims she helped save will be reunited with their parents. I'm sure Gwyn won't hear from them again. They've crossed to the other side."

Marti gazed out the window. "Hmm, sounds about right."

"Do you think all stolen spirits lose their way?"

"I have no idea. You think Diane and Rosemarie were stolen spirits?"

"Well, they couldn't cross to the other side until their murders were solved."

"Unfinished business?"

"Yes, unfinished business."

"That reminds me, next time you see Wisahkecahk I hope he's a trickster. We don't need any sign of the destroyer around here again."

"I'll say. Let's stick to him in legends shall we. You can include him in your stories but that's it."

Marti reached over to hug her sister. "It's a deal. I think the great news we had tonight calls for a celebration. Where are the girls?"

"Upstairs, I'll call them. Ice cream?" Marni confirmed as she hugged Marti back.

"I'd say double chocolate is in order."

"Make mine chocolate mint and you've got a deal."

Rosemarie's voice trembled. "Why did they kill us? Why did they hate us so?"

Diane stared into the distance. "They didn't bother to get to know us Rosemarie." She turned to her new friend. "They barely knew our names then they stole our spirits. They killed us because they never cared about who we were. They're immoral, unkind, cruel, racist individuals. They were incapable of love, that's why."

Diane shuddered, "They live in a world fueled by hatred." She grabbed Rosemarie's hand to lead her toward the light. "Forget about them. Let's work on getting our spirits back, shall we?"

They wandered hand in hand toward Rosemarie's Kookum and Diane's aunt who beckoned from the bridge.

"Is this the end?" Rosemarie wondered.

Diane squeezed Rosemarie's hand then smiled. "I'd call it our beginning."

Author's Note

I love mysteries. I love to read, write and unravel the plot lines of a compelling mystery. As I researched and outlined the story for *Stolen Spirits* I explored social media sites, articles and reports that promoted the awareness of missing and murdered Indigenous women in Canada. The statistics are disturbing. I'm shocked this national human rights tragedy doesn't play a larger part in media and hasn't warranted greater interest by the police, government and community.

As of May 2014, how can there be almost 1,200 documented cases (and the number rises monthly) of missing and murdered Indigenous women in our country without a national outcry to solve these disappearances and murders? This gave me the idea for the *'what if'* for my novel.

The first victim, Diane, was an outgoing, likable, friendly teen girl who gets murdered. Diane was from the city, while a second victim, Rosemarie was from a northern community. What did these girls have in common? They were both First Nations. This provided the basis of the *'what if.'* Were these girls murdered because they were Aboriginal or were their murders unrelated? You'll find the answer as you read the novel.

As a mother, writer and Métis woman, I wanted to bring the issue of missing and murdered Indigenous women to the attention of those who need to hear it. If women are vulnerable to violent predators because they're Aboriginal, society needs to protect our Indigenous girls and women.

Traditionally, Aboriginal women were respected, honoured and valued. They had quiet strength, were teachers, healers, nurturers, mothers, counselors and spiritual leaders. Women had power and equality as they supported the traditions and culture of the community.

Today, many Aboriginal women have lost their power, equality and self esteem as racism and sexism have become more prevalent. As a society, we need to empower Indigenous women, return to our traditions and provide opportunities to learn about our culture as women share their stories. Women are the strength and backbone of a community. They need to be recognized again as the teachers, healers, nurturers, mothers, counselors and spiritual leaders of Indigenous peoples. Aboriginal women need to move forward through empowerment, strength, education, and hope as they strive to regain their rightful place in society.

As an author, I feel stats, case studies and research are not the way to engage people. I wrote this as a murder mystery with the hope that girls and women would recognize themselves as a possible character. How would one react if faced with the choices the women and young adults made in the novel?

As you read *Stolen Spirits* I urge you to check out the links listed and read up on the issue of missing and murdered Indigenous women. The following social media sites and links provide a starting point:

Facebook sites include:

Families of Sisters in Spirit: http://ow.ly/wdvK6

Missing and Murdered Aboriginal Women in Canada: http://ow.ly/wdw6T

Missing Manitoba Women: http://ow.ly/wdwt4

Saskatchewan Missing Women & Children: http://ow.ly/wdwHi

Walking with our Sisters: http://ow.ly/wciUP

Missing and Murdered Native Women of Canada: http://ow.ly/wdwiX

Stolen Sisters Awareness Movement: http://ow.ly/wcjki

National Inquiry into Missing & Murdered Women in Canada: http://ow.ly/wdyfj

Other sites:

Amnesty International Canada highlights "Canada: No More Stolen Sisters": http://ow.ly/wdyur

Native Women's Association of Canada (NWAC) Sisters in Spirit Project compiled data from 1990 until 2010: http://www.nwac.ca/sisters-spirit

NWAC Fact Sheet – Missing and Murdered Aboriginal Women and Girls: http://ow.ly/wdzL1

NWAC Community Resource Guide: What Can I Do to Help the Families of Missing and Murdered Aboriginal Women and Girls? http://ow.ly/wdzYC

Maryanne Pearce, Ottawa PHD law student released a study September 2013. Her thesis '*An Awkward Silence: Missing and Murdered Vulnerable Women and the Canadian Justice System*' provides a public database that includes and documents 824 missing and murdered Indigenous women and girls: http://ow.ly/wdxi0

CBC News Article "*Research points to 'exhaustive list' of missing Aboriginal women*" - Refers to Maryanne Pearce's study and public database: http://ow.ly/wdy1n

House of Commons Committees –FEWO (41 – 1) – Ending Violence Against Aboriginal Women and Girls: Empowerment – A New Beginning – Missing and Murdered Aboriginal Women (Parliament of Canada): http://ow.ly/AfYCV

RCMP cross-Canada review *Missing and Murdered Aboriginal Women: A National Operational Overview* lists number of known cases at almost 1,200. Report was released to the public in May 2014: http://www.rcmp-grc.gc.ca/pubs/mmaw-faapd-eng.pdf

Acknowledgements

Thanks to my team of readers and editors Randy Semenek, Amber Semenek, Bill Barlow, Ryan Sigmundson, Tanya Johannson and Danny-Jo Sigmundson. I value your comments, encouragement and contributions. Thanks to Cathy Wickett for her spectacular cover art and design.

Thanks to groups, associations and individuals such as Maryanne Pearce who provided a database documenting missing and murdered Indigenous women and girls in 2013. The link to her research and others including the most current review released in 2014 by the RCMP are included in my author's note.

Special thanks to my family for their ongoing encouragement, love, patience and support throughout my writing projects. Thanks to my readers and reviewers for their generosity and comments.

About The Author

Penny Ross lives in Gimli, Manitoba with her husband and has two adult sons, Ryan and Dylan. Proud of her Métis heritage, she loves to create stories that appeal to all ages. In addition to *Stolen Spirits* Penny has published *Cave of Journeys, Bird of Paradise Drums Beating,* and *Mrs. Muggles Learns to Read.* She is currently working on a murder mystery, a fantasy novelette and a sequel to *Cave of Journeys*.

Visit her website at www.butterflydreamspublishing.com